KATHLEEN KORBEL

A ROSE FOR MAGGIE

Published by Silhouette Books

America's Publisher of Contemporary Romance

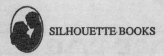 SILHOUETTE BOOKS

ISBN 0-373-60078-X

A ROSE FOR MAGGIE

Copyright © 1991 by Eileen Dreyer.

This edition published by arrangement with Harlequin Books S.A.

® and TM are trademarks of Harlequin Books S.A., used under license. Trademarks indicated with ® are registered in the United States Patent and Trademark Office, the Canadian Trade Marks Office and in other countries.

Printed in U.S.A.

Dear Reader,

Step into the Winner's Circle, with a set of special romance novels guaranteed to win your heart!

In this outstanding selection of Harlequin and Silhouette books, we've chosen to showcase award winners, those novels that professional lovers of romance are always talking about, and readers can never forget. Some of your favorite authors have contributed their works to this collection, including Anne Stuart, Penny Jordan, Curtiss Ann Matlock, Dallas Schulze, Kathleen Korbel and Glenda Sanders.

Look for the Winner's Circle insignia on a new title each month from January to June, and you'll know you've picked a winner!

Happy reading...

The Editors of Harlequin and Silhouette books

Because I can't find the words
to tell her how much I respect her,
this book is dedicated to
Lee, master gardener,
and Eric, her special rose.

From *The Story of the Binkley Brothers* by L. Wood Dowd

*J*ust this morning, in the Land Where Monsters Live, all the monsters were sitting down to their favorite breakfast of cornflakes and bat's wings. It had been a hard night spent frightening children and making adults turn to look when they didn't want to. So after breakfast, when people got up to work and play, the monsters would climb into their nests and snooze.

Now, there are many monsters. Monsters who are large and scaly. Monsters who are round and breathe smoke through their ears. Monsters who are as thin as snakes and hiss just like the wind. And each monster has his special job. Some monsters scratch at windows when it rains. Some live at the bottom of basement steps waiting to reach out and grab the ankle of people walking down into the dark. Some monsters curl up in closets and then push the door open, just a little, so all you can see is the dark inside, even though you know something is there.

But the most important monsters, the ones who live in the biggest houses and stand in the front of all the lines, are the *monsters who live under children's beds. Those are the busiest, the most feared, the sneakiest and creepiest monsters. Those are the monsters who reach up, very softly, and scratch the sides of beds, and very carefully pull the bedclothes off at night and then move toys around on the floor so someone just knows they've been there. They are the monsters who keep every little girl and boy awake at night for fear that if they do the wrong thing, the monsters will get them.*

Not just anybody can be an Underbed Monster. You have to be born into the family, like kings and things. You must be fierce and awful looking, so that even the other monsters tremble sometimes. And you have to be willing to eat one or two children every once in a while, just to keep all those other children afraid.

At breakfast this morning, in the biggest house on the biggest hill, with the biggest plate of bat's wings and cornflakes, sat the very most famous family of Underbed Monsters, the Binkleys. Mama Binkley, who looked very lovely in her green scales and pink dress, Papa Binkley, who liked to smoke cigars with his cereal, and revered Great-Uncle Ferocious Binkley, who was the most famous monster of all. Uncle Ferocious, you see, lived under Stephen King's bed.

And at the far end of the table, the lower end of the table, the very worst end of the table, because they hadn't quite yet lived up to the family name, sat the Binkley Brothers. Unctious, Noxious and Ralph.

Unctious, Noxious and Ralph were small monsters, apprentice monsters. Their scales were still unfurling and their teeth were still small and sharp instead of long and fierce. They were still learning the tricks of the trade, and it was their job to live under the bed of Billy Bartholomew. They were supposed to make Billy nervous. To make him not sure about sleeping with the covers off. They were supposed to make little hissing and scratching noises just when Billy was falling asleep, and wake him up again. Then, when he climbed out of bed to run to his parents, they were supposed to brush their scaly little claws right against his ankle and make him scream.

Unfortunately, the Binkley Brothers hadn't quite gotten a knack for their job yet. Other monsters laughed at them. Billy considered them his friends. And worst of all, the very worst, Uncle Ferocious considered them failures. And, I'm afraid, this is why...

Chapter 1

Allison Henley wasn't exactly sure what to expect. She'd driven to the address along the bluffs above the town of Alton on impulse. Allison was suddenly tired of trying to get the mysterious L. Wood Dowd to return her calls, and she was running out of time to arrange the publicity River Roads Publishing was requesting before his next book appeared.

Not that Dowd wanted the publicity. That was just the point. An invisible eccentric who hid behind an evocative fictitious name, the latest rage in children's literature, author and illustrator of the Binkley Brothers series, Dowd consistently refused not only to promote himself or his work, but to be identified period.

Even the publisher, a small regional house that had exploded into notoriety with these surprise bestsellers of the nineties, didn't *exactly* know who Dowd was. He lived in Alton, Illinois, where the publishing house was located, and corresponded via post-office box, answering machine and lawyer. And, until recently, the publisher had been happy with the arrangements because Dowd had been even more punctual than mysterious.

But, of course, that had all changed. Business being what it was, the new director of marketing wanted Dowd on the talk-show circuit. He wanted his cute, quaint picture on the book jacket along with his wildly imaginative creatures. He wanted him out there shaking hands with all those little tykes and their upscale parents who bought, read and cherished his family of monsters.

Much to Allison's chagrin, she had signed on with River Roads just in time to fall prey to the job of locating the mysterious author.

"Publicity should be doing this," she'd argued.

"Just how far do you think we'd get when we identified ourselves?" they'd countered.

If Allison didn't need the job so much, *this* job that had offered her not only income, but freedom and flexibility when she needed it the most, she would have told them to harass the old man themselves. Instead, she found herself pulling her car to a stop at the edge of a long gravel drive that wound up to a huge, three-storied brick Victorian perched high above the Mississippi River.

Shutting off the engine of the little compact that sported both briefcase and infant car seat, Allison took a moment to circle the wagons. Dowd wouldn't be happy, she knew, especially when he realized to what lengths she'd gone to uncover his address. If she were the old man, she'd feel violated and furious to find the boss at the front door. Especially when that had been one of the few stipulations in a contract that provided Dowd with his creative outlet and River Road Publishing with its golden egg.

"If only you'd answered my calls this last two weeks," Allison practiced instinctively, doing a quick check of her appearance in the rearview mirror and then raking quick fingers through close-cropped brown hair to push it back into order. The eyes that met her gaze were more troubled than she should admit, darker than she wanted. Changed irrevocably over the last few months from the bright sparkle she'd brought to her other jobs. "Ah, well," she said to herself as well as her phantom target. "Stuff happens. You go with it or you sink."

And then she smiled, and that, too, bore too much testament to be open and bright. Shaking her head ruefully at herself, she reached for her briefcase that held the latest Binkley manuscript, *The Binkley's Birthday,* and climbed out of the car.

For a minute, Allison didn't want to move. The soft spring air hovered with scent along the bluff. Far below, the wide slash of water glittered in an afternoon sun. Birds chattered and trilled in the gnarled oaks and chestnuts that were beginning to send out buds. Flowers exploded along the drive, along the walks and around the porch. Tulips, crocuses, jonquils, the first blush of azaleas. Startling color against the new spring green, a cacophony of life nurtured by a man too nervous to be seen in public.

Allison smiled. What kind of man was Dowd? she wondered yet again as she strode along the driveway, her heels scrunching in the gravel. Ever since her boss, Brook Donalson, had first placed a Binkley Brothers book in her hand, Allison had constructed one picture after another. The befuddled innocent from which he'd taken his name. A white-haired Samuel Clemens-type, his wry observations on life sketched with sometimes amazing precision. Santa Claus, with a hearty laugh and a great, huge lap for the children he seemed to love so much. His voice was quiet and restrained over the phone, deep enough to carry a heavy man, but formal enough to evoke visions of bow ties and suspenders.

She had to admit she couldn't wait to finally put face to name, and not just to win the pool that had sprung up in the office since the word had come down that Dowd must make his appearance. She wanted to know just who would hide so completely behind a pseudonym that he'd go to court to acquire it and then refuse his real name to his publisher.

L. Wood Dowd was Joseph Burgett. His identity had been discovered only because he'd put his real name and address on his request for a post-office box, and Allison, through some fast talking that a private investigator would have raised an eye at, had found it.

Probably his lawyer's great-uncle or something, since they shared the last name. An eccentric uncle who lived all alone in the big, red, opulent old Victorian house that went with every image of Dowd she kept in her head. Fussy, hearty, private. A Victorian man caught in a twentieth-century society, hiding behind his beveled glass and sketching his monsters by Tiffany lamp.

She couldn't wait.

Joseph Burgett wasn't home. Allison rang the bell half a dozen times, trying her best to peer in past the heavy drapes at the windows. She lifted the great brass knocker and slammed it against the solid oak door. Each assault echoed through the house as if it were an empty symphony hall. Still, there were no answering footsteps, no querulous voice.

"Wonderful," she sighed with a heartfelt grimace. "All that courage screwed to a sticking post for nothing."

That was when she heard it. A saw. A band saw, if she was any judge, from the back of the house.

Oh, well, no harm trying. Instinctively checking her watch, Allison climbed off the porch, her footsteps clacking on the wood. The sides of the porch were trellised, and morning glories overflowed the wooden slats. Allison couldn't help another smile as she stepped along the sidewalk that ringed the house.

She saw the truck first, an old battered white pickup piled with lumber and toolboxes. Pulled in back behind the back porch, it sat with its tailgate down. The sound of the band saw seemed as if it were coming from the detached garage beyond it. Fine. She'd come to meet a writer and come up with his handyman instead.

The sound stopped. Allison could hear the birds again, crowded into the trees that surrounded the yard and all querulous. She smelled wood shavings now, mixed with the heavy sweet perfume of hyacinth. She straightened a little, smoothed down the lines of her jersey dress, ignored the mud that had collected on her bone-colored high heels and approached the open garage door.

"Excuse me—"

Which was just about as far as she got. She'd been expecting—well, she wasn't sure what she'd been expecting. Someone middle-aged maybe, certainly with a potbelly and battered jeans that barely hung on below. Somebody with practical eyes and callused, dirty hands. Somebody normal.

The man who turned at the sound of her voice was definitely not normal. The eyes that appeared when he lifted his safety goggles weren't practical, and the belly wasn't pot at all. It was taut and glistening, sprinkled in wood shavings and hair. The jeans were precariously low, it seemed. But Allison was afraid that that was only because she hadn't expected to want to look at them so much. They molded taut legs and a very firm backside.

And his face.

"Hi," he said, greeting her with a smoky, sultry voice. "Can I help you?"

He was smiling a bit quizzically, his chocolate brown eyes just a shade shy. There were furrows in his lean cheeks and stubble on his chin. His hair, which she'd expected to be buzzed and gray, was thick, coarse, falling over his eyes in slashes of brown. There was a little gray there, but it was all at the temples where it belonged.

Allison dragged her own gaze back to his, trying her best to regain her composure. She smiled back, knowing exactly why she was reacting so strongly. At least thinking she knew why she was reacting so strongly.

It had, after all, been a long time. And, because of the decision she'd made—the decision made for her—it would be a lot longer. It would be forever.

"I'm...sorry." Her voice stumbled a little, her smile growing a bit rueful as she struggled to control her suddenly out-of-control hormones. "I'm looking for Mr. Burgett."

The man before her pulled the goggles off the rest of the way and lay them against a hip. Allison fought the urge to watch their progress. His arms rippled with movement. A workman's arms. Lean, well-muscled, decadent.

And then, just as Allison was beginning to regain some of her composure, when she was certain she could complete her conversation with Burgett's workman and get away with her lungs and brain intact, he smiled with devastating simplicity and tossed off the punch line of the year.

"What can I do for you?"

Allison shook her head. "Joseph Burgett."

"I'm Joe Burgett." His attention shifted fractionally. Took on a sharp glint. "I know you, don't I? You're—"

But Allison, still trying her very desperate best to get past that sweat-gleamed body and whiskey voice, dropped her advantage like a bad apple. "*You're* L. Wood Dowd?"

Buttoning the last button, Joe tucked his shirt into his jeans. He ran his hands through his hair, but that wouldn't make much difference. It was still wet, curling a little at his collar, that one hunk stubbornly dropping over his forehead.

No matter. He had to get back downstairs and face the problem perched on the single chair in his living room. He had to figure out how to contain the damage and protect himself.

He wasn't that upset that River Roads had finally found him. It had only been a matter of time all along, after all. But even before Allison Henley had said a word—he'd interrupted her earnest plea with a demand for a shower first, forestalling any confrontation long enough to regroup—he'd had a feeling that his days of anonymity were in perilous supply.

If only they'd sent somebody else. Somebody male and brisk and bristling with media jargon. He could have turned him down without blinking. He could have thrown him out of the house and threatened the whole lot of them with jumping ship to another publisher.

Joe had no illusions about his work. He wasn't Ernest Hemingway. He wasn't even Charles Schultz. The work he did with his hands would probably last longer than his books. But he knew that for some reason, he'd become a marketable commodity, which gave him a certain amount of leverage. It had also brought that very pretty, rather serious young woman into his living room.

And ever since Joe had first talked to his new editor on the phone, he'd been aware of the fact that he had a real weakness where that pretty, serious young woman was concerned.

The old, faded runner absorbed his footsteps as he descended the stairs to find her standing at the front window peering out toward the river.

"Great view, isn't it?" he asked.

She started, and the drapes fell closed again, blocking out the view, blocking out the sun.

Joe pulled the heavy red curtains open, suddenly impatient with the dusky light in the middle of the afternoon. "I have the Binkley Brothers to thank for that view," he admitted as the heavy red curtains slid open by yanks and starts. "I've wanted to live in this house ever since I was a kid and came up here to scare myself every Halloween. It was our local haunted house. Empty and full of cobwebs and creaky boards. The perfect place for a carpenter to buy and renovate."

She stepped back away from him as if he'd come too close. Still stiff, still surprised and hesitant. It made Joe want to reach out to her. To close the distance and soothe the furrow between those soft, green eyes.

"It's a wonderful old place," she admitted, her gaze drawn to the high ceilings and crown molding. There was still a lot of original cabbage-rose wallpaper in the front rooms, because Joe had decided to renovate the rooms he'd be using first: bedroom, bath, kitchen, workroom. The rest was waiting until he got to it.

"I'm working on the library now," he admitted, his own gaze following hers and seeing not the shabby remnants of someone else's lives, but the possibilities. The ghosts that still crept around in the shadows and the angular, rich beauty that the sun exposed. Real hardwood floors, great expanses of glass, sweeping staircases, a kitchen big enough to fit the family at Thanksgiving. "I'm building bookshelves. And, of course, a hidden bar."

"I shouldn't have come here," she said abruptly, turning on him, her dress flowing around her knees with the movement. "I'm sorry."

She was small. Petite, with hair that glinted like mahogany and skin as translucent as mother-of-pearl. There was a delightful roundness to her figure, a female fertility symbol, and a compelling depth to her large eyes and oval, fine-boned face. There was also a hint of sadness, of weight on those soft shoulders.

"What for?" Joe smiled instinctively with a shrug. "You were probably only doing your job."

Her quick grin made him think he'd surprised it out of her. "The pool money's going to have to go to charity," she said wryly.

"Pool money?"

Her grin caught and grew a little. "The office pool. The odds were heavily in favor of your looking like Captain Kangaroo and having half a dozen cats for pets."

His laughter echoed through the house. "Exactly why a pseudonym comes in so handy."

She shook her head, still not satisfied. "Your voice," she objected. "It's different than I'm used to."

Joe was completely unrepentant. "It's . . . nice to talk to you, Miss Henley," he mimicked easily, his entire posture folding instinctively into position, hands crossed, head ducked into submission.

Allison chuckled. "That's the L. Wood Dowd I know and love," she agreed with a nod.

Joe brightened up. "Not really," he admitted. "Mr. Wilson Maloney. My eighth-grade social-studies teacher."

She scowled at him. "Do me a favor and never take on a female pseudonym. I wouldn't want to see myself dissected quite that surgically."

"Oh, don't worry," he said. "I still have plenty of teachers to go through. Now then, if you're here on business, I'd suggest we go into the kitchen. It's the only room on this floor with more than one chair. And I'd much rather not try and duel with you from the floor."

"I brought your line editing with me," she offered, lifting the briefcase and following him through the hallway to the kitchen. "I thought we could go over it."

Joe turned his head. "Something wrong?"

"No. They just need to get in right away, and I hadn't been able to get in touch with you."

He nodded absently. "I've been out of town on a job and just got back. I figured I had a good couple of months on those, yet."

"Well, you did. But the publication's been bumped up a little. River Roads is celebrating its anniversary in publishing, you know, and the Binkley Brothers are going to represent the company."

"Interesting image," he obliged, flipping on the lights in the kitchen. "Have a seat and we can get to work. And then you can tell me why you really came out."

She stopped dead in her tracks, her face giving her away. Joe couldn't help a grin.

"Have a beer," he offered, turning to the refrigerator.

She barely moved. "I don't drink, thanks."

He turned back to her and lifted an eyebrow. "Soda? Tea? Milk?"

She just shook her head. "No. Thank you."

He suspected her stomach wasn't feeling very good right now. Deviousness did that to some people. Pulling open the door, he grabbed a beer and headed for the battered old Formica table he'd liberated from his parents' house.

"Manuscript." He nudged her on as he pulled out a chair for her.

"You're right," she acknowledged, still standing stock still with discomfort. "They do want something more."

"And if I say no?"

She shrugged. "I haven't gotten that far yet."

Joe nodded and let go of the chair. "Then let's start at the beginning." He held out his free hand to her. "Hi, my name's Joe Burgett. I write children's books as L. Wood Dowd. And you?"

She shook Joe's hand. "Your editor," she said, finally giving in and smiling back. "It's nice to finally meet you."

They both settled into their chairs as if at a business meeting. Allison brought the briefcase up and opened it.

Joe paid little attention. "Tell me something about yourself," he commanded, popping the tab on his can.

She paused, tilted her head a little. "I thought that was supposed to be *my* question."

Joe waved off the objection. "I've been working with you on this book for two months, and I don't know anything about you. The man you replaced kept me informed on everything from his homelife to the progress of his car loan."

She grinned. "It was his way to try and pry something out of *you.*"

Joe grinned back and knocked off a little of the beer. "I know. The quality of phone reception is phenomenal these days. I could even hear his teeth gnashing."

Allison dipped her head a bit. "I guess I wasn't quite as patient."

"I don't think I mind," he admitted, surprised by his own sentiment, his natural trust of this woman he'd only talked to enough to properly decline verbs and redraw monsters. "Have you had lunch yet?"

Her head came up at that. Joe saw the sudden defense in those eyes. "Yes," she lied badly. "I have."

Joe nodded as if to himself. "What about dinner?" he countered. "Have you had that?"

He could tell she was fighting a smile. "I guess I'm funny about that kind of thing. I don't like to eat dinner before two in the afternoon."

"Well, then, that'll just give us enough time to go over the manuscript and get that out of the way before I take you out."

"No," she said, certainly, simply. Finally. "Thank you, but I can't."

"You're married?"

"No."

"*I'm* married?"

"It wouldn't matter."

"I'm not." He waited for a reaction, any reaction. He saw it in the faint pink on her cheeks. When she looked back up at him, he smiled. "Just in case River Roads wanted to know."

"Are you ready to tell them?"

"You're not going to distract me."

Her smile was pretty and indescribably sad. "Yes, I am," she told him. "I'm your editor, nothing more. I'll be happy to work with you on *Binkleys' Birthday,* and *Showdown in the Binkley Saloon,* and all the rest of the Binkley books. I'll be your voice at the publishing house, and clear up your questions. But I don't consider it a good policy to go out with my authors."

"I wasn't asking for a date."

She didn't quite answer.

"A business dinner. Everybody does it. At least, that's what I've been told. Carpenters don't get to go to business dinners that often. The most we can usually hope for is a visit to the drive-through window at Burger Doodle. But now that I'm a nationally famous author—I *am,* aren't I?"

There was just a hint of humor struggling at the corners of her eyes. "You are."

"Then I should be able to have business dinners. Or lunches or breakfasts. I just choose dinner."

"In that case," she offered, leaning in a little bit so that the soft mauve jersey knit pulled across her breasts, "I have the perfect offer for you."

Joe leaned forward himself so that they were almost eye to eye. "You do," he countered, anticipating her.

She nodded, her hair whispering with movement. "All the free meals you want. In any city you want. All on River Roads."

"But I don't want to go out with River Roads. I want to go out with you."

"I told you," she objected instantly. "I don't go out with authors."

"For business," he amended just as quickly. "To discuss my newest idea."

She didn't even hesitate. "No. Thank you. Now, would you like to hear River Roads' idea?"

Joe finally sat back. "Only if you'll tell me why I'm so repugnant that you won't even break bread with me. Would you go out with me if I looked like Captain Kangaroo and had six cats?"

Her eyes crinkled again, the laughter caught there behind them. "L." She'd always called him L. on the phone. It had been their little joke about his pseudonym. Joe knew that her choice of salutation was intentional. Distancing. Final. "I don't mean to sound rude. It's not just you, believe me. I simply can't continue working with you if we have less than a professional relationship. If you'd rather, I can see if someone else can edit you in the future. Anything you'd like. Except dinner."

Joe took a second to assess her determination. She was awash in it. "And nothing I say or do can change your mind?"

She shook her head. "Nothing."

"Even accepting River Roads' request that I come out in public only on the condition that you go with me?"

He wasn't being fair. He hadn't realized it until he saw her reaction. Every ramification of his statement flickered in those sweet green eyes in the time it took him to lift a hand. "Never mind," he said, taking hold of his beer again and quenching a surprise fire in his chest with it. "I may be many things. Hell, I *am* many things. I'm not a blackmailer."

"Do you want a new editor?" she asked sincerely, no hint of rancor anywhere in her. Even so, Joe was tormented by the feeling that she was afraid of his answer. For more reasons than having a prestigious author on her résumé.

"No," he answered without hesitation. "I do not want another editor. I want you."

She started, a wild thing catching the scent of a hunter.

"For an editor," he amended, then held out his hand again. "Friends?"

It actually took her a moment to consider. Joe could feel the ambivalence shimmer from her like humidity in a summer sky. He could almost hear the argument raging in her head.

In the end, she gave in. Reaching out a hand, she met his gaze with certainty and nodded. "Friends."

Joe held on just a little too long. Just long enough to ingrain the feel of her soft palm against his, the small, strong fingers caught and quieted within his. And then he let go and cooled that hand with his can of beer.

"Now then," he said, reaching for the manuscript. "What have the Binkley brothers done now?"

The apartment was silent. Guilty for feeling grateful, Allison pulled out her key and quietly closed the door.

"Lucille," she called softly. "I'm home."

The afternoon light had waned behind a bank of thick clouds, leaving the rooms dim and soft. Allison dropped her mail on the foyer table and walked on in, shedding briefcase and purse to the soft green-and-peach-colored couch and kicking her shoes toward the rocking chair that was piled with picture books and furry animals. There were toys in the corner and an odd contraption that looked like an oversize cat's scratching post by the window. Instead of a coffee table, Allison had a ramp in the middle of her living room, homemade and scuffed, three feet long. Instead of a dining set, she had a card table and chairs and a big box filled with packing beads. Beyond the French doors straight through to the back, the yard was filled with sandbox and flowers—as many flowers as Allison could possibly squeeze into her eight-by-five square of grass.

The lines of her decorating were spare by necessity and pastel by inclination. The walls were hung with bright photographs of places to which Allison had once traveled, and posters of works by Mary Cassatt and Renoir, mothers and children.

The aromas wafting in from the kitchen would have made Allison's mouth water a few months ago. Instinctively now, they roiled in her. She'd eat, but then she'd spend the next three hours fighting nausea and heartburn. She'd tried to just not eat, but her stamina was more important right now than her comfort.

She was home now, and the weight of it settled back onto her like grief.

"Lucille?" she asked, leaning into the kitchen, a single, tissue-wrapped flower in her hands.

The room was bright and tiny, all white, plastered in huge primary-colored pictures. The refrigerator held a mosaic of snapshots. A big, soft, motherly black woman looked up from where she was checking the oven and smiled.

"You look tired, child," she admonished easily. "Get some of that tea from the icebox."

Allison stretched out a few kinks and bluffed her way past Lucille's concern. "It's been a while since I've had to do so much mental fencing. How is she?"

The woman's face dissolved into a broad, genuine smile of affection. "Asleep. She put me through my paces today, I can tell you that. Little imp."

Allison nodded. "I'll just..."

Lucille turned back to her work without needing Allison to finish the sentence. Both knew what she meant to say. Knew where she was turning to when she left the kitchen.

Down the hall, first door on the left, where the morning sun warmed the room and the hot afternoon light never reached. Where, instead of spare lines and pastels, the room exploded in color and light and action. Mobiles hung from the ceiling. Wind chimes danced in the rain-bred breeze. The walls were painted in animals and the ceiling in clouds. Another rocker claimed its place by the big front window, and pillows littered the floor.

There was a regular baby bed in the corner, but it was empty and unadorned. In the center of the room sat a white wicker cradle over which the mobiles swayed. Strung over the top, like the top of a carnival ride, was an arc of tiny silver bells so that every time the baby moved, the bells would sing.

Inside, the blankets were soft and handmade. Gifts of love, handspun dreams that had grown along with the life in Allison's belly. Declarations to a baby felt but not seen, each stitch accompanied by a different fantasy, a new dream. Sweet smelling and so very gentle against a baby, they had been Allison's promise to her child that no matter that her father didn't want her, had never wanted her, her mother did.

No matter what happened in her marriage, Allison would have her baby. She would have her dreams and her future, and they would grow together, there for each other even if there was never anyone else.

She saw her baby now, snuggled beneath the soft yellow shells of the blanket Allison had finished in the hospital, waiting for her to be born. A tiny, delicate child with her mother's brown hair and her father's dark eyes. A fragile life that had so utterly changed Allison's. The embodiment of every promise and dream Allison had cherished so defiantly when her husband had argued, then threatened, then finally left.

Tears burned her throat. Bitter, hot tears Allison had fought every single day of Maggie's life. She was so tired of crying, so very weary of fighting on alone, of fighting on at all. And yet, there she stood, her hands clenched to her chest where the pain always lived, her cheeks wet again, her heart breaking.

Because Maggie was her miracle. She was her child, the special, secret friend she had longed for late in the night when Brian had begun to grow apart from her. She was all hers, and Allison knew the singular, shattering joy every mother discovers when her very own child smiles simply at the sound of her voice.

But Maggie was also her heartache. Maggie, so precious, so reverently cared for from the moment Allison had first suspected her presence, so longed for, so welcomed. Maggie, the innocent victim of nature's capricious hand.

Because Maggie, born early and thriving slowly, had a heart defect. First a consideration, then a suspicion, and finally confirmation. In another two months, if Maggie could get her weight up to over eight pounds, she would face open-heart surgery.

But that wasn't the reason Allison cried. Allison cried because Maggie, her innocent, beautiful, sweet-smiling Maggie, also had Down syndrome. And there would be no surgery to ever cure that.

Kathleen Korbel

But that would be stored, Allison thought, while a part of her kept on humming the nonsensical little tune, stored away back in a chamber of memory where only pleasures belonged to see later.

Chapter 2

She'd had three hours with Maggie. Three hours of perfect joy, counting fingers and toes and reveling in the sweetness of her skin, smiling down into dark, open eyes and singing the love songs mothers of all history had sung to their children before her.

She'd even been able to hold a brief hope for her marriage. When the baby had decided to come early, Brian had been there for her. He'd stuck out the delivery and shared those first few moments with her, his expression torn between wonder, dread and anxiety. He'd held his daughter in his hands, the daughter he'd sworn he'd never wanted, and he'd smiled at her fierce little scowl.

And then, at four in the morning, the pediatrician had arrived.

"But she looked all right," Allison had immediately protested, seeing something on his face even before he spoke. "She's a little small, but she was breathing just fine."

"It's not that," he objected, pulling up a chair and folding his lanky frame into it. Still uncomfortable, still stiff with concern and a dread Allison thought now she should have seen. "She's breathing just fine. It's something else. Something I think she needs to be tested for."

"Tested." Brian had just gone home. They'd called her parents and his parents, and settled Allison in for sleep. And he'd gone home just before the doctor changed Allison's life.

The doctor had nodded. "There are certain...features we see in your little girl...uh, a crease across her palm. Slanted eyes, small, low-set ears. Poor muscle tone."

She remembered laughing in the delivery room. "The Parson eyes," she'd said to Brian. "Poor thing, they're probably going to be so small. But look how tiny her ears are."

"But she's only just born..." Allison had protested instinctively, faltering. Lost in this alien place with this only just-known doctor who couldn't seem to look her in the eye.

"I'll have a geneticist consult," he assured her, never bending into sympathy. "And a karyotype done of her chromosomes. But, uh, I'm pretty sure."

"Sure of what?"

Then, finally, he looked at her. And in his eyes, Allison saw her hopes shatter. "Trisomy twenty-one."

"English," she snapped, her voice high and terrible. "Tell me what the hell you're talking about."

He'd made a try for her hand, but she'd pulled away.

"I'm talking about Down syndrome, Mrs. Henley," he said. "Allison will be mentally retarded."

By the time they'd diagnosed the heart problem two weeks later, Brian had already been gone for good.

Allison had replayed that moment every day of the six months Maggie had been alive. That brief balancing between joy and terror just before her future had inexorably slipped from her and come crashing down. Sometimes she dreamed that Allison walked up to her, a full-grown woman, cured and whole. Sometimes she dreamed of Brian coming home, when she knew neither would happen.

And always she woke alone in the dark. Alone with the responsibility of not just a desperately sick child, but a forever fragile child.

Then, as always, the tears would come.

"You better get some food in you," Lucille offered from the doorway. "She's gonna be wantin' to play in a little while."

Quickly Allison swiped at her tears, frustrated at herself, just as ashamed. So many parents had it so much worse. So many parents never even had the chance to hold a child at all. Maggie was her heart, her soul, her life. And so, as she did every day, Allison unwrapped the flower and placed it, a tender, pink rosebud on the brink of blooming, in the vase on the chest by Maggie's bed.

"She taking her medicine all right?" she asked, stroking the baby-soft petals just once before bending to readjust the blanket around Maggie that needed no adjustment.

"Not all right," the other woman chuckled, "but she took it."

"Did you get any exercises done?"

They both tiptoed from the room and headed back toward the kitchen to savor the brief silence in the evening.

"She was kinda tired today. We only got in about a half hour."

Finally giving in and going to the refrigerator for iced tea, Allison scowled. "Really tired?" she demanded. "Or crabby? You know how good she is at avoiding work."

"Really tired, I think. All that eating does her in, you know."

Allison knew. Maggie had to get her weight up for the surgery, and eating exhausted her. Not to mention the fact that it was harder for her to do because of her poor muscle tone and shallow palate. It was a fight every time, one that had finally broken Allison's will to nurse and carried on the minute Maggie saw bottle or bowl. She might have been ill, often tired and quiet. But she did definitely have her own opinions about certain things, and the task of eating was one of them.

The tea was cold and quenching, all that Allison really wanted right now. Even so, Lucille pulled the casserole from the oven and began dishing some up for her. Lucille came over two days a week to watch Maggie when Allison had to get into the office. A mother of two disabled children herself, she had immediately adopted the little girl as one of her own, and Allison as another. And so it was that the only nights Allison really ate anything were those when Lucille did the cooking.

"Sit down, sit down," the big woman commanded, adding a crisp salad to the food already on the table. "Tell me if you got to see him."

For the first time since she'd walked in the door, Allison smiled. "I saw him," she admitted, taking a long sip of tea and following Lucille to the card table where they'd sit as she ate. It was Lucille's time away from her own children, and she often stayed just a little longer for girl talk. Allison, stranded in a new city by a husband who'd moved there for business and then run, knew she relied on Lucille too much. Her friends and family were fifteen hundred miles away in New York, and ever since Maggie's birth, most of them had fallen into a kind of chagrined silence.

Allison waited until Lucille dished up a portion for herself and eased into the chair across from her before continuing.

"We all lost," Allison informed Lucille archly. "He's not Mark Twain, and he's definitely not Santa Claus."

Lucille waited, her hand poised over her dinner. She'd been even more anxious than Allison to discover the secret identity of L. Wood Dowd. She'd wanted to know about the author ever since reading the first Binkley Brothers book, *Some Monsters Can't Be Scary* to her children. She was a Dowd devotee the way opera buffs followed Mozart. In fact, when Allison had first been assigned the author, Lucille had been the one to instruct her on his strengths and weaknesses. Strengths: wildly imaginative drawing with monsters that rivaled Sendak's, sympathetic characters— Lucille's favorite was Unctious, trying so very hard to be terrible when he was allergic to dust bunnies—and a gentle sense of how to defuse a child's fear. Weaknesses: a lack of real problems in his books. A veteran champion of disabled children, Lucille fervently believed in gently grounding all people in empathy.

"Someday," she'd said with knowing eyes, "that man's gonna know trouble. Then he'll write books that are real."

Allison understood those words in ways she couldn't ever quite explain, but for now, the matter at hand was simply girl talk, and Allison got little enough of it lately.

"The reason nobody knows just who L. Wood Dowd is," she announced with salacious delight, "is because he's a thirty-three-year-old, card-carrying union carpenter. He builds new houses and renovates old ones, and he's afraid that he's not going to still be able to do that once he's found out."

Lucille couldn't have been more surprised if Allison had claimed Dowd to be a ten-legged alien. After the way she'd finally met Joe Burgett, Allison understood perfectly.

"A carpenter?" the black woman demanded, hand on hip. "That man has the gift of words and he wants to play with saws and hammers?"

Allison shrugged. "It really seems important to him. I have the feeling that he sees it as much an art as writing and drawing."

"Well, no kiddin'." Taking a stab at her dinner, Lucille shook her head a bit mournfully. Lucille's money had been on the bow tie and suspenders. "So, what does he look like? No, on second thought, I don't think I wanna know. I don't think I can stand the fact that that man's probably got seven teeth and scratches his crotch."

Allison actually laughed. "Well, I can't speak for his scratching habits, but I can tell you that he does have all his teeth. He also has the most beautiful dimples you've ever seen, and eyes the color of dark chocolate."

Lucille's head snapped up as if Allison had just announced the arrival of the Pope. Her eyes grew wide. "You're blushing," she accused.

Allison had to admit that she was. Just thinking about Joe Burgett, about the sweet heat in his eyes, the brash humor in his propositions, the smell of wood shavings and sweat on him. Oh, to be able to dream again. If she could, she'd be doing it about him.

"Joseph Burgett is definitely the very last person I would expect to be writing children's books," she admitted.

Forgetting her food altogether, Lucille leaned in close. "So come on, girl. Tell me."

So Allison told her everything, from the way she'd accidentally come upon him, to his invitations, to her polite refusals. She didn't mention that he'd been the first person, except Maggie, to make her really laugh in weeks. That for just a few minutes she'd been able to forget her burdens and concentrate on his company, his humor, his seductive, laughing eyes.

But then, those were things that Allison didn't even want to admit to herself.

"So, what are you gonna tell all those people at the publishing house?" Lucille asked.

Allison stared a moment at the glass she held in her hand, not really seeing it, seeing instead the honest concern in Joe Burgett's voice, hearing the persistence in her co-workers'. Knowing just what the marketing department would say.

"I don't know," she admitted, looking back up at her friend. "I really don't know. He wants to keep his anonymity. And personally, I don't blame him. If the press got a load of his looks, he wouldn't have another moment's peace for the rest of his life."

"But what about the publishers?"

Allison's shrug was rueful. "I guess I'm gonna have to sleep on it. At least I don't have to give them their answers face-to-face."

"I don't mind comin' back tomorrow."

But Allison shook her head. "Maggie has a doctor's appointment. Besides," she amended with a wry smile, "this gives me the perfect excuse to chicken out and break the bad news over the phone."

"Is he married?"

Allison shrugged. "Doesn't look like it."

Lucille nodded with delight. "Good. Maybe he's just what you need, then."

Allison didn't bother to look up from the dinner she hadn't even realized she'd been eating. "Don't even start, Lucille. You know better."

"I don't know nothin', girl. Just because one man in your life was worthless doesn't mean they all are."

Allison did look up now, and her eyes held everything she'd faced alone during the past six months. "It doesn't matter," she said, yet again. "Worthless is one thing. My situation is entirely another. I've just begun to learn how to cope with this by myself, Lucille. I can't go through that again, no matter who it's for. Maggie and I are doing fine by ourselves, and that's just the way it's going to stay."

"Don't you think—"

Allison sighed. "I only have so much heart to break, Lucille. I don't have room for anybody else right now. I doubt I ever will."

Lucille didn't like it, but she dropped the subject. Allison didn't betray how relieved she was.

Allison Henley considered herself a realist. Raised in a small, formal family of college professors, she had learned early to rely on herself for entertainment and support. She'd attended Brown University, just as her parents had wanted, and then outraged them when she'd opted for the professional world instead of the academic one.

New York, specifically. For four years she'd worked her way from editorial assistant to assistant editor in one of the more scholarly publishing houses in Manhattan. Maybe she hadn't followed her parents' footsteps, but she had followed their inclinations, editing dark, solemn, sometimes terribly pretentious tomes aimed for library shelves and little else.

Brian had been the perfect date, the comfortable companion, the sharp mind that could challenge hers. She'd met him at a New Year's Eve party and been married by Easter. And for another two years, she'd been perfectly happy balancing their two careers and anticipating a future together.

She'd wanted children. He hadn't. It had always seemed like something the two of them could resolve sometime down the line. But when she'd discovered herself pregnant only weeks after finding out that Brian was up for transfer to Alton, Illinois, she'd found out that "sometime" didn't happen.

To be honest, when he'd moved farther and farther away from her, furious at her insistence to have the child, suspicious that she'd gotten pregnant on purpose, she'd begun to plan for the time when she'd be alone with her baby. She'd been realistic.

And now, even with the heavy, hot rock that sat in her chest twenty-four hours a day, even when the burden seemed too much to bear alone, she knew she would. She knew in her heart, after seeing the horror in Brian's eyes, the sudden coldness, the denial to even acknowledge his daughter, much less hold her, that she couldn't expect another man to assume a burden he wouldn't.

Relationships were tough enough as it was, and that was when all the dreams were still intact and the couple had time to grow together and support each other when the dreams didn't come true. Allison couldn't imagine how a relationship with her would look from the outside in, knowing that she didn't come with just a child, but a sick child, a child with a future no one could foresee.

So Allison refused to hope. She fenced in her future. She had said it all; she had only so much heart to break. And it would surely break for good if she let another man close just to see him run, too.

Which was why she'd set her limits with Joe. Politely, calmly, irrevocably. Which was also why she knew she'd only let him so close, keeping her private life that. The more she shared with him, the more she'd want to, and that spelled disaster.

Still, just because she'd decided to keep the relationship professional didn't mean she didn't empathize with the man. Everybody had secrets, small safe corners where they couldn't let anybody else in. Everybody had the right to privacy, and just because Joe was making River Roads money didn't forfeit that right.

Besides, she couldn't quite get past the real distress she'd seen in his eyes when she'd formally discussed River Roads' request. He hadn't made his decision to remain anonymous frivolously. He valued his friends in the carpenters' union, that unspoken bond that gave his work pleasure and made those job sites just as much his home as that big Victorian monstrosity on the hill. The minute the notoriety hit, all that would change. His co-workers would back away, would see him in a way that would eventually erode his ability to work there.

He'd be famous, and they wouldn't. And that would always, somehow, be between them.

And so it was that Allison had made her decision long before she actually picked up the phone to talk to her supervising editor.

Joe should have been out in the garage trimming the molding for the library. He had another job starting tomorrow, and a new book to start. The library should already be almost finished.

He couldn't keep his mind on it. Every time he marked the wood, he saw soft green eyes. He heard a wry chuckle in the wind and knew it wasn't the rain. He remembered her indecision when she'd left the day before and worried.

It had all changed yesterday. His bubble of contentment, his fantasy that he was successfully juggling the different parts of his life had vanished before a tentative smile. He'd been found out. Unmasked. L. Wood Dowd had been breached, and only time would tell if Allison could keep him safely hidden.

But that wasn't what had kept his hand from the saw. It wasn't what stilled his pen at his desk or propelled his feet as he paced first rooms and then lawn.

He was just heading for the kitchen phone when the door slammed open.

"Hey, Uncle Joe?"

His hand dropped. "Hey, Sam," he greeted his eight-year-old nephew. "What are you doing off school?"

"Teachers' conference." The boy sniffed. Towheaded and peppered with freckles, Samuel Burgett Peterson was the image of a Norman Rockwell child. He was also a gifted mathematician and crafty enough trader in baseball cards to be feathering his future college nest quite nicely.

"Soda's in the fridge," Joe offered. His sister didn't know, but of course, that was what uncles were for. "Let me make a phone call and you can help me fit molding."

"Can I see the new drawings?"

Sam was also the only one of a good dozen nieces and nephews trusted with the information that Uncle Joe was really L. Wood Dowd. Joe was sometimes amazed that the kids didn't see the connection between the little cartoons he was usually sketching for them and the Binkley Brothers, but then, no kid figured his uncle to be anything but what he seemed. Sam had always been too smart for all of them. He'd realized it by the time he was five. He'd also never breathed a word of it to anybody.

"Go on up," Joe suggested. "Maybe you have some ideas about what monsters do the morning after Halloween."

Sam was already clattering up the back staircase. "If I were a monster," he informed his uncle, his childish voice echoing up the stairwell, "I'd be stealing all that candy. After all, *they* don't ever get to go trick or treating."

Joe couldn't help a big grin. He'd have to dedicate this one to Sam.

Someday, he promised yet again, just as he did every time he saw his nieces and nephews. Someday he'd have kids just like that. Bright, happy, funny, full of life. Always keeping you on your toes, trying to keep up with them, their surprising insight stopping you dead in your tracks at the most unexpected moments. Noisy and rambunctious and exhausting.

Someday.

For the first time in his life, he saw the features of one particular woman on his children.

Turning back to the phone, he picked it up and dialed River Roads Publishing.

"Is Allison Henley in?" he asked the receptionist.

"No, I'm sorry, she'd isn't. May I ask who's calling?"

Joe hesitated, torn. Wanting to know what she might have done, wanting to just talk to her, feeling suddenly impatient with the ruse of L. Wood Dowd.

"I'll call her later," he said.

He knew her home phone number, after all. Had called it a number of times, always reaching an answering machine and then hearing from her in a matter of an hour. When he tried it this time, though, the line was busy.

"What do you mean you couldn't find him?" Brook was demanding. "I thought you said you had it all sewn up?"

"I thought I did," Allison lied, her eyes closed, her hands clenched. "But the post office thing didn't work out. I still don't even know where he lives."

She was only stalling; she knew that. Sooner or later, somebody would finally locate Joe Burgett. But Allison simply couldn't be the one to offer him up. She understood privacy. She understood the need for a facade. She wore one most of the time. And until Joe decided on his own to come forward, she couldn't do it for him.

"Well, Bill isn't going to be pleased at all," Brook groused blackly. "He's already begun plotting out the marketing campaign for the anniversary, and Dowd is definitely a part of it."

"Even if I do find him, that doesn't guarantee he's going to cooperate," Allison protested instinctively, wrapping her hand around a sweating glass of tea. Her chest hurt again. Her heart beat a thudding tattoo. It wasn't just the deception bothering her, although she wasn't a natural at it by any means. But every time she talked about Joe, she saw him—barechested, glistening, smiling, cocky as hell and shy as a child.

"All Bill wants is the opportunity to get close enough to lob in a few irresistible offers," her managing editor informed her.

"Bill has arms like an octopus. Once he gets ahold of that poor man, he won't let go long enough to let him breathe, much less say no."

Brook sighed. "I know. I actually feel sorry for the old coot. Maybe when you find him you can just...forewarn him a little."

Considering the fact that she'd done just that, Allison couldn't begrudge herself a smile. It broadened at the thought of calling Joe "a coot." That wasn't exactly the term she'd use to describe somebody who looked like he did.

"You're coming, by the way."

Allison's attention snapped back. "Oh, no, Brook, really..."

"Discussion over. If you want to keep your exalted position, you will get a baby-sitter and join us next Saturday for the annual River Roads Blues and Jazz Tour."

Brook knew all about Maggie. She'd been the first person, besides Lucille, who had greeted Allison's tiny daughter without hesitation and without pity. No embarrassing questions, no suppositions, no platitudes. Simply, "God, what a sweetheart." Coming from a woman who looked more like Elvira, Queen of the Night than Grandma Moses, it was quite something.

She heard Allison's hesitation and unerringly diagnosed it. "How long has it been since you've been out?"

"Yesterday," Allison countered. "On the great L. Wood Dowd Hunt."

"I mean for fun."

Allison didn't think this was the time or place to reveal exactly how much fun it had been.

"It is a time-honored tradition—" Brook began.

"Begun last year."

"Only because I was the first person in this mausoleum who realized the benefit of a bit of controlled insanity. Anyway, the bus leaves the office at precisely six. You will be on it, or we will swing by your apartment and harass you and your neighbors until you're evicted."

"Brook—"

"It's the wonderful thing about listening to blues, Allison. You can cry your heart out and nobody notices. See you."

Allison hung up the phone and stared at her tea. Brook knew her, all right. Brook and Lucille, the two people who had become her family in this small city so far from home; the people who had showered her with compassion and support when her own parents had offered nothing but stilted bemusement.

She'd go on the damn outing just to shut Brook up. And because Brook was right. There was nothing like blues to give voice to all that turmoil in her soul. If she could play an instrument, she thought with a wry smile, she'd be the best damn blues player of the century.

The cascade of bells interrupted her. Allison's smile grew, changed. Warmed. She finished her iced tea in a gulp and headed into Maggie's room.

"Hey, you little monkey," she sang to her as she approached. "Are you about ready to get up? It's been awfully quiet in there."

Maggie was silent, watchful, her dark eyes fathomless as they turned at the approach of her mother. There were bolsters on either side of her tiny body, propping up lazy joints and snuggling the little girl into the warmth of security. She wore a bright yellow sleeper today, which made her soft skin glow. When she saw Allison, Maggie smiled.

Allison laughed. That smile bubbled and welled in her, so impatiently awaited, so desperately needed when it had first blossomed on those delicate little features at three months. Recognition, response, delight. Maggie cooed and Allison sang.

"How's my baby girl?" she demanded, pulling the baby into her arms. "How's the prettiest girl in Illinois?"

She had to change her, doing Maggie's passive exercises as she worked. Speaking, naming, reinforcing cognition. She'd bounce a bright ball all around so that Maggie watched it, so that she would begin to reach for it. She would fold her daughter's hands over it, reinforcing Maggie's desire to grasp. She would name each item she used and then make it dance for the little girl, so she would know it. Later, out in the living room, they would work on Maggie's posture, on muscle control and balance. They would be cross-training, getting Maggie used to utilizing both sides of her body and brain, Maggie's least favorite exercise in the world. And then they would struggle through the eating. But for now, Allison simply held her daughter and sang to her.

It didn't matter what, whether it was *Sesame Street* or *Phantom of the Opera*. Maggie loved the sounds, her own voice mimicking with sometimes startling effect her mother's tones. Allison held her daughter's tiny body close, sating herself on her daughter's warmth, inhaling the sweet baby-powder scent that struck every mother down. Opening the curtains, she turned so she could watch the world.

"Only two more months," she promised, feeling that little head nestling against her chin and stroking her back. "Dr. Goldman promises. Then you'll have so much energy, I'll have to get track shoes. You won't get tired out doing exercising or eating or going to the store. You won't have to take your medicine all the time. When the surgery's over, you'll be a fat, sassy little girl."

If she made it through. She might have only two more months to hold Maggie in her arms. Allison couldn't stand it. She squeezed her eyes shut and clutched her daughter to her chest and prayed. And once again, didn't know exactly what to pray for.

"You and me," she whispered when the little girl sang to her. "Just you and me, kid. I'm not sharing you with anybody."

Just then, the phone rang. Allison wouldn't answer it. She never did when Maggie was up, preferring to wait until the little girl was safely occupied after exercising to take the time away from her. But even so she strolled into the hallway to hear the answering machine.

Maggie lifted her head at the sound of the bell and called to it, cackling. Maggie especially enjoyed sounds even more than she loved the bright colors with which Allison had decorated her room. She loved the sound of Allison's voice on the recorder.

"Telephone," Allison crooned from where she held her child. "Hear the telephone?" Her words were instinctive now, so ingrained, she sometimes identified coffee cups and paper clips in the office. In her arms, Maggie squirmed to get to the sound.

"You've reached 555-2120," Allison's voice said from the machine, the tone professional and crisp. "I can't come to the phone right now, but if you'd leave a message, I'll get back to you."

The beep echoed in the rooms, and Maggie tilted her head to it. And then, the sound of smoke.

"I bet you're home. I just called and the line was busy. If you call me right back, I promise you won't get my machine. L."

Allison hovered in the hall, uncertain what to do, her attention torn between the soft bundle in her arms and the hint of laughter that had escaped her machine. She had to talk to him. She had to tell him what she'd decided. She had to convince him to make the first move so he could deal with River Roads on his own terms.

But she wasn't at all sure she could do it now. It was like drinking. You should only do it if you want to, not if you need to. And suddenly, surprisingly, she needed to talk to Joe.

"Let's read," she said to Maggie, turning back to her room. "And then we'll take a walk and yell at the squirrels."

Behind her, the machine beeped into an empty room.

Chapter 3

"Are you avoiding me?" Joe demanded.

There was a short silence on the other end of the line that made him grin. She really needed to learn how to lie.

"Of course not," she said. "I never answer the phone when I'm working."

"Polishing old Unctious to a blinding gleam, were you?"

Then he heard the humor and was satisfied. "Don't get cocky, L. There are other writers out there besides you."

"I bet they don't draw as well as I do."

"Well, considering the fact that the book I'm editing right now is about the founding of the Precious Heart Sisters in the Mississippi Valley, I certainly hope not. I doubt the sainted sisters would like to see their foundress depicted with scales and wings."

"If she was anything like my third grade teacher, she should be."

Allison chuckled, a soft, throaty music. "Then when you write your memoirs, you can illustrate them accordingly."

Joe took a sip of beer, his grin knowing. "I can't write them until I come out of the pseudonym closet."

"Certainly a point to consider."

"A matter much on my mind the last twenty-four hours," he admitted, settling into the creaking oak chair by his kitchen table. Leaning back, he settled his feet atop the table and rested the can on his lap. "Has my cover been blown?"

"Sounds like the next Binkley Brothers book is going to be about monsters in the DEA."

Her voice was wry. Joe could just see the glint in her eyes, the sharp tilt of her head as she spoke. He watched the sun pouring in through the greenhouse windows that had once been a back porch and thought of sharing his house.

"*Miami Nice,*" he chuckled. "I like it. You deserve a cut of the royalties."

"I deserve that just for keeping my mouth shut."

He didn't realize he'd been holding his breath until he let it out, a funny low whooshing sound that decompressed the squeezing in his chest. He'd been ignoring the situation too long, blithely going about his life balancing all its different areas like bright balls as if he could keep doing it forever.

He couldn't. Especially not with Allison in the picture now. It had been different when his editor had been an anxious, middle-aged bald guy with bad dentures. Joe had never felt any particular loyalty to the man or sympathy for his wheedling requests.

But ever since he'd first heard Allison's voice on the phone, things had changed. He'd been delighted by her insight and intrigued by her polite distance. And even when she'd shown up on his doorstep, as sharp and witty as an O. Henry short story, she'd still maintained her restraint. She was as much a mystery to him as the first day she'd introduced herself, a pretty woman with a bright mind and sorrow in her eyes.

And no matter what Joe had promised her, he had the feeling he wasn't about to keep his distance.

"I assume that's why you called," Allison said.

"I was just a little curious."

"Your secret identity's still safe," she assured him. "So far, I've lasted through the whip, the rack and the thumbscrews, and they still haven't wrung it out of me."

"Brave girl. Your bribe will be in the mail." She was grinning. He could hear it. He recognized it because he was grinning, too. "What do we do now?"

"What do you want to do?" she asked.

That was the question, wasn't it? "How long do I have to answer that?"

"I was just the vanguard," she informed him. "The brunt of the marketing forces will attack within two weeks. That's when you're really gonna be in trouble."

He knew darn well he didn't need to offer up his identity. The publishing house could survive quite nicely on the various Dowd myths circulating the country. Every writer short of William Faulkner had been accused of hiding behind the Dowd label to save a reputation and build a new audience. Other popular myths included the eccentric hermit and the prison internee doing his sketches by flashlight after lights-out.

But the problem was that Joe didn't want to leave things status quo with Allison. He wanted to be able to drop in on her at the offices, to call her without disguising his voice. To sit down as they'd done in his kitchen and work together on a book. He wanted enough of an excuse to see her that she wouldn't instinctively shy away, and even though it was an absolute rarity that author and editor needed to even be in the same city to accomplish a book, he figured that the books would do it.

But revealing his identity would still sacrifice his privacy, his normalcy. He needed the security of his work friends as much as he needed his isolation in the workroom high above the river. He needed to be plain old Uncle Joe. Joe the master carpenter who knew all the current dirty jokes and could be counted on for a couple of rounds down at the local tavern. And the minute it got out that good old Joe was the reclusive author of bestselling children's books, that would all change.

"Did you tell them you'd seen me?" he asked.

A pause, as if the admission troubled her. "No. I told them I hadn't been able to find you."

"Can you give me another week?" he asked. "I start a new job tomorrow and my lawyer's out of town. And I don't really want to face that bunch in marketing without all my options lined up."

"Your lawyer also called Burgett?" she countered dryly.

"It's cheaper to keep it in the family. A week, Allison."

"A week," she mused, sounding as if she were checking some kind of calendar. "Yeah. I think I can do that."

"Good. A week from today, then. Where do you want to meet?"

"Ma Bell."

"No way. You want to do this, we do it my way. And I say we do it over drinks."

"I told you. I don't drink."

"Then one drink and a soda. No hassles, Allison. Just someplace I'm not renovating so we can discuss this whole situation uninterrupted by the phone or my family dropping in."

She sighed. "I'm not the one you should be doing that with."

"Well, that's too bad. You're the only one I trust over there."

"L.," she protested. "How can you say that? This is a good house."

"Unless River Roads is the only not-for-profit publisher in the country, it's still the bottom line that counts. And no matter how nice everybody is, that's going to weigh the most in the balance. One week from tonight. Six o'clock. Hawkin's Inn. I'll give you my answer."

Her chuckle was dry. "You sound like a distressed virgin succumbing to an abhorrent proposal."

"Consider me deflowered," he retorted with a grin. "Six?"

"No," she demurred quickly. "That's a bad time for me."

"Five? Four? Three?"

"One." She paused, her voice dying a little with what sounded like surprise. "It's the best I can do."

"Then one it is. I'll meet you there. On second thought, I'll pick you up."

"On third thought," she retorted, "you won't. Hawkin's Inn at one. Bye."

Joe shouldn't have been in such a good mood when he hung up the phone. His peace of mind was threatened. L. Wood Dowd's secret identity hung in jeopardy. Everything he'd been balancing for the past four years was poised to come tumbling down if he weren't careful. And yet, somehow, it wasn't mattering as much as it should.

As he got up to make himself something to eat, he tried to think about what course he should take with his career. Instead, he thought about what it would take to tap into Allison Henley's secrets. He planned his attack with even more care than River Roads had planned theirs and knew without a doubt that he would succeed.

There had been women Joe had been attracted to. Women he'd dated and a few he'd had deeper relationships with. None had so compelled him within minutes of meeting. None had that intriguing depth in their eyes or the darkness that weighted their laughter. None had matched wits so well or commanded such trust.

None had inspired Joe to look for their eyes on his children when he dreamed. Joe had long wanted a family of his own to rival the one into which he'd been born. In a matter of ten phone calls and one visit, he saw Allison Henley there with him.

"Come on, you stinker," Allison prodded gently. "This is good stuff."

Maggie obviously disagreed. No sooner did Allison put the apple sauce in than it reappeared, accompanied by a fierce grimace and a jumble of sounds that did not sound at all pleased.

"I don't care," Allison said, scooping up some more and slipping it back in, careful to compress the spoon against the center of Maggie's tongue so she could more easily process and swallow it.

Babies with Down syndrome were not overly fond of new tactile sensations. Maggie didn't mind playing so much in packing beads or rolling over her upholstered balance tube.

But she hated, absolutely hated, the textures of new foods. That was the reason Allison usually placed her high chair over a tarp on the kitchen floor during feeding time, and why both of them tended to get tired. Because if Maggie was going to eat enough to get her strength up, she was going to have to get used to different textures.

So, while Allison fed her baby, she sang to her to distract her from the less pleasant aspects of the meal.

"Come on, come on, you stinky little snot," she sang to the tune of "Row, Row, Row Your Boat." "I have got a bus to catch, and you are helping not."

God, she was alone in her house too much. It made her laugh. It made Maggie laugh. Allison slipped in more chunky sauce while the little girl's guard was down. It didn't do any good.

"Please, Maggie," she wheedled. "Two more spoonfuls and then I promise I'll quit."

Allison was tired already, and the evening hadn't even begun. She didn't want to go, even for jazz. It would be the first time she'd left Maggie like this for an evening, especially when she was going to be so far away—all the way across the river in St. Louis, which took a good forty minutes, by bus at that. She should have driven herself. She should have said no.

The only problem with that, of course, was that if she'd said no, Brook would have shown up on her doorstep with the entire busload of people.

But what if something went wrong? What if Maggie became ill while she was gone? They'd already been to the hospital twice with congestive heart failure since her birth, spent long agonizing hours separated by cold white walls and fluorescent lights, doctors spouting Latin and nurses comforting with harried hands. Allison couldn't bear it if Maggie had to go through that without her. She couldn't bear the guilt of being away if something happened.

Maggie was laughing again, her eyes sparkling and sly. She had her fingers in the apple sauce and didn't seem to mind the texture so much there. Her lips were as pink as her cheeks. And yet Allison couldn't help seeing her gray and struggling and taped to machines and monitors.

"Lucille's here!" came the call from the front door.

Maggie's head whipped around, her food forgotten. She called to Lucille, her other favorite person in the world.

"I'm not going," Allison said, dropping the spoon in surrender.

"Don't be silly," the woman argued, rounding the corner with her big knitting bag in hand and a scowl to match Maggie's on her face. "You haven't been out since this baby's been born. Don't you think you've done your penance?"

Allison whipped around in her chair, ready to argue. Too aware that Lucille had made her stab just a little too close to home.

Lucille had always been of the pragmatist school of parenting. She shook her head now, her grin broadening.

"How many times I got to tell you, girl? This baby is your blessing, not your judgment."

Allison grimaced, the guilt still sharp in her chest as she got to her feet. "Easy for you to say," she retorted easily. "You only have two kids with disabilities. And neither of them minds eating."

"It's the only thing they don't mind." Lucille bent to tousle Maggie's hair. Maggie reached to her with applesauce ladened hands. "Now, get your lazy behind out of that chair and go to your party. Maggie and I won't even know you're gone."

Maggie knew perfectly well. She waited until Allison was all dressed in her white stretch pants and oversize white-and-aqua-print shirt, grabbed her purse and slid into her flats. Lying on the floor, the little girl was busy batting at a stuffed toy, seemingly oblivious to the goings-on of the adults. Until Allison reached the front door. And then, with all the timing of a Broadway actress, she broke into the most heartfelt sobs a parent ever heard.

Lucille pushed Allison right out the door anyway. Allison told her that if something happened, she'd never forgive her and that she'd call from each place they stopped

along the jazz-bar tour. Lucille told her she wouldn't answer the phone and gave another shove. In the end, Allison
made the bus with ten minutes to spare.

Lucille did hang up the first three times Allison called.
After the fourth time in as many minutes, though, she gave
in and took the information. She took it again from the next
three clubs the tour hit and each time told Allison that the
only thing keeping her from having a good time was herself. Maggie was just fine.

Allison made that last call from a phone wedged in between a one-stall ladies' room and the swinging kitchen
door, a finger in one ear and her head bent as close to the
wall as she could to counter the noise around her. And the
band was still on break.

The bar was called B.B.'s Blues and Jazz, and it took up
the first floor of a brownstone. The walls were bare brick
and the wall decorations old music posters. The bar, a hand-
carved beauty of gleaming wood and hanging glasses, took
up one end and the postage-stamp stage the other. The atmosphere was close, dark and smoky, the perfect place to
hear jazz. Allison wove her way back through the crowd and
resettled herself on the high stool between Brook and Peter
Williamson from PR.

"She's fine, right?" Brook asked, sipping at her beer. Her
hair was as black as her dress, just about as short and
spiked. Huge multicolored earrings swung just shy of her
shoulders every time she moved.

Allison's smile was rueful. "Sue me. I worry."

Brook shook her head. "*I* worry," she corrected her.
"You obsess. But then, I guess you have the right. What did
the doc say the other day?"

Allison took a sip of her drink and looked out over the
crowd. They were all having a good time—laughing, nod-
ding, engaging in ancient mating rituals. Any problems they
might have had seemed to have been left outside the door.
Allison carried hers around with her. Her chest still ached
and her eyes stung. She wanted to be home with her baby
and she never wanted to go home and face the responsibil-

ity. She wanted what she couldn't have and felt guilty for not being more thankful for what she had.

Brook had been right. A blues club was the perfect place to be.

"We're right on target," she told her friend with a smile and a sip of her own soda, not realizing how much she looked like all the other people in the bar. "He'd like her to pick up another pound, but as it stands, surgery's scheduled for June."

Instinctively, Allison checked to see that Peter was busy arguing with the editorial assistant on his other side. Most of the people in the office didn't know the particulars about Maggie. She knew she was probably being unfair to them. They wouldn't act like her family had. But she was still too fragile to carry all their concern as well. Her composure was stretched thin enough.

Brook nodded. "Let me know. I'll be there."

"Oh, you don't—" Allison instinctively protested.

Her friend's expression brooked no argument. "And I'll bring pizza for the waiting room."

Allison's smile faltered, compassion sometimes more difficult to handle than insensitivity. "Thanks. I'd appreciate it."

Behind Allison the band was beginning to filter back onto the stage. She could hear the clatter of instruments being picked up and a quick rattle of a drum. Conversation was going to be quickly limited.

"Hey," Peter called leaning over. "Dawn over here says she knows somebody in the telephone company who could give us the name and address on Dowd's answering machine."

"I tried it," Allison lied immediately. "It's registered to his lawyer at his address."

Brook leaned in. "Have you made any other progress?"

Allison shook her head. "I think something may break this week. I still can't believe you never bothered to find out who this guy was."

Brook shrugged. "It never seemed important. He contacted us as L. Wood Dowd, the name was legal, the lawyer acted as his agent, and we figured it would be enough for a kiddie book that showed up at a couple of airports and grade-school book sales. Don't forget that the Binkleys was our first foray into children's books."

"And nobody minded this go-between situation?"

Brook shrugged. "Nobody really thought much about it. You know how books are written. You can work with an author for five years without ever seeing 'em. Dowd wasn't any different." Leaning in, Brook put on her best clandestine air. "What do you bet after all this that the guy really looks like Jabba the Hut and talks like Truman Capote. Wouldn't Bill just have a fit?"

Allison did her best to keep herself to a smile. If only they knew.

"I still have my money on the prison angle," Peter offered, taking a drag from his cigarette and then punctuating with it. "He's doing ten to twenty for murdering his wife and has tattoos of her face on his back." Fair and thin with a penchant for bomber jackets and jeans, Peter shuddered with the image. Allison thought she detected delight and smiled even more broadly.

"What do you think, Allison?" Dawn asked. "You talk to him."

"...welcome with us tonight," the lead singer announced out of the corner of Allison's eyes, "our friend J.D., who's sittin' in on the sax."

Allison had to wait for the applause to stop before answering, and then pitched her voice over the sudden crescendo of music. John Coltrane, she thought. Sax, keyboards, bass, drums. A tight band. She listened as she spoke.

"I think he's a very shy person who isn't going to want to come within twenty feet of Bill and his roadshow."

"I think I'm in love," Dawn said suddenly, her eyes nowhere near the conversation.

"Nothing unusual there," Brook retorted. "So, Allison, how are you going to convince our wayward scribe to march to the River Roads beat?"

Allison shrugged and busied herself with her soda.

"No, I mean it," Dawn protested, still watching the band.

Allison was amused, considering the fact that all she'd seen up on the stage were old black men who looked like they'd been playing jazz before it was invented. Dawn usually went in more for blond hockey players.

"*Look* at him."

Peter obliged. "He's not my type."

"I know you'll do River Roads proud," Brook threatened Allison over the syncopated wail of harmonizing saxes. "I bet shy little men drop like flies for you."

Allison lifted an eyebrow. "Why does that sound like a thinly veiled threat?"

"Probably because you know that Bill jumped on me with hobnailed boots today because he can't get his ad campaign into gear yet."

"Tell Bill he doesn't need my author to celebrate an anniversary."

Brook just smiled. "You tell him."

Allison was no fool. She knew a checkmate when she heard one.

"I've seen him here before," Peter was saying, stubbing out a cigarette, his attention still following Dawn's. "He's really good."

"I'd sure like to find out," Dawn sighed.

Allison finally gave in and turned to find out what all that hormone overload was about. She saw the drummer, keyboard player and bass player, all grizzled, eyes closed, intensely communing with their muse. And then she saw the two sax players. One black, one white.

Dark hair, just a little gray, furrowed cheeks. Deep brown eyes.

She almost fell right off her stool.

"Oh, my God."

"Didn't I tell you?" Dawn demanded, turning around to slap Allison on the arm.

He was wearing an unstructured charcoal gray suit and black T-shirt and wire-rim glasses. His eyes were closed, and his fingers danced over the keys on his sax. Allison couldn't quite get her mouth to close. He was moving with his music, slow and sinuous, like the snake doing his act for Eve.

"Now, *that's* what I'd like L. Wood Dowd to look like," Brook admitted.

And Allison burst out laughing. Because, of course, it was exactly what L. Wood Dowd looked like.

From *Showdown at the Binkley Saloon* by L. Wood Dowd

It all began when Noxious found the gun beneath Billy's bed. A six-shooter, just like Noxious had seen on the television when Billy had sat up late with the baby-sitter one night. He remembered hard-eyed men spinning the gun in their hands and shooting down the bad guys in black where they stood. He remembered them not being afraid when they had the gun.

"Don't be silly," Unctious said, and then paused. His fierce red eyes began to water and his snout scrunched up.

"Gausheunteit," Ralph said.

"Aa-choo!" It had been a week since Billy's mother had swept under the bed, and Unctious was allergic to dust bunnies. It was very embarrassing for a monster who lived under the bed to be allergic to dust bunnies. It always gave away the surprise when he sneezed just as he was about to reach out to grab ankles.

"God bless you, Unctious!" Billy called from above them.

"Thagyew," Unctious answered, blowing the four nostrils on either side of his head. It made Unctious very cranky that he wasn't able to sneak around. "As I said," he continued. "It's silly for a monster to have a gun. You have terrible claws and fierce teeth and a tail that can break bricks. Why do you need a gun?"

"B-b-because he's af-f-fraid of the d-d-dark," Ralph piped up in his wee little monster hiss.

"That's not funny," Noxious objected, his own slitty green eyes beginning to water up with shame. Because, of course, he was afraid of the dark. Great-Uncle Ferocious wouldn't even talk to him anymore. Mama Binkley had tried to convince him that there was nothing out there but the moon and owls. Papa Binkley had snorted so loud, he'd broken three plates and a window. But Noxious still trembled when the moon set. After all, he knew quite well that there were monsters out in the dark. He couldn't bear to think what else could be out there beyond the bed that could even be worse.

"It's not something monsters do," Unctious stated grandly. "Shoot guns. Only silly people shoot guns."

"Cowboys," Noxious disagreed, trying very hard to hold the six-shooter in his paw. The extra ten fingers kept getting in the way so that every time he tried to spin the gun, it fell on the floor with a thud.

"Police shoot guns!" Billy called out, of course, hearing the monsters' conversation.

Noxious nodded. "And police," he said.

Unctious sneezed. They blessed him.

"But I like cowboys best," Noxious admitted. "I want to be a cowboy."

"You c-c-can't," Ralph hissed the way all younger brothers do. "You're a m-m-m-. . . a monster."

"Can't a monster be a cowboy?"

Ralph and Unctious thought about that. "I think you can only be one thing at a time."

Noxious tried to pull himself up to his full height and hit his head on the bed, scraping off a few scales. "Well, I think that's stupid. I'm going to be a monster and I'm going to be *a cowboy, and if I want to be a ballerina dancer, too, then I will.''*

And so it was the next night that the Binkley Saloon was opened. Noxious was the sheriff. Unctious was Black Bart, and Ralph was the barkeep. Nobody was the ballerina dancer, of course, because that was just too silly.

Chapter 4

Allison listened to him play. Dark, smoky sounds, just like his voice, the instrument an extension of him, his whole body becoming part of the music. He was playing alto sax, riding the underside of the tenor next to him, weaving in and out of melody lines and dancing amid the cascade of keyboard and bass.

He'd been doing this awhile. He'd been doing it with his whole heart, just like he did his books. Just like he did his carpentry. It didn't seem quite possible that one man could have that much passion in his soul, that much dedication. Because each of his interests demanded work. Each cost sweat and grief and joy.

And there was no mistaking the joy in him tonight.

"Allison," Brook observed, "I don't think I've ever seen you like this. Is it your birthday soon? Would you like us to wrap him up for you?"

Allison finally managed to shut her mouth. She couldn't quite believe that nobody at the table could tell that this was the elusive quarry that had taken up so much of the office gossip effort. Here they'd been batting about their ideas of what L. Wood Dowd really looked like, and he was no more than seven feet away.

She wanted to laugh again. She wanted to turn and run before he saw her and gave everything away.

"I've sworn off," Allison demurred even as the song ended and Joe opened his eyes.

Dawn made a funny little strangled noise when he smiled. Allison stifled her chuckles with a fist against her mouth. When Joe began to scan the audience, she figured she was safe. After all, it was dark, and he had a light right in his eyes, a red spot that picked up ruby tones in his hair. Allison was one of a couple hundred in the smoky room.

His eyes went for her as if she were a magnet. They widened. His smile broke open and he waved.

Everybody at the table turned to her for explanation.

"Sworn off?" Brook demanded incredulously. "What was he, the cure?"

"Who is he?" Dawn demanded. "And where have you been hiding him?"

Allison was having a lot of trouble keeping a straight face. She was looking down at her soda, trying to think up a good lie, and then settled for any lie at all, when she realized it was already too late.

"Allison," Joe greeted her, coming around to stop between Allison and Brook. "What are you doing here?"

Allison looked up, trying to warn him with her eyes. It didn't help that his after-shave was distracting her. It was dark and smoky, too, and it made her want to bury her nose in his chest. "I'm here with my friends from work," she said, gesturing. "From the *publishing* house?"

The light in his eyes was mischievous. "No kidding." He nodded with pleasure, including everybody at the table in his greeting as he got comfortable, one foot up on the rung of the high bar table, his hand on the table's edge. "Allison's told me all about you. Glad you could come down."

"Allison didn't tell us she knew somebody who played down here," Peter accused.

"It's a secret," Joe allowed.

"That she knows?"

"That I play. My wife doesn't like it."

Allison was trying very hard to keep quiet.

Brook lifted a wary eyebrow. "What does she think you're doing?"

"Having an affair."

He got them there.

"She'd rather you have an affair," Brook finally managed to say, "than play the sax?"

Joe nodded brightly. "Oh, sure. She'd be divorcing me anyway. It's just the music that makes her mad."

Brook looked over at Allison now. "And where did you meet Allison?"

"Oh, years ago," Joe allowed.

Allison nodded. "Years."

"Here?" Brook asked.

"No, not here. California."

"She's never been to California," Brook accused.

"New York," Allison blurted out.

"That's right," Joe agreed with an easy nod. "New York. Columbia University."

Brook turned to Allison. "You went to Brown."

"I had a friend at Columbia," she said. "A...good friend."

"You went to Columbia, too?" Peter asked.

"I played there," Joe said. "On the corner. Allison dropped quarters in my sax case every day. I fell in love with her."

"What about her husband?" Brook asked.

Joe never hesitated. "I knew him."

"Jerk," Brook said.

Joe looked up.

"Her husband."

Joe nodded, an eye back to Allison. "The worst."

"I'm glad she divorced him."

"Me, too. That means she's available again."

Allison couldn't quite take her eyes from his, caught in their little bubble of laughter, united in their scam, intrigued by the new mysteries each had discovered in the other. Her chest, so long sore and empty, filled with the most delicious exhilaration.

"Allison is very rude," Dawn simpered, chin on hand and eyes fluttering like failing moths. "She hasn't even introduced you yet."

Probably because she wasn't exactly sure what name he wanted to use.

"J.D.," he offered easily, resting the sax on his hip.

Giggling, Dawn held out a hand. "Dawn Jenkins."

Joe shook the hand and turned for further introductions. Allison provided them.

"Allison told me you're trying to unearth L. Wood Dowd," Joe said to Brook, damn near giving Allison a heart attack. "I've always wondered who the hell that guy is. Having any luck?"

"None. Any ideas?"

Grinning, he shook his head. "I'll bet he's some scrawny, pimply-faced guy who has his mother buried underneath the rosebushes." Dawn giggled. Brook scowled. Allison held her breath. "I mean, after all, the Binkley Brothers are just a little too nice, y'know?"

"You don't like them?" Brook asked.

Allison came very near to closing her eyes entirely and wishing herself away.

Joe was shaking his head. "Give me some meat for my monsters. I want a couple of kids really chewed up for effect."

"Well, thank God you're not the one writing those books," Allison offered, figuring everybody would hear the strain in her voice.

Joe grinned like a bandit. "Yeah, I know. You'd all be broke, and I'd have every shrink in the country trying to reduce the size of my head."

"How did you two end up in Alton together?" Brook suddenly asked.

Allison hesitated a heartbeat too long. Joe had no trouble at all. "I was standing on a street corner," he said. "Playing my sax. The housing starts were down and I needed a little money. And suddenly, this quarter drops into my case. A quarter? I think. Who's cheap enough to drop a quarter into my case for the kind of music I play? And then I looked up and there she was.''

"Allison," Dawn sighed.

"No. Some cheapskate broad I'd never seen before with a poodle and a bad dye job. But Allison was standing right behind her. She'd moved here, and she knew I was from here originally.''

"And she began searching out street corners," Brook offered dryly.

Joe laughed. "The phonebook. My mother told her."

Allison almost believed him. No wonder he wrote books.

Joe straightened from the table. "Well, I have to get back up and play. You gonna be here for a while?''

"No," Allison answered.

"Sure," the rest disagreed. "The bus picks us up at closing.''

Joe leveled his gaze on Allison, and there was no doubt as to what he was thinking. "Good," he allowed, his voice as dark as his cologne. "Then I'll be seeing you a little later.''

Allison couldn't quite move. Her heart had begun to thud again, and she thought her palms were damp. Joe's eyes were so dark, so deep, so soft. She just wanted to slip in and never find her way back out again.

"It's good seeing you again, honey," he murmured. And before Allison could so much as protest, he bent to kiss her.

She could smell cigarette smoke and after-shave and Joe. She could feel the scrape of his beard against her cheek. She could swear she heard the sudden trip of his heart. She tasted coffee and Scotch on his breath. And she felt the slow, sweet melting heat of his lips.

He wrapped a hand around her head and held her to him. He teased her mouth with his tongue. And then he straightened, and Allison saw her own confusion mirrored in his eyes.

Brook at least waited until he'd made his way back to the bandstand to comment. "No wonder his wife's divorcing him.''

If Allison would have heard her, she would have laughed.

"And they had no idea who he was?" Lucille demanded two hours later.

Allison was still laughing. "None. They just thought I was hiding this oversexed, sax-playing carpenter somewhere in my past. I tell you, Lucille, I felt like I was in a Marx Brothers movie."

Shaking her head, Lucille downed the rest of her coffee. "I surely wish I could have seen that. I'm gonna have to meet that boy one of these days."

Allison slid off her flats and wiggled her toes, curiously content at having spent the past six hours with a group of twenty people in various states of inebriation.

"He's going to give me his answer Tuesday."

Lucille looked up from where she was stuffing an afghan-in-progress back into her bag. "You mean he may come out of hiding?"

Allison shrugged.

Lucille's eyes narrowed. "What do you want him to do?"

Allison studied the tops of her toes for a minute, seeing instead Joe's face as he'd played his music. Eyes closed, features intense, his whole body immersed in the rhythm and mood of the melody. She thought of what she should be trying to do and what she wanted.

She thought of the simple declaration of one kiss, and realized that her loyalties had definitely shifted.

"I don't know," she finally answered, looking up to find that her friend understood her answer before she did. "He's a really special man. I don't want him compromised just for an ad campaign."

With Allison's words, Lucille straightened with a sharp nod of her head. "Good girl. Be sure you tell him that Tuesday, 'cause it's a cinch nobody else will."

It was the only goodbye Allison got. Closing the door on Lucille's retreating figure, she padded back through the house, picking up the odd toy and shoe as she went.

The silence soothed her, cool and dim, passive. Nobody was demanding decisions or answers or loyalty. No one surprised or disappointed. No one slid in under her defenses and set her senses into a tailspin with a kiss.

No one interloped on her peace of mind.

But that wasn't true, of course. Tiptoeing into Maggie's room, Allison saw that the rose she'd placed that morning was just trembling at the edge of bloom, its fragile pink petals as soft as baby down, its scent haunting the quiet air. Maggie slept on her stomach, her hand curled up by her mouth where she could suck on it in a pinch, her little rump flat. Allison automatically repositioned her legs just a little and stroked the back of her head.

And uncovered all the dread and indecision and guilt that always awaited her in this room.

Her baby. Her life. Already so intricately entwined with her own heart that if Maggie's heart stopped beating, she knew hers would, too. Cherished beyond any gift or legacy she'd ever received. And still, sometimes, in flashes, in swift surges of rancor, resented. Grieved for. Frightened of.

These were the monsters that lived beneath Allison's bed, awful beasts no one else could see because Allison wouldn't share them. How did she tell someone that no matter how much she loved her daughter, she still yearned in a small place in her heart for the bright-eyed little beauty she'd dreamed of while she'd rubbed her belly and sung songs in the night. How could she admit that she was sometimes angry at her child for not being perfect? For not being the ideal that other mothers had? How could she express the dreadful shame that it might have been something *she'd* done that had hurt her baby?

Allison knew in her head the answers to all her dilemmas. She'd read books, talked to other Down syndrome parents. She was, after all, a realist. But the head didn't always communicate with the heart, with the conscience, and still the pain bubbled there, just below the surface. Just where she wouldn't let anyone else see.

Even worse, tonight, was the added burden of Joe Burgett. He was an intriguing, sexy man. She was attracted to him, and he, apparently, to her. In the normal course of events, the two of them would see each other socially—a movie, a meal, maybe a concert or a few sets of music down at the club. They'd talk and plan and slowly entwine in the dance of mating. Testing, tasting, tempting each other with the fruits of possibility. They might make love and they might fall in love.

In the normal course of events. But there was nothing normal about her situation. Allison had rationally made her decision not to date. She knew what she'd be asking of a man. She knew her chances that a man wouldn't be willing to accept her situation much less embrace it. After all, Allison hadn't even heard from Brian in three months, and it was his daughter who was scheduled for surgery.

But suddenly, tonight, after seeing the rare life in Joe Burgett's eyes, hearing his music, tasting his laughter, her decision ate at her.

Joe gave her laughter. He restored madness and whimsy to her life. He surprised her anew every time she saw him and enchanted her each time he smiled. He infected her with one kiss and an hour of silly game playing. She needed that, needed him. She wanted to be able to break down her own self-made barriers and let Joe close.

But she couldn't. And briefly, terribly, she resented Maggie for it.

The weather on Tuesday warmed into the seventies. The sky was dappled in fluffy white clouds, and willows draped vivid yellow-green steamers against the new grass. The air throbbed with life and swept the city with the smell of dark earth and brilliant flowers. Up on the cliffs overlooking the Mississippi, forsythia bloomed and trees whispered.

"You really expect me to believe this," Allison was saying, her hands on hips as she stood in Joe's kitchen.

Joe stood at the sink washing grease off his hands. His good black slacks and blue T-shirt were doomed for the wash, and another greasy streak decorated his cheek. An old compact car with its hood up sat out in his driveway.

"I swear," he assured her. "My sister had to get one of the kids to the doctor, and her car conked out on her. I tried, but..."

"You're a mechanic, too?"

Joe grinned and Allison felt her stomach skid. "I believe the term is 'Renaissance man.'"

He earned another scowl. "I don't believe I read anywhere that da Vinci fixed fuel pumps."

Joe was completely unrepentant. "He probably designed them. I promise I didn't drag you out here under false pretenses. The reservations are made at Hawkin's, and if I can do a quick change, we can still make it."

Shutting off the water, he grabbed a towel and slapped his hands dry. Allison dumped her purse onto the table and plopped into one of the chairs. It creaked alarmingly and swayed a bit, but held her.

"We can take care of this right here, you know," she offered.

He yanked his shirt out the waistband of his slacks and then over his head. "No, we can't."

Allison deliberately looked down at the table. "Why?"

As if in answer, young voices rose in protest outside and the screen door slammed. Allison looked back up to see one small clone of Joe and one of Opie from *The Andy Griffith Show.* Both looked to be in worse shape than Joe, but they didn't seem to notice as much. They were sweaty as six-year-olds get and arguing about baseball cards. That was when Allison realized that the one who looked like Opie was a girl.

"Allison," Joe said, swiping at his face with his shirt and then tossing it over his shoulder, "I'd like you to meet Marcy and Bobby. Niece and nephew respectively, of my little sister."

"I thought she was at the doctor's."

"The other one."

Allison tilted her head. "How many sisters do you have?"

"Three. And three brothers. The count on nieces and nephews right now is twelve, with two on the way."

Allison looked at the two bright-eyed imps and let out a breath. "Good Lord."

"Tell him, Uncle Joe," Marcy demanded, red faced. "A Bob Gibson is too more valuable than an old José Canseco."

"Oh, Marcy, you're such a dweeb," Bobby snapped. "Bob Gibson didn't even have a nine hundred number."

"Last I heard," Joe offered evenly. "Nine hundred numbers don't affect sale prices of baseball cards."

"See?" Marcy shrilled with delight.

Allison watched with unspeakable envy. For just that brief moment, her heart broke all over again. She bet nobody had to pull that little girl up from her back twenty times a day to teach her to sit. They didn't have to teach her to crawl, bending unwilling knees, flattening palms, moving one side and then the other until it seemed the only thing her mother did with her life for months without seeing any progress.

"Does Uncle Joe take you to the ballgame?" Bobby suddenly demanded of her.

"Nope," Allison admitted. "He sure doesn't. Does he take you?"

"Yeah, all the time. There's a special nieces-and-nephews night at the ballpark, and he takes all of us."

Allison blinked. "All twelve?"

Bobby grimaced as if Allison were surely the most stupid person on the face of the earth. "Well, not the babies. Just the big kids. Marcy and me and Ted and Ellen and Betsy and Sam. And Mike when he's not grounded for sneaking downstairs after everybody's in bed and playing video games."

Allison nodded. "Sounds like fun."

It sounded as if Uncle Joe doted on his family, especially on the children. It sounded as if he had good reason to.

"Any more questions, you guys?" Joe asked. "'Cause if there aren't, Allison and I have to get going." He leaned close, confiding. "She's taking me out to lunch."

Obviously the brother and sister were still years shy of interest in the opposite gender. The general consensus was a pair of scowls and yuckie noises. Joe scooted the pair of them out the door and headed for the stairs.

"Does your sister live close?"

"The whole family lives close," he admitted.

He came back down in gray slacks and a cream-colored V-neck sweater. Allison had been nervous enough facing this meeting. Every few minutes, he kept making it worse. She couldn't take her eyes off him, off the gleam of water in his hair, the strong arms that flexed beneath pushed up sleeves, the wicked glint in chocolate brown eyes. Allison saw the bemusement in his eyes when she grabbed her purse and led the way back outside, but she didn't say anything. All she could think about was self-incrimination.

"So," she said as she turned the car back onto the road. "Have you made up your mind yet?"

"Oh, no you don't," he retorted, seat belt snapped and window rolled down. "I said we'd have that discussion at Hawkin's, and that's where it's going to be."

Allison rolled down her own window and let the wind pick through her hair and blouse. "All right, then," she suggested, unable to help but be invigorated by the sweet spring air. Maybe by the company as well. "Tell me about your family."

Joe turned to her. "I thought I just did that. Three sisters, three brothers, twelve new generational members. Remember?"

"Do *they* know what Uncle Joe does when he's not taking the kids to the ballgame?"

"Which?" he asked. "The carpentry, the books or the sax?"

Allison scowled. "Any of it. All of it." She turned on him. "Is there anything else you do I should know about, just so I don't trip over you by accident again? Brain surgery? The priesthood? Ambassador to the U.N.?"

His laughter was deep-throated and easy. "I figured I'd put off my race for the senate until I finished *There's a Monster in My Bathroom.*"

It was Allison's turn to laugh. "And the sax? Any road tours? Record dates with the Rolling Stones?"

"Just B.B.'s. They're all friends there."

Allison heard the emotions simple words could hold. History, loyalty, passion. It added to the oddly sweet ache in her chest.

"Did you really play on the street corners at Columbia?"

His grin was mischievous. "Did you really have an old friend who went there?"

Allison shook her head with amazement. "I still can't believe I let you get away with that."

"*Let* me?" he retorted. "In this county, they call that aiding and abetting. That one gal who looked like Vampira wasn't sure whether to shake my hand or spray it with disinfectant."

"She's my boss—who, by the way, is even smarter than she is nice. The guy in early motorcycle was in PR."

"And the blonde with trouble breathing?"

"Editorial assistant."

"Are you really divorced?"

"Are you really having an affair?"

Allison couldn't believe she'd said it. What was worse, she couldn't believe that she really wanted to know. Attached? Interested? Available? It didn't made any difference. It never had.

But Joe didn't seem to hear anything but the irreverent humor in her voice. "Only with Ruby."

Allison found it more difficult to look noncommittal than she'd anticipated. "The gal with the poodle and the bad dye job?"

"The sax."

"Ah." She shouldn't feel that quick slide of relief. She shouldn't have such a silly grin on her face.

"And the divorce?"

She shrugged, her attention ostensibly on traffic as she neared town. "Old news."

"Are you really from New York?"

"Born and bred. I worked at Wilson Walters Publishing before striking out for the great midwest."

There was a small silence as Joe absorbed that latest information. "If you'll pardon my saying so—"

"It's not exactly a giant leap upward on the publishing food chain from Wilson Walters to River Roads?" she finished for him. "I know. But it's more intimate. I have more autonomy. And I get to do more than just existentialist treatises on the futility of life and man's general inhumanity to man.''

It was an excuse that didn't always wash, but Allison wasn't the kind of person to explain that she'd stayed in Alton after her divorce because she was too afraid to interrupt her child's medical care this close to surgery. That the sudden upheaval of a move back home wouldn't benefit either of them, especially when Allison wasn't really at all sure of her welcome back there with a disabled child. Her parents hadn't been much on parenting her. She couldn't really see them suddenly struck down with a call to grandparenthood.

''Why Alton?''

''My husband had been transferred here in the distant past,'' she admitted. ''I came, I liked, I stayed. He didn't.''

''And you don't secretly dream of the big city?''

Allison did look over this time, hearing something new in Joe's voice, something she couldn't quite identify yet. ''Not enough to get restless.''

As she and Joe lapsed into a comfortable silence, she realized New York was the farthest thing from her mind. Ever since Maggie's birth, she'd been lucky to set foot from one day to the next. Gaging her life by seconds, then minutes, and finally days. Dreaming now of tiny miracles where she'd once taken big ones for granted.

But that wasn't something she'd tell Joe Burgett. If she did, he'd already be too close. He'd insinuate himself into her life with his soft brown eyes and quirky smile and then leave again when the going got too tough. He'd give her hope when she knew that hope was something measured in precious drams.

But she liked him. He made her laugh. He betrayed a joie de vivre most people only aspired to, and it was as intoxicating as the spring wind that rushed through her window. Maybe, she thought as she pulled her car into the parking lot of the Hawkin's Inn, she could settle for that. Hold him carefully at arm's length, their relationship a comfortable professional one. They'd talk on the phone and send funny little notes back and forth with line editing and galleys and contracts. And maybe, on occasion, when Maggie was stronger and Allison braver, she'd venture back down to B.B.'s and listen to him play his saxophone again.

But nothing more. No more surprise kisses that seduced with their sweet life. No more visits to that funny, big, handsome house up on the hill where he was comfortable enough to forget his shirt and encouraged his family to wander in unannounced. No more gentle forays into her past, because that would be disastrous. She might just tell him. And then, no matter how much he tried, he wouldn't be able to keep it from his eyes. The pity. The revulsion. The disappointment.

It would be the one thing that would kill Allison. So she simply wouldn't chance it, which seemed an easy enough decision when made in the parking lot of a busy restaurant.

Joe was feeling reckless today. He'd slept badly last night and the night before, plagued with half-remembered dreams and painful physical results. He'd replayed that kiss in his mind over and over, the taste of sugar on Allison's lips, the scent of mysteries and dusk on her skin, the whisper of her hair against his fingers.

An impulsive move, that kiss. A miracle. Joe wasn't a romantic. At least, he didn't consider himself one, having successfully fended off some pretty intense involvements born of hormones and loneliness. He was one of the last of the family to remain single, and until about two months ago, it had suited him just fine. He did what he wanted when he wanted, and nobody but his mother and sisters hassled him about it. Since he didn't have to face any of them first thing every morning, that didn't bother him at all.

But ever since that soft, patient voice had first called him ''L.,'' he'd been finding that his rooms were getting larger, emptier. That all those kids who hung around his house weren't enough, and that the Binkley Brothers demanded being read to children of his own.

He'd been intrigued. From the moment he'd met Allison face-to-face, her eyes wide and alarmed at the sight of a half-naked man standing in front of her, he'd been enchanted. The better he knew Allison, the more he was becoming ensnared. After all, he'd never intentionally disabled his sister's car for *any* other woman, just to make sure he could spend more time with her.

"You really haven't moved more than five miles from home in your entire life?" Allison was demanding after Joe's rendition of "My Life in Alton." They were seated on the patio behind the original nineteenth-century inn, sharing the sunshine with the lunchtime crowd and a sprinkling of brave birds cadging free crumbs.

"No real reason to," he said. "Besides, I'd miss the kids, and without them there would be no Binkleys."

Allison conceded the point with a tilt of her head. "You've never been married yourself?"

"Nope. Not yet. I'm waiting for somebody who can put up with odd hours, odder habits and the influx of family members anytime, day or night."

"You know you've set a dangerous precedent with that nieces-and-nephews night at the ballpark, don't you? They're going to expect that until they're twenty-one."

"No problem. I'll take 'em when I take my kids."

"What your kids? Is that something else your wife's going to need to know about?"

"Only that she gets to have them. I want to fill the house. That's why I bought it, so all the Burgett grandkids can fit inside on Christmas morning, and the noise level will be deafening. I want to get a piano in there for them to pound on, just like I did, and a swingset and a basketball net and maybe a train track."

"When are you going to have time for all this?" she asked, and Joe didn't notice that her voice had grown quiet. "You have a pretty full schedule."

Joe shrugged. "You can always fit in something important."

She studied her glass intently. "Children are important to you?"

"Let me put it to you this way," he explained, because something this vital had no real words. "I had to cancel a gig down at B.B.'s last month because it coincided with nieces-and-nephews night. And those weren't even *my* kids.''

If the waitress hadn't arrived just then to take their orders, Joe might have admitted more. He was glad he didn't. Allison didn't seem the type to be railroaded, and that was just what he felt like doing.

Joe also knew that it was time to pay the piper the minute the waitress sauntered off with the orders for French-dip beef and salad.

''All right,'' Allison said, the sunlight dappling her through the trees on the restaurant terrace. ''We've sat down, we've ordered, we've discussed weather and families and the state of television. It's time to talk business.''

Joe was perfectly happy just drinking his iced tea and watching the breeze play through Allison's hair. It was a perfect afternoon, warm and bright, the world muted and distant beyond the tree-ringed restaurant.

''Well,'' he said easily, ''unless there are any more problems with *Saloon,* I'm going to concentrate on the *Bathroom* book. I'm about a third of the way finished with the story. Illustrations begin next week, probably. What do *you* think a gremlin looks like?''

She tilted her head a little. ''Don't you know?''

Joe grinned. ''I've polled the kids. The general consensus is that they're short and dumpy and have big noses. But, of course, this one has to be a fairly attractive gremlin. At least by monster standards.''

''Then give it blue hair.''

''Blue? Why?''

She shrugged. ''I don't know. It seems kinda fun.''

Joe nodded. ''Blue it is. Billy's mother also gets new shoes in this book.'' Billy's mother had never been seen except from the knees down. New shoes was quite an event.

Allison's smile was wry as she took a sip of her iced tea. ''A woman couldn't ask for much more.''

''Except to know whether her author is going to come clean in public, I imagine.''

''I imagine.''

She didn't betray her sudden tension. Still, Joe could feel it, something more than company coercion, something tight and heavy in her eyes that made him set his iced tea back down without another taste.

"What are you going to do, Joe?" she asked gently.

Her brow was furrowed, serious, intent. Sincere. Joe wanted to take a finger and rub away the crease that seemed much too set between her eyes. He wanted to caress her eyes closed and let them rest. He didn't know why, but it seemed they never did. There was always something they carried, some unspoken burden that stole the light from Allison's eyes.

"What do *you* think I should do?" he asked.

Her eyebrow quirked just a little. "Seriously?"

He nodded.

Briefly she looked around. Then she dipped her head, as if gathering courage, tact, maybe wisdom. Her one hand clutched her glass and the other lay flat against the oak table. "I think," she finally said, lifting those serious eyes back to him, "that you should only forfeit your privacy judiciously. Once you lose it, you won't get it back. And as much as I like them, the people in publicity won't really care."

Joe couldn't help smiling. His lawyer had been adamant. Nobody, he'd insisted, would look out for Joe's welfare. Joe was a commodity now, and the bottom line for commodities was profit. Joe was the only one who would look out for Joe. Joe was going to have to introduce his lawyer to Allison.

"I did check my contract," he said. "The company doesn't have any rights to my face. I would be perfectly justified to walk if they insisted on it."

"Would you?"

He didn't answer right away. Fingering the beads of sweat on his glass, he considered what he'd already decided. "Yes," he finally admitted, meeting her gaze head-on.

Then Allison smiled, and relief washed through Joe. "I'll tell them," she said.

"I could have my lawyer do it," Joe offered. "He lives for stuff like that."

But Allison shook her head. "No," she disagreed. "I'll do it. After all, they might not take L. Wood Dowd's lawyer's word for it how very distressed the poor little old man was over the company's request. They might think the lawyer's making it all up—in his client's interest, of course. I, on the other hand, don't have any interests in mind but River Road's."

"You're sure?"

"I see L. Wood as about sixty-five, with a bow tie and suspenders, who lives with his mother and two cats, and who watches *Jeopardy* in the afternoon. He's a widower, poor thing, and writes the books for his grandkids. But, of course, none of that is for publication."

If there had been any question in Joe's mind about Allison, her delight in her own fabrication dispelled them all. He didn't have to keep seeing this woman, he had to marry her. And if there was one thing Allison Henley didn't appreciate yet, it was that Joe Burgett didn't understand the meaning of the word *no*.

Chapter 5

Allison hoped that Joe was acquainted with the word *no*. He was going to need to repeat that word a lot the next time they talked, just so she had an official reaction to Bill's hysterical demands....

She actually hadn't minded walking into Bill's office the day before. He'd been on the phone when she'd knocked, but he'd waved her anxiously into one of the wing chairs on the other side of his desk. Most of the paint and gloss of River Roads had ended up in this office so Bill could court the public. He had a corner office with two sets of windows looking out over the rolling town of Alton from what had once been a warehouse. High ceilings whirred with ceiling fans, and pristine white walls were covered in posters of some of River Roads' regional successes, from *Women of the Civil War* to *St. Louis Blues*. The ficus were fake, but the leather on the wing chairs wasn't.

"You've seen him?" he'd asked without preamble as he dropped the receiver back into place. Bill was middle-aged, overweight and chronically agitated. Somebody forever wasn't doing something right—never Bill—or was costing too much when they did. Even before Allison could answer, he'd lit a cigarette from a butt in his ashtray and had run a quick hand through thinning brown hair.

Allison took a deep breath and settled herself more comfortably into the chair. "I've seen him."

Absurdly, she felt as if they were speaking of religious visions—or maybe an Elvis sighting.

Bill nodded briskly and leaned forward, his hands clenched on his desk. "And?"

"The long and short of it is, he has no real interest in changing the status quo."

Bill almost came right off his chair. "You obviously didn't make it clear enough how important this is to him, Allison."

Allison would have smiled, but she knew Bill would take it the wrong way. "He doesn't even talk to his mailman, Bill. I can't imagine him getting down and dirty with Geraldo."

But Bill shook his head, still not hearing an answer he was happy with. "What kind of person is he? Is he weird or something? A pervert?"

She actually considered telling him yes. It was the only surefire way to make him back off, because if she came up with an author who had an unholy interest in rubber and chains or lived with the corpse of his Aunt Millie, the last place Bill would want that information was in the national press.

"He's frail," she said instead, forming again her illusion of the bow tie. "An eccentric, maybe, but no pervert. He just needs his privacy, and he knows that he won't have it anymore if he agrees with your proposal."

But Bill wouldn't stop shaking his head. "Not acceptable. He's a folk hero now. He can't hide behind his health."

"He did mention invoking his lawyer, if necessary."

A brief wave of disbelief. "It's a matter of romancing the man, Allison. Sweet-talk him."

Allison shrugged. "Be happy to, but it's not going to help."

Bill was suddenly taken with a new idea. "We could actually use the hermit thing, if necessary. Frail old man who can only express his love for children through his work."

"I wouldn't," Allison suggested diffidently, getting to her feet. "Don't forget the lawyer. His anonymity is part of that contract, and if we break it, he has every right to go across to Red Apple."

Red Apple was the national benchmark for children's books, lots of money and gloss and promotion. Just the mention of the company sent Bill's hand into a desk drawer for antacids.

"I don't want to change this ad campaign," he insisted. "I don't want to sound threatening, but you know how important Dowd and this campaign are going to be. It would be to your best interests to get an affirmative out of him. You have until June."

She didn't care if she had until the turn of the century, Allison thought now as she sat at her dining room table poring over the drawings for *Showdown at the Binkley Saloon,* she wasn't about to force Joe Burgett into offering himself up.

There was such magic in Joe's creatures, such a wonderfully empathetic sweetness. How could you not like a monster who had an imaginary playmate? The thing Bill didn't understand was that it was Joe's imagination that sold these books, not his personal appearances. Oh, people would be fascinated for a short while if he came clean. Book sales might lift for a bit. But after the first rush of publicity, it would still be the books that would make the difference. And by then the fine balance Joe kept in his life that enabled him to produce these little masterpieces would be shattered. He'd be too famous to slip back into his life and too busy to reclaim his peace....

"Mamamama," Maggie crooned from where she was playing in the living room.

"Hello, pretty girl," Allison instinctively responded, her head still bent over her work, her thoughts of the day before interrupted.

"Mamama," Maggie repeated more insistently.

"Yes, sweetheart." The last four times Maggie had interrupted her, it had been to show her the teddy bear she had in her hands. She was on her tummy, and was at an age to scoot a little. Her little brow pursed up in concentration, her natural curiosity overcame her disinclination to work hard. So Allison put everything just a little bit out of reach.

"Mamama-a-a!" Insistence had turned to something that sounded suspiciously like distress, and Allison turned around.

Her jaw dropped. Her chest caught fire.

"Oh, my God, Maggie," she whispered, coming slowly to her feet. "Oh, my God."

Every step a baby took was precious to her mother, but when a baby with Down syndrome mastered a new task, it was like a gift. A reward for the slogging, tedious work that the parent did for the baby who had been deprived of its natural drive to develop.

The accomplishment was one thing. The fact that Maggie had gained a new skill prematurely to predictions was almost a blow. Kids with Down's had trouble with balance and muscle control. Therefore the big moves like rolling, crawling, sitting and walking were usually delayed. Sometimes a little, sometimes a lot, depending on the child. That average was always lengthened when a baby had the extra handicap of a dicey heart to stifle energy and enthusiasm.

The average age for a normal baby to roll over was four months. For a baby with Down's, the average was closer to eight, with some not mastering the task until their twentieth month. Maggie was six months old.

Allison walked up to her surprised baby and crouched down above her, her eyes filled with tears even as she smiled. "You rolled over. You're on your back!"

Maggie still wasn't sure she was pleased about it. Her arms and legs waved a bit awkwardly so that she looked like a tipped over turtle. But an accomplishment was an accomplishment. The minute the baby saw her mother smile, she burst into delighted laughter.

Allison scooped her up into her arms, laughing and dancing with her startled little girl, the tears she spilled sweet and heartfelt. Hope came in the tiniest of drams, but sometimes the measure overflowed.

One of the most frustrating, frightening things about Down syndrome was that there was absolutely no way to predict how affected the child was until she began to develop. No one could say how slowly they would speak or walk or run. At least today, Maggie was beating the odds.

"You are brilliant," Allison sang. "Brilliant and beautiful and a great singer to boot."

She wanted to call someone, to share their success. Allison danced over toys and through the dining room and to the phone in the kitchen. With Maggie still in her arms, she picked up the phone and began dialing. And only realized halfway through the number that she'd been dialing Joe.

She slammed the receiver back into place, her hand trembling. What was she doing? Why would she have instinctively called Joe? She didn't know him well enough. Certainly not as well as Lucille or Brook. And yet it had been *his* excitement she'd wanted to hear, *his* praise for Maggie's accomplishment.

He didn't even know she had Maggie. How could he celebrate her achievement? How could he even understand its magnitude when he was surrounded by children blessed with health and normalcy. He might have the insight to draw monsters who betrayed a child's fears and yearnings. But those were normal children, normal little monsters who didn't have to battle a faulty chromosome.

Suddenly, for the first time since Maggie was born, Allison missed having a partner. Someone to buffer the fear and celebrate the successes. Someone who had as much at stake in this little girl of miracles as Allison did.

She felt the loneliness of those quiet little rooms even more acutely than when she paced in the hours before dawn, because for the first time since making her decision, the cost of her isolation had a name. She hadn't been on the verge of calling just anybody, but one person in particular.

"Tell you what, munchkin," Allison promised, nuzzling her daughter's downy neck and producing a new cascade of giggles. "We need to go out and get you a new rose. I'd say this calls for a detour for ice cream at Lucille's."

"Mamamama," Maggie answered, settling in against Allison's chest, and Allison wondered if her daughter could feel the ache in her own heart.

She missed Joe's call by five minutes.

Joe was upstairs in the third-floor workroom staring out big windows into a trilling, chirruping spring night when Allison called him back. He'd spent the day on the job, finishing up a half-a-million-dollar house in the hills overlooking Alton, and had come home to a decision. Spread out before him were several quick sketches he'd done for his next book, a tome about monsters, bathtime and clean ears. In the last week or so, his concept had changed.

"I guess you want to know if it's safe to come out of your house," Allison said without much preamble.

Joe stepped over to turn down the Marsalis brothers on the stereo and then settled into his rocker, where some of his best monsters had been hatched.

"I haven't seen any minicams lurking about today," he admitted. "So I assumed that the meeting with the marketing people went well."

"Well," she countered with a little smile in her voice. "It went. I came very near to telling him that you had a penchant for whips and chicken entrails just to quell his enthusiasm."

Joe chuckled as he closed his eyes and conjured up the sly humor in Allison's eyes. He didn't question the easy companionship he felt when talking to her on the phone, or the sudden, harsh ache for the feel of her in his arms. It was a natural evolution, or so he'd heard from every family member who'd been down this particular path. The curious contrast of pleasure and pain just the sound of a person's voice ignites.

"Is the company giving you a lot of trouble over this?" he asked in all sincerity.

"No," she said quickly. "Nothing an old campaigner like myself can't handle. I have kind of let it slip a little that you do have a heart condition and a bad prostate, though."

"Hey, and I appreciate it," Joe retorted. "That kind of rumor will do so much for my popularity."

"It won't ever get out of the publishing house. If it does, you can sue us all. Of course, you'd probably have to show up in court, and the press would end up covering the trial, and Bill would get his publicity after all...."

"Thanks. I'd rather have a bad prostate."

"Think nothing of it."

"Will you tell me something?"

"Sure."

"Now that you know who I am, just how long do you plan on keeping it a state secret?"

There was a pause, and then Allison's voice, a little smaller, as if disappointed in him somehow. "Don't you trust me?"

He instinctively shook his head, frustrated at his own clumsiness. "With my life, lady. That wasn't what I meant. What I was trying to say was that it seems unfair that you have to keep that kind of secret from all the people you work with."

"They don't have a right to it," she retorted easily, honestly. "Come to think of it, *I* don't have a right to it."

"You have my personal dispensation. Are you sure you don't mind?"

"I love secrets. Especially secrets that make Bill Frazier sweat. Besides, you shouldn't presume that yours is the only secret with which I've been entrusted. I'm a veritable repository of trust."

He'd been grinning at her, soaking in the cool water of her voice on this soft spring night, washing in her dry humor. Something, though, changed in those last words. Something intangible shifted in the sound of her voice, forcing Joe's eyes open.

"It doesn't sound like you're particularly happy about it," he offered softly, his forehead creased with sudden, inexplicable concern.

There was a brief throb of silence, as if she were holding her breath. "Some secrets weigh more than others," she finally admitted.

"Then don't keep them."

The smile he heard this time wasn't funny. "Life just isn't that accommodating."

Their conversation slowed, the intermittent silences more pregnant than the words. Outside, the night throbbed, and far below on the river, a tugboat blew a low, sad call into the emptiness.

"Want a strong shoulder to help carry the load?" he asked, wishing suddenly that he knew what weight it was Allison was carrying, what pain had slipped from her eyes into her voice.

"Thanks," she answered sincerely, "but I'd rather have those strong fingers get that bathroom situation whipped into focus so I can present it."

Pause, wait, regroup. They both did it, consciously or not, the offer made and refused without acrimony and new business attended to. Joe felt the frustration of missing something, of coming very close to the truth in the dark and passing it right by without recognizing it.

"Well, I wanted to talk to you about that," he admitted, his eyes drifting back over to the table where Unctious could be seen blushing at the sight of a rather rumpled, short, blue-haired female with a big nose.

"What about that?" Allison asked.

"I'm redesigning the bathroom, and I wanted to get your ideas on it."

"I'm partial to whirlpools and skylights," she offered.

"What about gremlins?"

"I thought you already had gremlins in that book."

"This is going to be different," he admitted. "I don't think I'm going to have Wanda Wartwhistle be a bad guy after all."

Allison made it through the rest of the call without giving herself away. She sat alone in her kitchen, eyes focused toward the quilt of Maggie photos on her refrigerator, and thought of secrets even as she discussed the merits of gremlins over trolls. She squeezed a fist to her chest where the weight lived, holding it in, holding it up as it grew in her.

And when she hung up after throwing off a few quick lines about beauty being in the eye of the beholder, she walked dry-eyed through the house and ran herself a hot shower, because somehow the hot water seemed to dissolve knotted tears.

She was going to have to come to some kind of decision. Joe was edging closer, easing his way so effortlessly into her confidence that she'd almost accepted his offer tonight. She'd almost opened up about what her life was, what it wasn't, and how damned lucky he was. She'd almost shattered the fragile veneer over their relationship and let loose the truth.

She stood where she was, her face lifted to the hot water, the steam clouding the room, dimming the world beyond, the shower shushing her, the tile cool and impersonal beneath her feet. Tears bubbled from that hard knot in her chest and coursed down her cheeks, and slowly the fierce fire in her receded.

Somehow, she'd broken her own rules. Without knowing how or when, she'd crossed the boundary of isolation and let Joe matter. She'd begun to count on the sound of his voice on her machine, had caught herself wanting to share herself with him. Desire, so long buried beneath a mountain of grief and guilt and effort, was pushing up just beneath the panic. A slow, curling heat in her belly, an addictive effervescence in her blood. She'd held her breath tonight waiting for him to pick up his phone, like a teen agonizing over a date or a woman wanting a lover.

Even now, numbed by the pounding water, she still felt the narcotic of his voice seeping through her, coursing life into cold fingers and an abandoned heart. Even alone, she felt him with her. It terrified her, because she'd heard the same life in his voice when he'd recognized her on the phone. He wasn't going to let her back away again. There was nothing to do but go ahead, and that meant giving him the whole truth. Forcing reality on him.

This man who had made his world to his own design, who was lucky enough to be surrounded by health and happiness and normalcy, who dreamed passionately for a family just like the one in which he'd been raised, had to realize now before it was too late that Allison couldn't be part of that dream. She already had a child, and that child would never be allowed to share all the wide-open dreams of Joe's nieces and nephews.

Joe's future was still all possibility. All dreams and plans and imagination. Allison's was Maggie. And for Joe's benefit, she was going to have to tell him. She was going to have to *show* him so that he understood. So that he left her alone. So that she could still survive the heart he broke.

Allison stepped out of the shower already knowing what she had to do. All she had left was to gather the courage to do it.

Three days later Allison still hadn't brought up the subject. She and Joe had talked twice more, each time abusing each other with familiar humor, discussing the new book, the new rumors swirling around the company, and springtime in general. And then Joe managed to open the discussion all by himself on Thursday afternoon.

"Another business lunch," he proposed in that brash voice of challenge that sounded a lot less serious than it really was.

"No, thank you," she demurred, hearing the bells from Maggie's room and fighting indecision.

"Oh, come on, Allison," he objected. "Nobody from the company will see us. We can go someplace dark and intimate just so we're not recognized. Of course, you won't be able to see my drawings for Wanda Wartwhistle, but I guess that's just the way it's going to have to be."

"Joe—"

"A simple business lunch."

"Dinner," she said instead, closing her eyes, her stomach heaving with dread.

"Dinner?"

"My place," she said. "After all, I owe you for lunch."

He didn't answer right away, obviously taken aback by her abrupt change in tack. Allison couldn't say she blamed him. She was just as unsettled as he was.

"You're sure?" he asked, and there was just the first note of hope in his voice. "After what you said when we met—"

"There's something we need to talk about," she explained. "And I don't think I want to do it at a restaurant."

"We can do it here, if you want," he offered. "If it would be more comfortable for you."

Instinctively she shook her head. "No. I think I'd rather do it here. What about Sunday?"

"What about tomorrow?"

"No can do. I'm . . . not available." She was going to be at the doctor's checking out Maggie's cold. It didn't do to let those things go. But Allison couldn't explain that quite yet.

"Anytime's fine," he assured her. "I'll bring the wine."

"I don't drink," she reminded him gently.

He laughed. "I do," he said. "And from the sound of your voice, I think I might just need it."

Allison couldn't help a wry smile. He had no idea how right he was. "Seven o'clock Sunday, then," she said. "And bring along Wanda. I'd love to see her."

Joe was not amused on Sunday when he walked down the stairs from dressing to find his two sisters loitering in his kitchen.

"You haven't run far enough," he advised them dryly. "The kids will still find you here."

Maria was shaking her dark head with an expression of mock severity. "Sam was right," she marveled, crossing her arms across her chest and leaning against the counter. "I had to see it for myself."

Joe stopped mid-stride and stared. "Right about what?"

Elizabeth, taller and prettier, pointed at him. "The last time it took you this long to get ready for a date was your senior prom. She must really be something."

Joe scowled heartily. "She's my editor. We're going to talk print runs and word counts."

The last thing he needed was to betray to these two just what kind of state his stomach was in. Of course, knowing them, they probably knew. He pulled out the bottle of Chardonnay he was bringing anyway and pulled his car keys off the keyholder Mike had fashioned for him out of a coat hanger and string.

"And for that you're missing Mom's Sunday dinner for the first time in twelve years?" Maria retorted. "These must be some print runs she has."

Joe made it a point to ruffle her hair on the way by. "They are, baby. They are."

They were still standing in his kitchen when he walked out of the house.

"Turn out the lights when you leave!" he called over his shoulder.

"We're going to want details!" Elizabeth retorted, leaning out the door.

Joe just laughed and climbed into his truck.

It was going to be another spectacular spring evening, the sky a sharp peacock blue and a breeze ruffling the burgeoning trees. Joe had been alternately anticipating and dreading his visit to Allison's. She'd made a definite decision in letting him enter her territory. She'd let down a barrier, one she'd constructed long before ever meeting Joe. He could hear it in her voice, the instinctive reserve every time they wandered too close in their conversations. He'd felt it in her body when he'd breached her defences with that kiss at B.B.'s.

And now she'd made it a point to both literally and figuratively let Joe close.

He should be more nervous. After all, Allison had hardly sounded breathless with anticipation over the proposed dinner date. He was sure she meant to set him straight. To try once and for all to convince him that for some reason or another—maybe the jerk of an ex-husband, maybe because dating sax players was against her religion—she wasn't sure a relationship with him was a wise idea.

What she didn't seem to understand was that wise had nothing to do with it. Warm and loving and compassionate did. Enticing, addicting, unforgettable. When he woke sweating and aching in the dead of night, Joe's first thought was hardly that his attraction to Allison wasn't wise. Nor did he worry about that now.

He was going to sit down at her place where they could relax, be themselves. Where he could convince her that she was wrong. That no matter what her ex had done or what her inclinations were, Joe was the man she needed in her life.

By the time he pulled into her complex, he had himself convinced that there wasn't anything Allison could say that could possibly deter him. She'd allowed him the first step, and he wasn't about to waste it.

Her apartment was set back from the road a little, located in one of a collection of whitewashed boxes with a lot of windows in front and a tiny fenced patio out back. Joe rang the bell and waited, smiling to himself at the thought of Allison at the Burgett Sunday dinners.

She must have been busy. He rang again, listening hard for footsteps and not hearing any.

"Come on, Allison," he mumbled, jabbing the bell again, the bottle of wine he held in one hand almost forgotten. "You're not allowed to change your mind after I'm already here."

Suddenly the door opened. Joe started, not having heard even her approach.

"You decided to let me in after all." His instinctive smile faltered and died. Something was very wrong.

"Oh . . . J-Joe," she stammered, rubbing her free hand against her pant leg. "I tried to call, but you . . . you'd gone."

She was already turning away, her hand now raking through her hair. Instead of the flowing, sexy dress Joe had half envisioned, she was in T-shirt and jeans, and her features were taut.

Joe immediately forgot wine and romancing and determination.

"Allison, what's wrong?" he demanded, stepping in. Dropping his gift and his portfolio on a nearby table, he reached out to her. She never noticed, her hands busy, her movements brisk. She was collecting things and stuffing them into a bag.

"Allison!"

She turned on him. "I can't...I have to go. I'm sorry. Maybe we can do this later."

"Why?" he demanded, his hands on her shoulders, pulling her to a stop, forcing her to face him.

That was when he saw the fear in those liquid green eyes.

She tried to smile and failed miserably. "I have to get to the hospital," she said, pulling away and turning from him.

"What for?" he demanded, following.

He didn't even realize that he trailed Allison into a child's room until he heard the wheezing.

"It's okay, munchkin," Allison was crooning, bending over a cradle in the middle of the room and making the tiny bells over it dance. The baby inside was whimpering. "We're going now. We're going to make you feel better."

"Allison," Joe insisted, suddenly sinking beneath the shock. The room was a riot of whimsy—clouds and animals and stuffed animals. "What's this all about?"

"She is," Allison said, picking up the baby and turning to him. "This is Maggie, Joe. My daughter. She has a problem with her heart, and it's giving her trouble tonight. I have to get her to the hospital. Please, I don't have time."

He saw the baby, dark eyes and wispy brown hair, delicate features. Pale, struggling to breathe. So small, so fragile.

"I'm sorry, Joe," Allison apologized, her voice as tight and anxious as her face. "I wanted to explain all this to you. To help you understand. I'm just not going to have time now."

Allison was right. This wasn't the time to be dealing with that. Maggie was sick, and Allison had to get her help. Ramifications would come later.

"Let's go," he said, pulling the bag from her shoulder and shepherding her out the door. "You take care of her. I'll drive."

And later, much later, when that little girl could breathe easily again, Joe would have to come to grips with what Allison had told him.

But all that would wait.

Chapter 6

Joe hated hospitals. He hated the sights and sounds and most of all the smells, all conspiring to unsettle his stomach and make him sweat. As the family designated driver for injuries he'd been in emergency rooms before, but he'd always retreated straight to the waiting room to concentrate on televised baseball until the time to go home.

This time he didn't get the chance to escape. By the time he'd pulled the car to a stop in the garage, the baby had begun to look alarmingly blue, and Allison was crooning nonstop in a voice that was just a shade too desperate. It didn't even occur to him not to accompany Allison to the desk. He helped her out and held her all the way in, that too-pale little girl in her arms taking all their attention.

Inside, it was chaos, children screaming, phones ringing, radios crackling and barking, alarms shrilling. A nurse swooped in on them the minute they stepped inside, immediately sensing the baby's distress, and steered them straight back to a room. Allison held tightly to her child, and Joe held on to Allison.

"How much does she weigh?" the nurse was asking, punching buttons on a monitor and pulling out equipment as Allison settled the baby on the cart and began to undress her.

"Seven pounds, ten ounces," Allison said, her voice deceptively calm. "Maggie's six months old. She's had a cold the last three days and just got worse tonight. I think she's in heart failure. She has a ventricular septal defect."

More people came into the room. Allison tossed medical terms back and forth with the staff as they swarmed over the baby. She stood rigidly by the bed, her hands clenched together, her eyes on her child, calm and purposeful. Joe wondered if the nurses and doctors knew how very frightened she was.

He looked down on Maggie. On Allison's daughter.

Joe felt as if he were suffocating, drowning beneath the surprises and shocks of the past few minutes. An hour ago he didn't know Allison had a baby. She was so small on that big table, so frail amid all the people and equipment. The staff was inserting wires and intravenous lines and hooking up monitors. They were applying oxygen and taking tests, and all the while Allison stood quietly by, every so often reaching a tentative hand out to her child, most often standing perfectly still where Maggie could see her.

"It's all right, baby," she crooned along with the nurses. "They'll take care of you. Mommy's here. Mommy's here."

"Dr. Goldman's on his way in," one of the nurses said, reaching out to touch Allison's arm. She jerked a little, as if startled by the contact. She nodded. The nurse turned to Joe and continued.

"We're getting Maggie a bed in intensive care, and we'll give her some medicine that will make her feel better, Mr. Henley." Then she smiled. "But I imagine you know better than I do how this works."

No, Joe thought wildly. He didn't. He had no idea what was going on, what congestive heart failure was or why it should happen to a six-month-old infant. He wanted to know what he could do to help, but there was nobody there who was going to tell him. He'd left his house on his way to a date and ended up at the hospital mistaken for Mr. Henley, suddenly responsible for a woman he'd just found out he didn't know at all *and* her sick daughter.

"Excuse me," someone said, her hand on Joe's arm now. He turned to see a secretary at his side. "Your car. You need to move it."

He looked back at Allison where she stood in front of him. He didn't want to leave her alone to face this. It was all too numbing, too overwhelming. The staff was talking about doses and oxygen levels and rhythm strips, a different language spoken by a different species, and Allison had to offer up her child to them.

"Please," the little woman urged gently. "You can come right back."

Joe reached out to Allison. She stiffened and turned to him. Her eyes widened. She'd forgotten that he was there.

"I'll be right back," he promised.

She nodded, her eyes still huge. And then she turned back to Maggie.

Joe had to skirt two ambulances and a family of six to get to his car, but he still managed to make it back to Allison in five minutes. Sweating. His stomach churning. Wondering just what else he was going to have to deal with tonight.

"Excuse me, Mr. Henley," the little secretary called to him when he walked back in through the sliding doors. "We need your insurance cards."

Joe was beyond explaining. He saw Allison standing down the hall just outside the door to Maggie's room, and his stomach tumbled again. She was so pale. So tightly controlled, her face a mask, her posture rigid. He had to get down there.

"I'll...uh...get them," he promised vaguely, and turned away.

"Best thing for everybody if they'd just wait a little too long one of these times and just let that poor thing go," somebody was saying behind the front desk.

"Who, the Henley baby?" was the answer.

"Well, sure. She's got Down syndrome. I mean, what are they trying so hard to save her for?"

The words brought Joe to a halt. He turned to see two secretaries standing behind the partition to the desk area. When they saw that he'd heard them, one blushed. Joe couldn't do anything but turn away again, back to Allison.

Down syndrome. Oh, God.

What more? he thought. What more? He was numb, shaken, sick. How could he not have seen? Hadn't guessed that those soft, dark eyes were just a little different? How hadn't he known all these weeks that Allison had been carrying a weight that size around with her?

Suddenly, he needed to get away. He wanted to turn away again from the tight strain of her beautiful face, to run outside and suck in great lungfuls of night air, to hide in the dark and let the isolation wash over him. He wanted to deal with this alone before he dealt with it with Allison.

Instead, Joe took a slow, steady breath and raked his hands through his hair. Took a few steps, and then a few more. Reached Allison's side and silently slid an arm around her shoulder.

Allison didn't have to look to realize that Joe had returned. She knew, even with her eyes glued to the door, that he was approaching before he slid his arm around her shoulder.

It still surprised her. She'd never had anybody help her through one of these sessions. It had always just been Maggie and her, alone except for each other. Allison had stood by her baby, helpless in the glare and bustle of the hospital, torn to shreds by ambivalence and guilt. Forcing her child to be all right with only her will, frustrated that she didn't know more, couldn't step right in there and stop them from hurting her daughter, couldn't give the medicine that would make her breathe better.

She had learned to gird herself to battle alone for Maggie. Having Joe there, even for these few hours, changed things.

"How is she?" he asked softly, his touch gentle and his presence solid and supportive.

The tears swelled in Allison's throat. Just his touch might make it all unbearable when the isolation hadn't. "Better," she admitted in a too-small voice, not able to move, not comfortable enough to return Joe's gesture of support. She wanted to sink against his strength, to bolster herself with him. But she couldn't take the risk. "They've already given her some medicine, and they're x-raying her now. She'll be going up to intensive care."

"Are you going with her?"

Allison looked up then to see nothing but concern in those bottomless brown eyes. "Oh, you don't have to stay, Joe. I'm an old hand at this. I'll spend the night here and probably head home tomorrow when I know she's stable."

His smile was indescribably tender, hurting her even more. "Hospitals fascinate me," he offered. "I think I'll stay and see how things go. How 'bout some coffee?"

"Mrs. Henley?" the nurse called, leaning out Maggie's door. "We're gonna head on up. Wanna meet us on the fourth floor?"

Allison nodded with a thin smile.

"We're going to stop for something to eat on the way up," Joe said easily, his arm still confining her.

Allison turned to protest, but both the nurse and Joe were ahead of her.

"Good idea," the nurse approved. "She forgets sometimes when Maggie pulls these little stunts. It's nice to see somebody around to take care of her."

"He's not—" Allison protested, but the door was already swinging shut. So Allison turned on Joe. "You are *not* taking care of me."

Joe grinned and steered her down the hall toward the elevator and cafeteria. "Wouldn't think of it. By the way, they need your insurance cards."

She knew she should pull away from him. She should stand alone and straighten him out about just what she was capable of. After all, this was her third trip here, not counting exams and tests and one evaluation after another. Allison could navigate this hospital blindfolded and send anybody in the building scurrying for cover if need be. She didn't need a strong shoulder to lean on, a knight in shining armor to lift her up over the muck of life. She didn't need his compassion tonight when she knew it would wither into discomfort and, finally, distance.

But she couldn't quite do it. Her chest was on fire. Her hands shook and her throat knotted up. Sometimes it was just too much to expect herself to do everything. Sometimes it would be nice to buffer the fear.

"Why didn't you tell me?" Joe asked when he sat them both down with dinner trays and coffee at a table in the half-empty cafeteria.

Allison looked at the food he'd heaped on her plate and forced the nausea back down. There was just too much roiling around in her right now.

She settled into her chair and faced him, wishing yet again that she could have done this better. Or maybe not. Maybe he needed the full dose right away so that he could be sufficiently warned off.

"That's what I'd been planning to do tonight," she said.

"Why not before?"

She ducked her head a little, wondering how she could make him understand in a few words. She was too tired to be diplomatic, too shaken to be patient.

"I'm not the kind of person to wave Maggie's problems around like a flag," she said, staring defiantly at her congealing soup. "I don't usually introduce myself to prospective co-workers by saying, 'Hi, I'm Allison Henley, and I have a six-month-old daughter with a ventricular septal defect.'"

She squeezed her eyes shut, knowing that she had to tell Joe the rest, realizing that he didn't recognize the facial features that would identify Maggie as a child with Down's. She had to give him the real dose—now or never.

"What exactly is a ventricular septal defect?" Joe asked, giving her soup bowl a little push in her direction to remind her of its purpose there.

Allison tried to drag in a calming breath, lifted her eyes to meet the care in Joe's. "The heart has four chambers," she explained, as it had been explained to her. Joe nodded her on. "Two atria and two ventricals, right and left each." Another breath, control costing her. "The blood on the right side of the heart is the stuff coming back in for oxygen. Right atrium accepts, then the right ventrical pumps that into the lungs for a recharge. Back to the left atrium, and the left ventrical pumps the rejuvenated stuff back out. Well, Maggie has a hole in the septum in between the two ventricals, and the bad blood and the good blood get mixed."

Joe's features pursed in concentration. "What can be done?"

Allison shrugged. "Open-heart surgery. We're waiting for Maggie to put on some more weight for it. Until then, we try and prevent overloading her heart's workload so that it doesn't throw her into failure. The heart doesn't stop beating. It just can't keep up with an increased demand or illness."

"Like now."

She nodded. "Like now."

"Is this common?"

Allison couldn't answer right away. She couldn't bear to see it again, to lose that strong arm that had held her even when she hadn't needed it.

"It is for children like Maggie," she admitted. "Over forty percent have heart defects of some kind or other."

Joe became very quiet. "Children like Maggie?"

Allison couldn't even breathe. "Maggie has Down syndrome, Joe. She'll take longer to develop physically and will be mentally retarded."

She watched his face for reaction. Revulsion, pity, disgust, anything. Instead, she saw a certain sadness, and it unnerved her.

"You didn't think you could trust me with that?" he finally asked, his voice so quiet.

The pain of fresh tears was brutal. Allison simply couldn't put her emotions into words. She couldn't make Joe understand here in a hospital cafeteria. She didn't understand herself, sometimes.

"When my husband left," she finally said, "I decided that it would be easier all around if I simply didn't allow myself to become involved with another man. Especially since it probably wouldn't happen anyway. I don't have any delusions about what a burden Maggie can be, so I simply maintained a careful distance when I dealt with men. Until I met you, I never had any problems maintaining it."

"And now?"

She struggled to fight the despair in her voice. Who ever said it was better to have loved and lost? Even though she'd sworn she'd never forget, she couldn't remember it hurting this badly the last time. And she didn't love Joe. She was sure she didn't. She simply couldn't imagine never hearing his laughter over the phone again. Never seeing his quirky smile or challenging his much-too-sharp wit.

"Now I'm more convinced than ever that I was right."

She wasn't exactly sure what she expected Joe's reaction to be. Instinctive denial, maybe. Uncomfortable agreement. Instead, he merely watched her, his thoughts well hidden behind those empathetic eyes, his callused, carpenter's hands embracing his coffee mug.

Good hands. Strong hands, the tools of a craftsman, not a magician. Solid, squared off with large knuckles and a few scrapes. The kind of hands that could fix anything, could cradle anybody, could build up or tear down. Allison couldn't take her eyes from them, thinking how she'd felt them on her shoulder, imparting Joe's silent strength, his comfort. Thinking of how she'd never missed a hand on her shoulder until Joe's had been there.

"You're so sure I'd do the same thing as your husband?"

Frustration propelled her own hands, lifting them in aimless flight. "I've heard you talk about the children you want," she protested. "The family you want. A house full of children who'll baffle you with the knowledge they have, who'll play the piano and star in major-league baseball. You want the same kind of children you're surrounded by, bright, inquisitive, challenging children who will grow up to reshape the world and give you grandchildren who are just like them. And you should have that. Well, I'm not the person who can give it to you. Maggie isn't that kind of child. She never will be, no matter what we do. That's a hard enough reality to face when you're a child's parent. I can't ask someone else to volunteer for duty.''

"You're *afraid* to ask."

She faced him, baldly and rigidly. "Don't forget, Joe. I saw what became of one of Maggie's parents. It doesn't take much to extrapolate that a little."

His hands still clasped around his mug, he shook his head. "You never gave me the chance to make up my own mind."

It was a battle to get past the ache of unshed tears. "I never had any intention of it getting to the point where it would be necessary."

"Well it did," he informed her.

Allison went very still, his words warring in her chest along with every other shock and stress of the day. "It can't," she objected, her voice small and frightened.

His smile was more resigned than ecstatic. "My sister says I don't exhibit much sense. She's probably right. I think I'm falling in love with you."

"But we've only known each other—"

"Two months."

Still she shook her head. "But you can't. Not with me."

"What do you suggest I do?" he asked with a little tilt to his eyebrow. "Do some comparative shopping? I've done that already, and the rest of the products left me uninterested."

This was why she'd never attempted love. This battering, burning, breathtaking ambivalence. The terror of hope. Dear God, she wasn't going to make it through this.

"No," she insisted out loud, her hand up, her eyes wide and dry, her fragile balance shattering. "I just can't do it, Joe. Maggie's upstairs and I have to be with her. I have to concentrate on her because there isn't anyone else who will. Until she's better, I can't divide myself. Don't you understand?"

"You haven't eaten yet," he informed her, impossibly prosaic.

Allison didn't even bother to look down at her tray. "She's all I have."

He nodded, taking a sip of his coffee and giving her soup another gentle shove. "Then when you're finished, we'll go back upstairs."

Still Allison shook her head. "No, really. I'm not hungry. I'm just going to go upstairs."

Joe nodded and climbed to his feet.

Allison held her breath, praying. Again, not sure for what. Terrified that he would stay. Terrified that he would leave. "Thank you, really," she said anyway, knowing she had no other choice. "I've done this alone twice already."

"Well, this time you're not. So live with it."

And he held out a hand.

Allison froze, unwilling to want more, unable to admit to less.

"Not another word," he promised gently, his hand still outstretched, still steady and solid. "Just coffee and company. If you want, I'll go get Wanda and we can do some work while we wait."

"I'm not going to change my mind."

"Then just accept the help and shut up."

Impossibly, incredibly, Allison smiled. Not much of a smile, since her empty stomach was still fighting itself for something to chew up. But a smile nonetheless. When she got to her feet, though, she refused to take hold of his hand. That would have been too much.

"Go get Wanda," she instructed. "It's going to be a long night."

From *There's a Monster in My Bathroom*
by L. Wood Dowd

*M*onsters did not, as a rule, live in bathrooms. Bathrooms weren't scary. Closets were scary, right after dark when all the shadows moved inside. Basements were scary at any time of the day, but especially when it was raining out and the lightning flashed through the little windows way at the end of a dark basement room. Outside was scary at night when the animals made their snuffling noises in the bushes so that you could never turn off your flashlight when you camped out.

But bathrooms, on the whole, were not scary. In fact, they were fun. Bathrooms were where you could float boats in the sink and have water fights in the tub. There were fluffy towels in the bathroom and toothpaste that squeezed out of the tube in a funny way. There were Band-Aids for scrapes, and soft washrags to clean yourself with.

So Noxious and Ralph were surprised one night to find Unctious in the bathroom.

"B-b-but the lights are on," Ralph protested, his hiss quite insulted. After all, what good was a monster in the bright light? Especially a very small monster, because monsters were scary precisely because people thought they were so big and terrible in the dark.

But Unctious wasn't paying attention. He was busy looking very intently into the bathroom mirror, which was quite a feat since he had to balance by his tail on the toilet. Since Unctious didn't know about closing things, there was always a chance he'd slip right in.

"What are you doing?" Noxious demanded, paws on his hips.

"Go away," Unctious demanded, patting at the scales on his face. There were several that wouldn't lie down quite properly, and he was using some kind of lotion that smelled like fruit to get it right. It looked silly on scales, but there you are.

"I b-b-bet he's t-trying to look good for Wanda Wartwhistle," Ralph teased.

"Am not!" Unctious protested.

"Are too!"

Noxious pretended like he was sticking a finger down his throat. "Ugh!"

"Yeah," Ralph agreed with a nod of his head that made his ears wiggle. (Being a very small monster, he had little pointed ears, like a collie.) "Ugh."

But Unctious wouldn't answer them. He just went on flattening down the stubborn scales. He really hoped his brothers would go back under the bed soon because he wanted to finish looking good and get back off this sink (he secretly hated heights). And then, he wanted to just very casually, very slowly, as if he didn't have anything better to do, creep on by the little space behind the washer and dryer in the laundry room where Wanda Wartwhistle lived.

He'd done it three nights in a row. Just walked right on by like he was going to take a quick look outside to check the weather, and then said something like, "Hi there, Wanda," to Wanda.

He had no business liking Wanda, of course. Wanda wasn't a monster at all, which would make his parents really mad. She was only a gremlin. She was the one who *snuck off with all those things that children think they lost during the night. Wanda lived on a cozy nest of unmatched socks and had her tomatoes planted in a brand-new pink tennis shoe that Billy's sister Missy had lost two weeks ago. Wanda decorated her wall with homework papers and ate school lunches. And Unctious thought that she was the prettiest thing of all.*

But Wanda didn't really notice him. Oh, she said, "Hello there, Unctious," but she said it to everyone who passed her nest. She was a very friendly gremlin who laughed a lot. Unctious dreamed of the day when he would see her very lovely pink eyes flutter when she saw him, so that her "Hello there, Unctious" sounded different than it did to any of the other monsters she greeted during the night. He wanted so very much to tell her how he liked the way the fluorescent light bulb shone in her fluffy blue hair, and that he thought warts on the very tip of a gremlin's nose were very becoming. But Unctious just couldn't say those things. Besides, he'd probably just sneeze instead, since there were a lot of dust bunnies in back of dryers.

And so he walked by her nest every night, real slowly, real cool, and said, "Hi there, Wanda." And not one of those nights, even with his scales slicked flat with that fruity-smelling stuff, did Wanda really notice him. Not once did she look up from her book of odd lots and really smile.

But Unctious kept walking by, and each day he felt smaller and smaller. But he kept trying.

Chapter 7

Maggie was in the hospital for four days. She spent the first night in the intensive-care unit where they flushed out the fluid her weakened heart had let build up and regulated her medication. The entire time that Allison spent there, wandering from the waiting room to the stark brightness of the ICU, Joe stayed with her.

He discussed Wanda and played a couple of hands of cards. He cadged pillows and blankets and forced Allison to at least lie down in a dim corner where all the other exhausted mothers slept as their sick children were being cared for down the hall. Then, when she woke up, needing to peek in on Maggie to reassure herself, he'd silently handed her a cup of hot coffee, as if he'd anticipated her. Sometimes he'd followed her in to check on her sleeping baby, and sometimes he'd waited behind, never crowding her, never making demands or insisting on inclusion.

He took Allison home in the morning so she could shower and change, and he went to work. But he showed up in the evening with home-made dinner from one sister or another, and watched Maggie while Allison took a little time off.

He was the perfect companion, funny, easy-going, silently supportive and strong. By the third day Allison expected to see him. By the third evening, when he hadn't yet shown up, she was afraid he wouldn't, and then, that he would.

She didn't want to need him. She didn't want to count on his being there. She didn't want to let him fill the void in her life and then find out that he'd never intended to, but had just been charitable to a person in trouble.

They hadn't said a word the entire time about Maggie. The book they'd talked about, other books, the situation in health care, Allison's friends, Joe's family. They had argued world politics and literature and simply let long bridges of silence stretch between them, the stillness comfortable and friendly rather than stiff.

But they hadn't talked about what Maggie meant to them.

Allison couldn't do it, not yet. She knew she should have simply made the decision Sunday evening. She should have told Joe to go home and expect to hear from her next week when they had something to discuss about the book. Now, it was too late. She'd spent the past months steeling herself for isolation, and the past forty-eight hours forfeiting every ounce of fortitude she'd amassed.

She wanted him near. She wanted that strong shoulder, those practical hands, those delicious eyes that could say so much without a word. She wanted just a few hours when she could share her burden before she had to shoulder it alone again.

Soon she would have to discuss the situation with Joe. She'd have to get a truthful response from him, not just platitudes delivered to soothe anxious mothers, and then she'd have to deal with it. She'd have to let him leave gracefully, and it was already too much to bear.

His stomach wasn't handling the hospital any better than it had Sunday night. There was just something about those warm chemical smells that made him queasy. Stepping off the elevator on Tuesday night, Joe found himself wishing that he hadn't had dinner. However, he wished that Allison had.

He could see her at the end of the hall, talking to one of the other mothers, and she looked worn out. Thin, pale, her hair dull and her eyes just a little hollow. Just as it had every other time he'd come upon her in the past couple of days, the sight of her sent a sharp ache through him.

He couldn't stand to see her hurting, to see the strain in her eyes or hear the careful disregard of the situation in her conversation. He wanted to help. He wanted to make everything better. But he didn't know how. He didn't know whether he could.

"I can see I'm here just in time to take you down to dinner," he offered without preamble when he reached her. "I don't know about you, but I'm starved."

When Allison looked up at him, Joe could have sworn he saw relief in those dark green eyes, a fleeting lightness that was just as suddenly repressed.

"You know Peggy Williams, Joe." Allison introduced him casually, unconsciously taking a swipe at her hair. Joe thought the tense action was more telling than her voice.

Even so, he turned to greet the small, plump lady with the too-bright eyes. "Hi, Peggy. How's Justin?"

The woman shrugged, her movements as jerky and brittle as everyone else's in the place. "He's on a respirator."

Joe couldn't do more than nod. He had no easy words for a mother whose son was dying of AIDS.

"Why don't you come on down with us?" he asked instead.

She shook her head. "You go on," she suggested. "I'm waiting for my husband."

"Oh, I'm not—" Allison started to say, but Joe took hold of her arm and guided her toward the elevator. She went with barely a whimper of protest. "I suppose I should."

"You've lost at least five pounds in the last three days," he accused, punching the elevator button, his hand still on her too-thin arm.

"Nothing like a stretch in the ICU waiting room for taking care of those extra inches," she retorted, her voice just a bit too strained to be funny.

"How's Maggie doing?"

The doors opened and they stepped on board with a couple of nurses. Joe hit the button for the lobby where the regulation cafeteria food would do even more to ruin his appetite.

"She's been sleeping a lot," Allison admitted. "This kind of thing wears her out."

"Wears *me* out," Joe admitted. "And I'm not six months old. Why did they move Justin out of ICU if he's on the respirator?"

Three days and already he was beginning to understand how the place worked. He didn't think he liked it at all.

Allison sighed, and Joe heard the pain of one mother for another. "Because there isn't really anything else they can do. They'll probably turn the machines off tomorrow and just let him go." She shook her head, her eyes glittering, and Joe slid an arm around her. "Y'know, just when I think I have the weight of the world on my shoulders, I meet Peggy and feel ashamed."

Joe didn't know what to say to that, either. There was so much he wanted to tell Allison about her own courage, her strength and purpose. But there was a taboo on that kind of discussion, and until it was lifted, he couldn't make a move.

Not that he was sure what his move was going to be. He hadn't slept in two nights, and half-finished sketches of gremlins laid untouched on his table. At work, he'd pounded the hell out of a lot of white pine and then come home to pace the bluffs, purging the shock, hoping for inspiration and finding none. Wanting direction when he had nothing by which to guide himself.

He hadn't been frivolous Sunday night. He was falling in love with Allison. His sisters had diagnosed it in his kitchen when they'd watched him get ready for dinner with those superior smiles married sisters tend to have for unmarried brothers. If things had been different, he would have courted Allison with every ounce of charm and attention he could dredge up. He'd introduce her to the things that mattered to him and ask her to reciprocate. In the normal course of events, the two of them would discover compatibility, respect, passion. They would walk carefully into commitment.

The last three days had changed all that. Maggie had suddenly redefined Joe's picture of the future, bursting his illusions, scattering his dreams. Joe had never had the experience to anticipate anything like Maggie.

And then there was Allison. Allison, who'd intrigued him on the phone, sly, just shy of serious, with mysteries in her soft voice. Allison, who'd enchanted him in person with her ingenuity, her curiosity, her sharp eyes and sweet laughter. Allison, who had awed him in these past three days with her quiet strength, her singular will and loving tenderness. What Joe had suspected, had half anticipated before, had coalesced when he'd seen what kind of woman she was, what kind of mother she was. He couldn't help but love her. And that, he knew, was the problem.

The cafeteria was crowded this time, and the mealtime conversation was about the rainy weather and the stalled book. Joe actually got Allison to eat a sandwich and some chocolate cake before she gave up. She didn't seem to notice that he was the one who was just picking at his food.

"It's going to be a great sunset," Joe offered. "Why don't we go outside for a bit?"

Outside was a busy boulevard, but the park across the street wouldn't be too much risk at this hour of the afternoon. To Joe's surprise, Allison agreed with alacrity. She didn't say anything when he took her hand.

The rain clouds had moved off toward the east, and the sun was setting behind the towers of the hospital. Traffic was heavy and impatient, but a soft breeze cooled the evening, and beyond the trees a rainbow arched into the mist. Joe led Allison to a bench that overlooked the park and settled her in.

"I don't have much time," Allison protested without noticeable heat. "Brook is going to be stopping by tonight."

"Brook from the *publishing* company?" Joe countered with a small grin as he settled his arm around her shoulder. Allison didn't seem to mind.

She managed to grin back. "Yes, and don't think for a minute that she considers me safe or sane while in your company."

Joe chuckled. "She's probably afraid of jealous wives and mistresses attacking you on the street."

"She says it just doesn't pay to trust a jazz sax player. Whatever that means."

"It means that she would be much happier if you could hook up with a nice, respectable lawyer," he admitted. "Are you sure she's only your supervising editor and not your mother?"

"Definitely. My mother never really noticed who I married."

Joe looked at her, but she didn't seem to realize how odd her statement was. She was watching the sun gild rain clouds, her face more peaceful than he'd seen it in days. The breeze ruffled her hair and plucked at her blouse, and Joe could smell the fresh scent of her shampoo. The clear golden light of dusk warmed her skin and gave it back the color the hours in the hospital had taken.

Suddenly, Joe ached for her. Fierce, sharp, shattering. He wanted to pull her into his arms right there with the taxis honking over their shoulders. He wanted to soften the strain on that face with small caresses and ease the line of her mouth with a long gentle kiss. She was so alone, so taut, like a young tree before a horrible wind. She needed sheltering, care. She needed the support of more than just his words and his presence.

But he knew what would happen if he demanded she accept his love now and then found he couldn't stay. He couldn't do that to her. He couldn't insist on rights when he wasn't certain yet whether he had any.

His hand clenched against the damp wood of the bench. His jaw scraped with sudden tension, and he dragged in a surreptitious breath to still the staccato of a frustrated heart. He held his place. He held his silence.

She must have known. Somehow she sensed his frustration and turned to him, her eyes dark. She lifted a hand without seeming to realize it and almost touched his cheek.

At the last minute, she held back. "I'm being unfair to you," she admitted, her voice as dark as her eyes.

Joe couldn't seem to move, to breathe. She dropped her hand into her lap and he almost groaned with the separation. "Have I been complaining again?" he demanded gently. "I keep telling you, the stuffed cabbage in the cafeteria isn't your fault."

But Allison would have none of it. She turned away briefly, clasping her hands together in her lap as if that would somehow give her purchase on what she needed to say. Joe couldn't take his eyes from the glint of the setting sun on the crown of her head.

"I've been taking advantage of you," she admitted. "It's been so easy to rely on you, and I promised myself I wouldn't."

He was going to say something flip like, "Rely away." Knowing what she wanted to say, what he needed to, he kept quiet and simply watched her bent head.

"It's just that I can't do it any longer," she said, and her voice, if possible, seemed smaller. "I can't keep putting off talking to you about Maggie just because I don't want you to leave." She looked up briefly, her eyes impossibly vulnerable, and then shied away, dropping her gaze to her lap. "I know what you're going to say, so we might as well get it over with."

"You know what I'm going to say?" Joe couldn't help but ask. He was amazed, especially since he didn't know himself.

Allison finally managed to face him without flinching, and Joe saw the pain in those eloquent eyes of hers, the memories. "You didn't count on Maggie when you started seeing me. It's not something people automatically expect."

Joe nodded. "True."

"See, the problem is that if I begin to rely on you here, I'll keep doing it later. And I can't afford that, Joe, because it's unfair to you."

"Unfair to me?" he retorted. "Why?"

"Because I can't expect you to automatically want to take on a burden like Maggie just because you think you might be attracted to me."

It was Joe's turn to look away, to seek wisdom in the soft grass, to afford silence at the edge of hurtling traffic as he formed some of the most important thoughts he'd ever considered.

"When you found out about Maggie's condition," Joe finally said, turning back to her, "how long did it take you to come to grips with it?"

Allison's smile was at once wistful, rueful and bitter. "I'm *still* coming to grips with it. There's just so much to deal with when you consider her. Not just the Down syndrome, but the heart problem, too. It's a day-to-day roller coaster."

Joe nodded slowly, carefully, holding his breath, hoping that what he was going to say would be the right thing, that she would understand and listen.

"I just found out Sunday," he said. "I can't say I wasn't surprised or upset. I haven't slept for two days because of it."

Allison's smile was telling. "I know."

"The other reason I haven't slept for two nights," he continued, "is you. This may come as a shock to you, but I don't follow just anybody to the hospital. I've been worried about you. I've begun to realize just how much you mean to me. And I don't think I want to just throw that away."

She was already shaking her head. Joe withdrew his arm so that he could take hold of her hands with both of his. To anyone passing, he looked suspiciously like a man proposing, but neither he nor Allison noticed.

"Allison," he insisted. "I don't know anything about Down syndrome. I don't know about ventricular septal defects. Hell, I don't even know Maggie. How do you expect me to make any kind of decision two days after I find out you have a little girl—much less a special child like Maggie—if I don't even know everything that's involved?''

Allison's eyes swelled with harsh tears. ''I was hoping it wouldn't ever get to that. That I could spare you that kind of decision.''

''And if we'd courted and gotten married and had Maggie as ours and she'd had Down syndrome,'' he retorted. ''Would you spare me then, too?''

She shook her head again, the words not enough for what she'd lived through. ''Maggie's mine, Joe. First, last and always, I'm the only one responsible for her. That's because her father walked out on her when she was four days old. He couldn't deal with the fact that she was abnormal. He couldn't face a future with a retarded child. When he left, I knew that I'd have to raise Maggie alone. I've almost reached the point where I'm resigned to it. Where I can survive it. And now, you come along and expect me to offer myself up again? I'm just not sure I'm strong enough for that.''

His hold tightened. ''Don't put me in his mold until you give me a chance.''

She could only seem to shake her head, her eyes huge and tormented. ''You just don't understand,'' she protested.

''Then make me understand,'' he demanded. For a minute Joe couldn't say any more. He just held Allison, both with his hands and his gaze, frustrated for the information she hoarded, the emotions she held in check, for just one brief peek into her soul to help him understand what she was facing.

''I want to know everything,'' was all he could say. ''I want to find out what your life is like, to try and come to grips with everything that Maggie means, both the good and the bad. I want the myths cleared up. I want to know what her day is like, what her future holds and what our future would hold. I'm not going to fool you, Allison. This isn't what I've always envisioned for my life. You know that. I'm not sure yet how to concede that to the reality, but I have to know if I can.''

"But don't you see?" she demanded, the tears silently coursing down her cheeks. "I don't know if I could survive if you failed."

"Think it over before you decide," he said. "Talk it over with your friend Brook. She's sensible. See if she doesn't think it's worth the chance." He paused, the frustration sudden and hot, overwhelming his command of words. "I can't just walk away without at least trying. You mean too much to me."

Allison trembled in his hold. She ducked her head, afraid. Joe released one hand to gently wipe those tears away. Then he lifted her face back to him and saw the depth of her fears, and knew that he couldn't offer any more words to soothe them. So, bending carefully to her, one hand still caught between them, the cacophony of traffic lost to them and the breeze dying between them, he kissed her.

Sweetly, gently. Offering promise and begging favor. Calming, quieting, commanding. Slipping his hand back to her neck, he held her to him. She started, protested, stilled. Joe tasted the salt of her tears on her lips and heard the hope in her half-stifled sob. He felt her hand against his chest and knew she could feel the thunder of his heart.

"This isn't the time to answer," he whispered into her hair, holding her to him, soaking in the tumble of her heart as well. "You still have to get Maggie home and get yourself taken care of."

"You're not making any promises," she accused half-heartedly.

He kissed the top of her head. "It's still too early for promises, Allison. Except that I'll do my damnedest not to hurt you."

There was a silence, a shudder through her as if she were assimilating, processing, protecting. "I know," she finally said. "I just wish I knew whether it was enough."

"A chance," he repeated. "Just give me a chance."

"I'll... talk to Brook."

It was the most he could hope for. He held her quietly, eyes closed, heart slowing, his hand stroking her soft, silken hair. And there, in the park across from the huge children's hospital, he knew for the first time in his life what real fear was. Because there in the softening light of dusk, he was really afraid that he wouldn't be what this woman needed. And he wasn't sure he could face that.

"Let me get this straight," Brook said from where she lounged on the sole armchair in Maggie's room, only her eyes moving as they followed Allison as she wore a groove into the terrazzo floor. "After getting burned by an accountant in a big-eight firm, you want to trust a jazz-playing carpenter who has a wife *and* a mistress?"

The surgically precise evaluation of the situation actually brought Allison to her first temporary halt since Joe had left an hour earlier. Her hands shoved into her slacks pockets, she faced the amusement in her friend's face with a brief resurgence of her own humor.

"It's not really as bad as it sounds," she demurred, wondering how she could get Brook past Joe's lurid imagination to the meat of the issue without giving him away, and then thinking that maybe it would be a nice distraction to leave things as they were. "We've known each other a long time." She never realized she lied so easily.

"Which was why he had no idea about Maggie."

Allison couldn't help letting her gaze slide over to where her daughter slept peacefully, unaware of her mother's turmoil. "Well, we haven't talked . . . in a while."

Brook gave her one of those slow nods that betrayed her own skepticism. "Of course."

Allison grinned halfheartedly and resumed pacing, the movement instinctive rather than deliberate, the image of Joe chasing her back and forth across the room without respite.

"Well, I have to say that he's certainly made quite an impression in a few days," Brook observed dryly.

Allison smiled when she wanted to sob. Somehow, she'd ended up by the window—the window that looked down onto the park where they'd sat at sunset. It was dark out now, the landscape muted into ghosts and shadow by the streetlights, the traffic still lurching along.

His arms. They were all she could think about as she looked down on the crowns of those trees. So strong, so capable, so very patient. He'd held her for three days, unobtrusively, gently, keeping her up when she thought she'd crumble into a little pile of ambivalence. Always there, never demanding more, never pressing where he knew she couldn't yet go.

She'd seen it in his eyes, of course, those deadly soft brown eyes that seemed to soak in the world and carry all its weight, even as they looked back with outrageous humor. Eyes brimming with life, with caring, with a heart-stopping, unconscious sensuality.

Allison had never seen such eyes before, so sweet and hungry and strong that she couldn't seem to drag her own gaze away, as if by simply meeting them, she could tap into the life that seemed to bubble from him like a freshwater spring.

Her body still tingled from him, shimmered in memory and anticipation of his touch. He had meant that kiss out on that bench to be a promise, a pact. When he'd pulled away, she'd almost sobbed with loss.

"I said—" Brook repeated, nudging Allison back to the present.

Allison didn't bother to turn away from the window. "I know what you said," she retorted quietly. "And yes, he has made quite an impression." More than even Brook realized. More than anyone could realize could they see the withered, sere remnants of Allison's trust.

"And you're going to tell me just why it is you can rely on this paragon of respectability."

Allison couldn't help a wistful smile. "Because he was the one who told me that I couldn't rely on him."

Brook actually shuffled to her feet with that one. Wandering over to resettle Maggie's blanket, she obviously spent the time searching for tact. "I'm sure that makes sense to someone."

Allison finally turned from the window. "He was honest with me, Brook. He told me that he wanted a chance. That it wouldn't be fair to either of us to sabotage a relationship until he knew exactly what it would entail. He wants to know all there is about Maggie. He wants to find out what having a child with Down syndrome might entail. All he asked was that we try.''

The two women faced each other, silent and uncertain.

''And are you?'' Brook finally asked quietly.

''Going to let him know just what it's like having a child with Down's?'' Allison retorted, head dipping a little. ''Yes. I think I'd like to.''

''That means everything,'' Brook challenged, not relenting at all. ''Not just your patented speech on Down's progress and the joy of having a special child, but all those private, dark, painful little places you won't let anybody else go. Are you willing to offer those up, too?''

Allison came very close to flinching. Brook wanted her to uncover her monsters, to acknowledge them and consider them in the harsh light of reason. Brook wanted her to admit the things she didn't even admit to herself. Was she really ready to chance that yet, even for Joe?

''Do you think he's worth it?'' Brook prodded, closing in without moving.

Allison shrank away a little, afraid of the imminent decision, even though she'd been the one talking Brook into it. ''He's been really wonderful with Maggie,'' she hedged.

''And is kind to small animals and gives to charity,'' Brook countered impatiently. ''I know. What I want to know is, deep down where it counts, is he worth the chance he's asking you to take?''

Allison retreated into herself for a moment, into her memory of the past three days, when Joe had anticipated her needs, bullied her into taking care of herself, when he'd simply held her without being asked, without making demands. She pictured him, sprawled out on the waiting-room couch at four in the morning, his features as young as life, as vital as earth and granite. As suddenly familiar as her own.

She'd stood there before him for ten minutes, not speaking, afraid of losing that selfish moment of possession. Assailed by the urge to lift that fallen lock of hair from his forehead and smooth a cover over him. It was then, oddly enough in sleep, that she could finally understand how the Binkley Brothers had been born.

"Yes," she admitted. "He's worth it. He's ... special."

Brook's eyebrow quirked. "He must be, with a wife, a mistress, and now you. I should have spent more time talking to him."

"Knowing you," Allison offered dryly, "you'll make it up quickly enough."

Brook's smile was knowing and unrepentant. "Does this mean you've come to a decision?"

Allison opened her mouth, closed it. Looked over once again at Maggie, still sleeping. The baby's face was pursed as if in concentration, her limbs loose, the telltale Down's features softened in sleep. She was a beauty, Allison thought, aching for her. She was too fragile to be offered up as a pawn in a game of chance. But she deserved the opportunity to have somebody as unique as Joe in her life.

Allison's chest was on fire. Turmoil knotted in her throat and took her breath. She'd never made a more important decision in her life, a decision so fraught with peril. Because simply by giving Joe her answer, by inviting him into her life, she was asking to have her hopes shattered yet again. She was risking Maggie's well-being as much as her own.

Every day since she'd first discovered she was pregnant, she'd had to make tough decisions about her daughter, choices without guarantees. Yet none had carried with them a consequence she couldn't overcome. This time she wasn't so sure.

Tell me, she wanted to beg Brook. Give me the answer that's right for all of us. An answer that would give me the chance and protect me from its failure at the same time.

But there was no answer like that, and Allison had known it all along. All she could do was choose and pray that she was wise enough to choose well.

In the end, she took a slow, deep breath and looked back out into the shadows that had earlier been a park, at the indecision that had once upon a time been hard-won certainty.

"I think," she said, closing her eyes against it all, and hearing only the staccato of her heart, "that I have."

Chapter 8

"So, *you're* L. Wood Dowd."

Joe considered the sizable black woman standing in the doorway, hands on her hips, head tilted to one side and a wicked smile in her eyes. She wasn't exactly who he'd been expecting to answer Allison's door.

Joe grinned a greeting. "If this isn't Allison Henley's house, my secret's out."

"Your secret's safe long as those flowers are for me," the woman assured him without moving.

He considered the bouquet of spring flowers and then her again. "I had you pegged more for a diamonds-and-fur woman."

"What I want fur for?" she demanded. "I'd just look like a bear, and some fool'd shoot me in the street. Get in here before she escapes out the back door."

"Allison?"

She moved to the side. "Of course, Allison. She been twitchin' around here ever since she got home from the office. Cleaned up three times, and I already did that this morning."

Joe stepped into the living room, much more aware of the scenery than the last time he'd set foot inside. A peaceful place, all pastels and uncluttered soft furniture and the mouthwatering aroma of roast heavy on the air. It sure beat the last time he'd eaten a meal with Allison.

"When are you gonna let Ralph have a book of his own?" the black woman demanded as she shut the door.

Joe turned, surprised. "You read the boys?"

She snorted brusquely. "I know 'em by heart. Got babies of my own."

"Lucille's a connoisseur, aren't you?"

Joe hadn't heard Allison arrive. He turned back to find her standing at the edge of the hallway, barefoot and smiling, a filmy flowered cotton dress drifting about her legs and leaving her throat and arms bare.

"You changed again?" Lucille demanded incredulously.

"Shut up, Lucille," Allison smiled, never taking her eyes from Joe.

Joe couldn't help but smile back, the sight of Allison bumping into him like a surprise. He'd forgotten how much he'd grown to like pixy brown hair and smoky green eyes. He'd forgotten how anxiously he'd waited for word from her. He'd forgotten how much he'd ached for her in the middle of the night.

He'd forgotten, hell.

"I brought some more sketches," he greeted her, casually lifting the portfolio that had come with the flowers. "Since this is a business dinner and all."

"Sketches?" Lucille demanded, noticeably brightening. "Like from a book?"

"You can see them later," Allison promised, still not turning from Joe, a curious effervescence in her gaze. Joe felt it skimming him like a tide and decided he didn't want to pull clear. "Tomorrow, maybe when you come back. Since you're leaving."

"Who made your dinner?" Lucille demanded, hands back on hips. "Who rocked that child to sleep when she got so cranky she wouldn't settle and I was afraid she'd end up back in the hospital? Is it too much I ask just to see some—''

Without a word, Joe handed over the portfolio. When Lucille grabbed on to it, Joe headed in.

"Would you like a drink?" Allison asked, whirling before him toward the kitchen.

"I think you still might have a bottle of my wine here," he offered.

She grinned over her shoulder. "I was saving that for the roast."

Joe could see close up how brittle that smile was, how purposeful her enthusiasm. She was as terrified as she was excited. Well, he couldn't really blame her. It had taken a lot for her just to call and make the invitation. It was going to take more to give him her decision.

"Beer, then," he allowed.

Allison produced his beer and her tea while Joe perused the collection of snapshots on the refrigerator. Ninety percent of them involved Maggie, from her first hospital shot against a backdrop that looked like a baby quilt, to some that looked pretty recent. Smiling, laughing, concentrating, sleeping. Alone or with Allison or Lucille, but not any other adults. A normal composite of first-child photos, all amassed right where Allison couldn't miss them. Or escape them. Joe wondered which.

"Where's Maggie?" he asked, lifting the bouquet back into sight.

Handing over his beer, Allison lifted a dry eyebrow. "Those aren't for me?"

"Did *you* just get out of the hospital?" Joe demanded playfully, deliberately setting the tone for the evening, knowing perfectly well what Allison was facing. Knowing what he was facing.

She scowled. "Yes," she retorted. "I not only got out of the hospital, I paid the bill and played ambulance on the way home. So she gets flowers and I have to cook dinner?"

"*I* cooked dinner!" Lucille immediately yelled from the other room.

Allison bent over and produced a vase from a cabinet.

Joe rewarded her by pulling out one of the paper jonquils from the center of the haphazard bunch of jonquils, tulips, hyacinth and Japanese iris and handing it to her. "I grew this one just for you," he teased gently, fingering the faint rose tint of the center. "It's blushing, just like you."

"I am not blushing," she protested with a tremulous grin, accepting the jonquil all the same. "I'm . . . flushed."

Joe just nodded. "In that case, it's flushed." Then he caught her with a smile. "Just like you."

He didn't let go of the flower quite quickly enough so that he had to brush against her fingers. She jumped, startled by the contact. Joe could feel it all the way up his arm, the sudden jolt of anticipation. Desire. She curled her fingers around the stem, and Joe curled his around the cool neck of his beer, but the tingling didn't abate.

"Is Maggie asleep?" he asked, handing over the rest of the flowers for placement.

Deliberately busying herself with her task, Allison nodded. "For the moment." She didn't seem to notice that her hand trembled. "She'll probably wake up just as we're sitting down to eat. Come on in and take a peek."

The two of them carried the flowers to where the little girl's room lay in dim afternoon shadow. Again Joe took in the bright colors, the cacophony of visual and auditory stimulation. Bells, chimes, birds, clouds, enough to keep a child dreaming for a decade.

Except, he knew, that this child didn't yet know how to dream. He wondered if she ever would, and he ached for her.

She was so tiny, so soft and downy, with her wispy brown hair and delicate hands. Propped on her side in the little bed where bells cascaded if she moved, Maggie Henley looked like a precious doll.

Just as he did when looking at any baby, Joe smiled. He loved babies: their smell, their gurgling laughter, their nonsense chatter that was so intensely communicated with pursed foreheads and serious eyes. Bundles of energy and potential. Innocence and amazement.

It was unfair, he thought with sudden venom. Obscene, that this should happen to Maggie, that she should have her future snatched from her before she ever had a chance at it. That she should suffer and struggle before she even knew why.

How, he wondered for the hundredth time, would he cope with that? How would he live with her limitations, her fragile hold on life?

"Hard to believe she's sick," he mused, looking down on the pink cheeks.

Allison looked over from where she was setting the bouquet on the white dresser. "There are some days I can almost forget it," she admitted.

Joe looked over at her to find her scooting over a bud vase with a single live pink rose in it to accommodate his gaudier offering.

"What's this?" he demanded playfully, indicating it. "Another man?"

Allison looked up and then at the single flower she'd held. Almost unconsciously, she reached out a hand to caress the just-opening petals. "No," she said. "That one's from me."

Joe heard so much in those words. Sadness, longing, pride, determination. She touched that rose as if it were a talisman.

"A welcome home?" he asked.

She turned to him, then, and her eyes darkened unbearably. "A promise."

Joe could do no more than wait, knowing that she needed to say more, not sure whether she could. Allison dipped her head a little, her eyes on her baby, her attention torn, her hand still seeking out that flower.

"You grew those flowers in your garden, didn't you?" she asked.

Joe nodded. "Yes."

She continued to consider the flowers side by side, one a riot of color and texture, the other a pastel blush of grace and simplicity.

"Every flower grows differently," she finally said, her voice low and fragile. "Some can grow anywhere, with no help. Others need mulch and fertilizer and a lot of talking to. Well, the rose needs the most care of all. It needs acid levels and rose dust and trimming and the right kind of sunlight. It's hard work to grow roses. And when they bloom, they do it slowly, so that the process is all the more beautiful. The rose is the most precious flower in the garden because it is that blooming itself that is the beauty.''

She briefly looked over at her daughter, and then turned her attention to Joe. There in her eyes he could see the battle that must be raging. Even so, she sparkled with gentle pride and fierce love. "Children are a lot like flowers in a carefully tended garden," she said softly, her words familiar, the emotion still thick. "And because you have to work harder and wait longer for the bloom, the rose in that garden is a child with Down's."

Joe saw that frail pink rose, just on the brink of opening, trembling so close that it made you want to watch and wait. He thought of the struggle to bring a child with Down's to blooming, and knew what kind of courage and compassion Allison had. He saw that the rose was a day old, and thought of all the roses Allison had bought and brought home and placed in her daughter's room, a solitary gift, a gentle reminder.

"It's hard to remember that sometimes, isn't it?" he asked Allison just as gently.

Allison's smile was heartbreaking. "Sometimes once a day."

He didn't know how to offer his own support, how to add his promise to hers. There were neither the words nor the understanding. He still had to find out what that daily struggle was. He had to know just what kind of bloom Maggie would become. And he had to know whether he had the patience to be that kind of gardener.

Even so, he gave Allison what he could. "I'd say Maggie has a pretty special mother."

Allison took a second to recover her baby, stroking that downy head and murmuring to the sleeping infant. When she turned back to Joe, there was the glitter of tears in her eyes. "Not nearly special enough for her."

Before Joe could protest, she walked on out of the room. He was left behind for a moment, in that soft nest of color and shape, where the hyacinths had already begun to anoint the air with their heavy spice. He watched the sleeping infant. He thought of promises and chances. He wished he knew whether he would make it better or worse for Maggie and her mother, because they had it hard enough. And then, bending over just as Allison had to rearrange a blanket that needed no rearranging, Joe reached out and stroked that soft cheek, much the way Allison had caressed the lip of the rose.

Allison was waiting back in the kitchen, sipping at her iced tea with tense, jerky movements. Lucille was still poring over sketches at the card table where two place settings had been laid out on a lace tablecloth.

"I hate to ruin dinner," Joe offered as he picked up his beer and faced Allison. "But I don't think you're going to digest anything if we don't talk abut the decision you invited me over to announce."

Allison was already shaking her head, gesturing briefly toward the dining room. "Later. Please. I'm really hungry now."

Joe almost laughed. She looked almost as hungry as he had back at the hospital.

"Get it over with quickly," he advised dryly. "Like pulling off a Band-Aid. It doesn't hurt so much."

Allison actually scowled with a modicum of humor. "It does when I have a peanut gallery not five feet away."

"When did you decide Unctious should fall in love?" Lucille suddenly demanded from the doorway, right on cue. "I thought the bathroom book was going to be an adventure in the wilds of the Amazon."

Joe turned to see the sketches in her ample hands and acquiesced to a higher power. He wasn't going to get a decision until dessert, after all. "It was. Wanda was going to be the evil tribal priestess demanding the boys be boiled in oil."

Lucille nodded, her eyes a lot sharper than her desultory movements. Joe had a feeling that she already knew perfectly well when Wanda had changed from villain to lead.

"I like the wart," was all she said, stuffing the papers back into the portfolio. "Does he get her?"

Joe offered a slow smile that he knew she understood perfectly well. "That remains to be seen," he retorted. "Doesn't it?"

Lucille smiled right back and handed over Joe's work. "I guess it does." Shaking her head with delight, she reached down to pick up her things. "I guess it does."

"I imagine you two had some vague idea of what you were talking about?" Allison asked a few minutes later, after showing Lucille out.

Standing by the glass doors to Allison's patio, Joe managed a smile for her, too. "She's something," he acknowledged. "Is she your cleaning lady?"

Allison afforded him a quick laugh. "Hardly. She has a master's in art history. She quit nine-to-five work to take care of her kids. In her spare time she likes to help take care of special children."

Joe found himself chagrined at his own dismissal. "How did you find her?"

Allison laughed. "She found me. Two of her kids are disabled. They go to the same school Maggie does, and Lucille heard that I was suddenly single and probably in need of a little 'friendly assistance,' as she calls it. I call it despotism."

"And you hired her?"

Allison shook her head. "She adopted me. I couldn't have said no if I'd wanted to."

Joe couldn't do much more than shake his head, amazed. Unsettled by his complacent ignorance of the world Allison and Lucille inhabited. He'd always been lucky. Healthy and able to follow whatever dream he'd set out for himself, happy with his work and his accomplishments. Comfortable with his family. He'd never had to look for someone who might be willing to take care of a child with developmental problems and a heart defect. He'd never been tested to see if he had enough strength to not only take care of his own children, but someone else's.

He'd asked Allison to be allowed in. Once again, he wondered if he were not strong enough, but wise enough to manage it.

"Why don't we go sit in the living room and appreciate how clean it is?" Allison asked.

Joe looked down at her and realized that she knew exactly what he was thinking.

"Just promise you won't patronize me," he demanded with a soft scowl.

She actually chuckled. "This isn't a subject that's covered in high school health class, Joe. I can't expect you to understand it by osmosis the minute you walk in the door."

"Just remember, I'm willing to learn."

Allison waited to answer until they'd settled themselves onto the couch. One of the table lamps was on, spilling a pool of buttermilk-colored light across Allison's features. Joe thought her cheeks were a little too hollow, her eyes a bit too stark after her stint in the hospital. But still she radiated a sweet life that was intoxicating. She enticed with that wry smile and unsuspected strength.

Even a rosekeeper needed company. Even a saint needed help. Joe wanted that to be him.

"I guess you're wondering why I called you here," she abruptly began, eyes down, drink clutched in her hands. She had nail polish on tonight, a muted berry shade that made her look elegant.

Joe lifted an eyebrow. "I thought we were going to do this after dinner."

Her grin was halfhearted. "We were going to do it after Lucille left."

Just as a precaution, Joe drained his beer. He figured that no matter how this went, he was going to need a little fortification. "So that she wouldn't be embarrassed when I sobbed on her shoulder?"

A grin tugged at the corners of Allison's mouth. "So that she's not so insufferable the next time I see her. She never lets me forget when she's right."

Joe went very still. He'd been anticipating this answer, but still wasn't sure he was ready for it.

"She voted with me, huh?"

Allison shook her head a little, her eyes more troubled than her voice. "She seems to think I'm stronger than I am."

Joe reached out and took her hand. "I have a feeling she thinks you shouldn't have to do this all by yourself."

"But in the end, I might anyway," Allison retorted sharply, pulling away.

"I promise—"

"No," she interrupted. "Don't promise. Don't tell me things I want to hear just because they'll make me feel better—not until you know everything, just like you asked."

"And you're going to tell me."

Her eyes glittered with emotion, fear and frustration—and a terrible hope. Joe held his breath, careful not to touch her since he knew damn well she'd splinter into a million pieces just then if he did.

Finally she took a sighing breath, a capitulation more than a decision. "You're damn right I'm going to tell you," she said.

Allison didn't remember eating her dinner. She must have. When she looked down, her plate was empty. She felt raw, exposed, every one of her nerves screeching in protest of what she was doing to herself. Common sense battered at her. Hope ached in her chest more unbearably than despair, and she wasn't sure she could take it.

Joe had stayed. When Allison had dropped two plates into explosions on the kitchen floor, he'd taken over getting dinner out, sitting her firmly on her chair and setting out dishes and opening wine. He'd entertained her and cajoled her and seduced her, never once coming closer than the far side of a casserole dish when he'd passed food.

Maybe that was the biggest surprise of all. Not that she'd actually given in and trusted Joe enough to let him get to know Maggie. That, after all this time, since well before Maggie's birth, she should recognize the first stirrings of desire.

Before this, Allison simply hadn't allowed it. She hadn't had the energy, the will or the time for attraction. She'd known since the day Brian had walked out that she wouldn't get another chance, that her focus had to be her daughter. So she'd simply, almost surgically, cut out her body's natural inclinations.

And now, suddenly, in the matter of a couple of weeks and one tentative promise, Joe had set all that loose. Slipping in beneath her defenses with his brash humor and sweet, sharp eyes, he'd let loose that most deadly of emotions, the undercurrent for excitement and hope and possibility. He'd opened her up to anticipation, and that was something Allison had closed her heart to more fiercely than anything else.

The dreadful hope Joe had unleashed by demanding inclusion was more terrifying than the void of desolation she'd been left with after Brian's departure. Allison felt its insidious tendrils snaking around her limbs, compelling her, intoxicating her, and she was terrified that instead of setting her free, it would pull her under.

"Carpentry grounds me," Joe was saying in answer to a question. "Hands-on, sweaty, hard work that shows results and lasts if you do it right. Nothing feels quite as good as running your hands over well-fitted wood. Nothing smells as good as fresh shavings in the morning when you take your first coffee break."

His eyes gleamed with satisfaction. Accomplishment. Completion. Allison couldn't seem to pull away from the sense of wholeness he projected. A proud man, a man whose success was measured by his own skills rather than anyone else's opinion. A rare and striking man for his own lack of pretension.

"What do you want to know about Down syndrome?" Allison asked abruptly, baldly.

Joe didn't seem in the least fazed. Allowing the smallest of smiles, he reached for her plate. "Do you have coffee?"

Allison blinked, following his movements. "Uh, yes. It's already made." Ashamed, she shook her head. This wasn't the way to handle it. But she didn't know how else to break it off before she really began to love him. She didn't know how to discourage him except with the truth. "No, never mind. I'm sorry."

He got to his feet, both plates in hand, his eyes knowing. "We can talk over coffee. All right?"

"Really, Joe. You were talking about your work. I'd like to know."

"And I'd like to know more about Maggie. I've got plenty of time to bore you with brad sizes and load-bearing stress."

No, she wanted to say, you don't. You can't stay that long. You can't make yourself more important to me. You can't. Oh, God, you can't continue to seduce me with those earth brown eyes and knowing smiles.

She shouldn't have told him to try. She wasn't going to be able to survive this. Halfway up to protest Joe's assumption of her duties, Allison heard the bells.

"Looks like we've run out of time," she hedged, and slid into Maggie's room before Joe had a chance to argue.

Maggie needed changing, and Allison took as long as she could at the task, trying her best to distance herself from Joe's insidious charm. She played all her games with her daughter, naming, repeating, singing. Maggie crooned along, waving her little arms aimlessly as Allison worked, and crinkled up into a toothless smile when her mommy lifted her up.

Allison hadn't seen Joe come to stand in the doorway. When she turned, Maggie filling her arms, he was leaning against the doorjamb, coffee in hand, expression enigmatic.

"Whenever I do something for Maggie, I identify what I'm doing," Allison said, her voice flat. "I repeat words constantly so that, hopefully, she'll be able to begin identifying objects sooner. I enunciate carefully, because she'll have trouble enough talking due to muscle control and the shape of her mouth. The better she hears things, the easier it might be. Everything I teach her has to be repeated again and again every day, just to impress it on her. Every exercise, every book I read, every song I sing. Over and over and over again."

Joe dropped his gaze to the little girl for a moment and then gave it back to Allison. "How slow will she be?" he asked.

Allison hated the term, but knew she had to use it. Had to impale Joe on it if he were to understand. "How retarded?" she asked. "There's no way to tell. There's a wide range with children with Down's, from mildly to profoundly retarded. Most kids with Down's fall into the moderate range. There's never any way to guess in an infant how severe her retardation will be, because every single task a child has is a developmental crapshoot. No two are alike, and no child has a recognizable pattern. Maggie just rolled over for the first time. That's really good, especially since her heart has temporarily set her back. But she's way behind on hand-eye coordination. We simply won't know until she begins to grow and learn."

She saw the impact of her words strike Joe. No one with any kind of compassion could possibly be unaffected. No one who loved children could imagine what kind of struggle Maggie was up against and not feel for her. Joe was no different. His eyes darkened. His jaw tightened. His silence was taut and painful.

Allison steeled herself against the first sign of what she dreaded most in the world. The uncomfortable distancing. The pity. The platitudes and unknowing barbs couched in terms of concern. *Well, she'll be your baby forever, won't she? These children are always happy, so that's all right.* Or, the worst, the one her mother had so disastrously tried to comfort her with. *You know, I've seen those kind working at burger joints.* Sincerely offered, unadvised, more painful for their bland disregard of the scope of the truth.

Joe, though, didn't say a word. He simply held out his arms for Maggie. And Allison, still torn, still ravaged by doubt and guilt and exhilaration, handed her daughter over.

Joe weighed the little girl in his arms. He looked right into those fathomless dark eyes and smiled. And Maggie, who didn't know a stranger, snuggled right into his embrace.

* * *

B.B.'s was still crowded at closing. The music had been good for a Wednesday night, the band tight and sweet, the air thick with blues. Caught in the glare of the lights, Joe was bent over his sax, his eyes closed, his fingers stroking notes out of the instrument that glided and moaned with an almost human need.

He was in all black tonight, his hair brushed straight back, the perspiration from the close room sliding in rivulets down his temples and staining his shirt. He didn't see the considering glances from his fellow musicians as he stroked out Eric Clapton's "Running on Faith." His mind was closed to the room, the people. Only the music mattered, dark, deep notes that echoed and shuddered through him. Slow minor progressions, the tone of tears, the voice of confusion and pain and need. Keening in the wind.

He almost didn't hear the applause, so intent had he been. The band swept in on the heels of his solo and ran together to the end. They ended the set with Dave Brubeck's "Take Five," and the lights came up. Joe blinked a couple of times, still gliding back down from the adrenaline rush of good music. His heart was pumping and his veins fizzled with it. He was sweating and exhausted, as if he'd just run a mile, purged in a way he'd never been before, even by this.

Little William Washington, the other sax player, turned to Joe with a hand on his shoulder.

"Boy, you been places tonight you *never* been before."

Joe offered him a wry grin. "Yeah," he admitted in amazement, wiping away the perspiration with a towel. "I think I have."

Little William shook his large grizzled head, black eyes glittering in the lights. "You musta lost your woman."

Joe's answering laugh was sharp and wry. "No," he disagreed, knowing exactly what had fueled his music tonight. "I think I got her."

Chapter 9

"What do I do?" Joe asked, his voice faintly tinged with alarm. He was crouched before the balancing wheel, both hands tight enough around Maggie that she was beginning to complain, his own expression not much more confident than the baby's.

Allison almost laughed. Men made things so complicated. "Just rock her from side to side. She's not going to break."

They were at early-infant stimulation class at the local Society for Retarded Children Center. Around the room about a dozen other children were working on other tasks, from balance to coordination to tracking—following objects with their eyes and hands to improve hand-eye coordination. The predominant sound in the room was encouragement, mother's voices high and singing, repetitive in a syncopated chorus, punctuated by one or two irritable wails of protest and the calm instructions of teachers and therapists.

For the first time since Joe had met her, Maggie was in a snit. Maggie hated to work. Like any child, she could instinctively find just the right chain to yank, and she was definitely yanking Joe's.

"She's terrified," he objected, seeing the swelling tears, the pitiful demeanor, the tiny hands flailing for support.

"She's nothing of the kind," Allison assured him easily, getting things started herself by placing her hands over Joe's and moving them, Maggie and the rocker. A big horizontal tube covered in corduroy, the piece of equipment served to develop balance. Maggie didn't particularly care for it. Her balance wasn't all that good.

"You'd never know she rolled over," Ellen Barlow commented from behind them.

Allison turned to the teacher and scowled. "Once. She rolled over once. If I don't get proof soon, you're all going to believe I was hallucinating."

Ellen smiled. "You know she's bound to regress a little after that stint in the hospital. Be patient."

Allison's answering smile was wry. "I should cross-stitch that into a sampler."

"Am I doing this right?" Joe demanded, still rolling Maggie from side to side so that she looked inches away from slipping over onto her ear, and then lifted back the other way. For her part, Maggie was whining.

"Hard to do it wrong," Allison assured him.

He scowled at her. "Easy for you to say. You're trained in this."

Maggie hit full pitch and Joe winced like a man who'd just had to spank his first child.

"Hold her any tighter, she's going to pop," Allison advised quietly, her hands stuffed deep in her own pockets.

Joe didn't even look up. "She's so unwieldy on this thing. I mean, her head isn't even that stable. I'm afraid I'm going to hurt her."

"She's tougher than you think," Allison reassured him.

She kept wanting to pull Maggie away from Joe, to do this herself. It surprised her, considering all the times she'd rocked Maggie herself or worked on tracking or grip or eye-hand coordination and had wished desperately that there were somebody else who could take some of the grinding repetition away. Suddenly, with her daughter firmly in Joe's hands, with Maggie's eyes turned first her way and then his for rescue, Allison wasn't so sure.

After all, this had been all her job. Maggie had been all hers. And within the space of a few days, the little girl was recognizing Joe. She was cooing along with him and waving her arms at him when he approached. Allison was terrified. She was ambivalent. She wanted someone else for her daughter, *and* was afraid her daughter would need them more than her.

"Okay, now, lift her up and let me turn the thing around," Allison commanded, holding out her hands. Maggie made an immediate attempt to reach for her, tears now coursing down her cheeks.

Joe lifted and Allison turned.

"Now," Allison commanded, wondering whether she was trying to scare Joe deliberately, "you have to put her on her tummy on top and roll her forward until she almost falls on her nose."

Joe snarled at her. "Hey, you're a nice guy."

"Babies with Down's have a slow reaction time. Because of that, they can't catch themselves as quickly when they fall, and it takes them longer to get up the guts to get up and walk. We're teaching her how to fall."

"Hell," Joe retorted, settling Maggie in place anyway. "Why don't we do it like swimming? I'll just throw her to the floor and see if she can manage."

"This way saves on Band-Aids."

He pulled Maggie toward him, whereupon she immediately screeched in protest. After a long moment, she did, however, stretch her arms in the right direction. Progress.

"Great," Ellen crowed from behind them as she came around again.

Joe looked over his shoulder with a brash grin. "I'm a quick learner."

"Not you," she laughed. "Her. That's the first time she's gotten it right."

Joe looked back at Maggie. "Gotten what right? What did she do?"

"She reached out for the floor," Allison informed him. "It's an instinctive response in most children. A millisecond reaction. But we have to teach it to Maggie."

Joe nodded. "Wonderful. Now she knows it, can we do something she likes better?"

"Now that she knows it," Allison corrected, "we have to do it about a thousand more times to get her to remember it."

Joe crooked an eyebrow at her.

Allison smiled with very little humor. "Progress comes in inches, Joe. She won't suddenly wake up one morning and have all these skills we're teaching her. We have to fight for every one. Every day."

"I still think it calls for a celebration," he challenged.

Allison waved at him. "Don't stop now, for God's sake. Get that movement imprinted. Improve her reaction time."

He snorted. "Taskmaster."

He pulled, Maggie howled and Allison grimaced. "Tough being the bad guy, isn't it?" she asked. "Every time she wants to quit, so do you. But you can't, or she'll never know what fun it is to run down a hill or sit on a horse."

"What do we get to do after this?" he asked, still rocking the little girl back and forth, taunting another response from her, ignoring the protests and the wide, beseeching eyes. "See how fast she can crawl over hot coals?"

"That's the advanced class. Next we do a little time with a high chair and finger food. Which, actually, she does like."

She did. Allison and Joe ended up decorated with pudding and Maggie cackled at the cool substance on her hands.

"Pudding," Allison sang to her again and again, hands still in pockets as she rocked on her heels before her daughter. "Pudding, Maggie. Isn't that good pudding? Chocolate, mmmmm."

Maggie liked that. She held out her hands for inspection. "Mamamama."

Allison chuckled. "Good girl. Good girl. Now put it in your mouth." She mimicked the action, then took Maggie's hands and accomplished it for her. Maggie seemed incredulous. She had no idea how to copy her mother's actions, though. A lot of pudding ended up everywhere by the end of the session.

"How often do you do the exercises?" Joe asked, cleaning his neck off with a towel as Allison did the same to Maggie's face.

"Every day," Allison said. "Not necessarily everything, but I try to incorporate range of motion when I change her, the language skills all the time and the equipment stuff when I have a good half hour or so at a stretch. I also play a hell of a lot of peek-a-boo and patty-cake."

Joe brightened. "Finally. A course I've already passed."

Allison grinned. "Be my guest. It's good for her socialization and cognitive development."

Joe scowled. "It's peek-a-boo," he protested. "Do you have to be so clinical?"

Allison sighed. "Takes the mystery out of things, doesn't it?"

Joe bought the ice cream and they sat outside, with Maggie tucked in her car seat amidst bolsters to prop her joints and a rolled towel to support her head. Joe was crammed with information, bursting with questions, anxious to know everything.

The session at school had produced mixed results. Joe had seen the work being done with the children, all retarded, some with Down's, each at his or her own development stage. Maggie's was the youngest class, starting at two months and going to two years. He'd seen dedication and love and the price of progress. He'd recognized that Maggie had a sparkle that was missing from some of those sweet wide eyes in that room, and then found himself comparing her progress to others. Allison caught him and shot him right down.

"Measure Maggie by Maggie," she'd instructed, echoes of past hurts in her own voice. "Or the next time you have a niece, you're going to find yourself judging Maggie's progress against hers, and you'll always end up frustrated and disappointed."

Against whom had Allison measured Maggie, Joe wondered. What quick, precocious child had innocently in-
jected that hurt into her voice?

Joe had also seen the older kids there. Not quite as cute
anymore, all working hard, every one at a different level of
accomplishment. A few had been reading. Some had diffi-
culty making themselves understood. One, a tall, raw-boned
boy with the most beautiful blue eyes, simply stood and
rocked back and forth most of the time.

The truth, like a cold shot of water. Maggie wouldn't
grow up to be prom queen or anchorwoman for the nightly
news. She wouldn't change worlds or discover new ones. She
would, at best, manage in her own. Joe was stunned at the
fierce rush of grief that thought provoked. She wasn't his
own daughter. She might never be his. Still, he wanted to hit
something, to break it, to let loose the anger at an imper-
fect world.

"Pralines for you," he announced heartily, setting down
Allison's dish before her. "Rocky Road for me, and—here's
a surprise—chocolate for Maggie."

Pulling over an extra wrought-iron chair to the little table, he settled himself in, all the while still wondering how
Allison looked on those children every time she saw them.
With hope? With dread? With fatalism? He wondered if he
would ever get used to it.

"Wait till you see this," Allison was saying, tying a bib on
Maggie. "She hates cold stuff."

Joe crooked an eyebrow. "Maybe we should clear a few
tables."

Allison grinned. "Nah. You'll stop anything she spits."

"What does she like?" he asked.

Allison took a second to think, the sun washing her hair
and settling into her eyes with a sparkle. "Games, reading,
cuddling, and her toys. And singing…ice cream, baby," she
automatically crooned, the spoon extended. "Mmmmm, ice
cream."

Joe couldn't take his eyes off her. When she faced her
daughter like this, she glowed. Her smile, unreserved, unaffected, undimmed, was bestowed on Maggie like a bounty.

Her voice lulled and lifted, a musical instrument as it taught. Her eyes crinkled up at the corners, the green as sweet as spring grass. Joe could sit like this for hours, for days, and watch her, a woman who came to life as a mother. Who gave unstintingly to her daughter even as she fought her own private battles.

"Tell me about what you plan for her," Joe asked, his Rocky Road melting away untouched.

Allison never looked away from Maggie, never changed her expression, but Joe could see the darkness peek out. "I can't plan," she allowed. "Right now, all I can do is get from one day to the next. One doctor's report to the next. Maybe if she comes through the surgery okay, I'll begin to think farther ahead than June . . . come on, you little snot. Don't spit that on Joe. He's not a wall, y'know. And this is the expensive stuff. . . . Chocolate, chocolate."

"What are her chances?" Joe asked quietly.

The spoon arrested in midair, Allison looked over at Joe, and he saw the chasm widen. "About fifty-fifty."

Another punch in the gut. Another step closer to the precipice, a mile closer to the edge of the flat world beyond which lay dragons. Joe didn't know this territory. He didn't want to. It was tough enough bringing children up into the wild confusion the world had become. It was unthinkable to have to face the fact that after all your effort, all the love you poured onto them like rainwater and sunshine, they could die anyway.

It was incomprehensible that this scowling, sweet, beautiful little girl might not live long enough to see Christmas.

"How do you deal with it?" he asked.

Allison looked over at him, and the spoon fell back onto the table. "I don't," she admitted quietly, her gaze dropping to her hands. "Not always. I find that if I don't look any farther than today, then I can't be excited or disappointed. I can manage. And I don't have to face the fact that Maggie might not be with me next year. I just ignore it." She looked up now, and her eyes were stark and dry. "I don't know if I told you, but Justin died. I couldn't even go to the memorial service . . . it was just too frightening."

Joe reached out a hand to take hers, words not enough for what he saw in her eyes, what crept into her voice.

For the first time, Allison held onto him, her fingers as taut as her words. She drew a deep breath, as if summoning courage, and went on. "I distance myself from it. And, sometimes, I distance myself from Maggie. Like if I don't love her quite so much, I won't…miss her so much. I won't hurt so badly if…"

For a moment, only the mutter of passing pedestrians filled the silence between Joe and Allison. Even Maggie went still, as if she knew what this conversation meant to her.

"It's a horrible thing to do," Allison said, her gaze falling with the weight of her words. "I'm all she has, and I'm trying my best to be far enough away that if she dies, I won't be sucked in behind her."

Joe held on tight, communicating with only his voice and his hand. "I don't think you're being fair to yourself," he offered quietly, his throat tight with grief.

Allison's eyes blazed with challenge. "I've been praying for somebody to come along and take her off my hands," she snapped. "To share her so I won't have to bear it all alone."

Joe shook his head. "Is that so wrong? You're only human, Allison. Why should you expect more of yourself than other people can deal with?"

"Because I don't have a choice. There's nobody but me. I have to give her everything I have, because if she doesn't live past the surgery, she should at least have the best eight months on earth a child can have."

The air was brittle with rage, with fear and frustration. Joe wanted to give her so much, to ease the deep creases that marred her smooth forehead, to calm the splintering emotion in her voice.

"How do *you* feel about it?" she asked, and her voice still held challenge.

Joe took a slow breath and thought of the surprises in the past few weeks, the turmoil, the sleepless nights. Finally, he offered the truth with his eyes. "It scares the hell out of me," he admitted. "I've never had to deal with this kind of thing before."

Her smile was wry and sad. "Neither have I."

He lifted his other hand and swept a gentle finger down her cheek. "Well, you're sure teaching me. She's a tough little kid," he offered, reassuring himself as much as Allison. "I have a feeling she'll sail through this much more easily than we will."

Joe saw Allison's sharp glance at his choice of pronoun. He didn't explain or amend. He simply left it where he'd laid it, his own small promise. A statement that lay more heavily on him the longer he thought about it.

Falling in love should have been so easy. It should have been fireworks and summertime. Unfortunately, with Allison it was also an inescapable ache. A heaviness that wouldn't dissipate just because Joe didn't want to face it. Along with promise came loss. With the dreams came the reality.

He needed to move. To pace away the frustration that suddenly bubbled in him. He wanted to talk about how he felt, and wasn't sure Allison trusted him enough yet, no matter how truthful she'd just been.

"So, we have about four weeks for me to get used to the idea of spending more time back at the hospital?" he asked instead, letting Allison take her hand back and returning to his half-melted ice cream. Careful retreat, wounds to be attended to.

Allison's gaze was piercing. "Unless Maggie surprises us again."

For Maggie's part, she was beginning to whine, tired from the exercise and the traveling. Her bib and the table decorated with most of her ice cream anyway, she reached out to Allison for rescue. Joe smiled at her and couldn't bear the thought of facing another stint in the ICU waiting room.

"Well, there's only one thing to do about it then," he announced.

Allison crooked an eyebrow.

Joe grinned brightly at her. "Fatten you up. I figure I have twenty-eight days to get you up to fighting weight."

She grimaced almost as dramatically as her daughter. "It's Maggie who needs the weight," she objected. "I'm perfectly all right."

"And you've taken in your belt two notches," Joe retorted.

"You've been talking to Lucille behind my back," she accused.

He grinned. "I have to get the truth from somebody. She agrees with me. That's why she's watching Maggie tomorrow night so you and I can go out."

Allison immediately stiffened. "I can't go out tomorrow."

Maggie heard the stiff protest in her mother's voice and turned to her, eyebrows puckering in question.

Joe merely finished his ice cream. "Of course you can. I figured we'd go out to dinner and then down to B.B.'s. I'm playing there again . . . unless you really don't like jazz."

"I shouldn't—"

It was Joe's turn to scowl. "Even parents of children with Down's go out on occasion, Allison. Paying penance won't change things."

Allison stiffened as if she'd been slapped. "Now I know you've been talking to Lucille," she accused, her voice soft with hurt.

Joe shook his head, wondering how he'd suddenly ended up in this conversation, thinking that it was surely too soon. She didn't know him well enough yet, didn't trust him. And yet, he suddenly couldn't go back, even with the path ahead littered with mines.

"I've been reading," he corrected her. "Everything I could get my hands on. I know more about Down syndrome now than I did last week. And one of the things all the experts say is to be careful you don't forfeit your life for your child's, no matter what. You're not doing them any good."

"I'm not forfeiting my life."

Joe wanted to hold her, wanted to shake her. Her eyes were so dark, so full of hurt and fear. He wanted to possess the words that would open all those dark little places to him so that she wouldn't feel she had to suffer alone anymore.

"You are the most patient, loving, giving mother I've seen," Joe admonished sincerely. "And I've seen some of the best. You also suffer twice what Maggie suffers. You can't keep doing it without any kind of reserves when you need them the most. You're going out with me, and there's not a damn thing you can do about it."

A reluctant grin tugged at the corners of Allison's mouth. "I bet Lucille told you that this was the only way to deal with me."

Joe grinned back. "Actually, she said not to waste my breath on explanations. Just throw you in the car and drive off so fast, you couldn't get back out."

Allison shook her head. "I should have run while I had the chance."

Joe kept his voice light, but he knew the real message lay in his eyes. "You couldn't have run far enough."

Her eyes suddenly glittered. Joe saw the fleeting exhilaration, the hope and then the fear color her eyes. Fragile, frightened, so raw that Joe could almost see the pain skitter across her skin. He wanted to reach out to hold her and knew that here in public, he couldn't. He couldn't touch her because it would be a promise she couldn't accept yet, and she would shatter. Allison, who walked a precarious edge each and every day, balancing between hope and despair, hungry for communion and yet terrified of it, would see her precious control disintegrate and would not easily forgive him.

So he held her with his eyes and hoped that, at least for now, it was enough. Knowing that, for him, it never would be.

Joe helped Allison put Maggie to bed. He played peek-a-boo during her bath and sang nonsense songs while she was changed. At first Maggie wasn't sure how to react to his baritone. She went very still, her forehead puckered and her hands still. Joe laughed. Maggie wasn't convinced. She looked over to Allison for a reaction.

Allison couldn't help a chuckle of her own. "The only man who sings to her is her pediatrician," she informed Joe. "And right after he sings, he sticks cold things in her ears."

"Is that right?" he demanded, and immediately swung the little girl into the air. "Well, I'm not sticking anything into your ear, young lady." Instead, he rubbed his nose in her belly.

Maggie shrieked with delight. Allison fought the surge of joy in her chest. It ached to be freed into laughter, but she held on to it tightly, still not trusting it. Not trusting the warm comfort she felt in Joe's presence in her house or the sweet agony of trusting him with even a small portion of the truth.

Suddenly, her rituals were changing, adding a new dimension, new sounds and shadings—Joe's laughter and his spontaneous affection. The sight of strong arms lifting Maggie toward the clouds. The smell of woodshavings and cologne. The bright gift of flowers. The suddenly coy smiles of her little girl. It took Allison's breath away, taunted her with happiness.

God, but she wanted nothing more than this every night. She wanted Joe's eyes to light up when he saw her. She wanted him to bully her into going out with him and then to spoil her just a little. She wanted to hear him sing to Maggie and then fall asleep nestled into his arms. She wanted to be able to let his strong beauty reduce her to giddy incoherence, to be able to savor the liquid heat of his touch. Just as she'd feared, Joe had opened the door to possibility, and there was no way to close it again.

"If you get her wound up," she warned, turning away to close drawers, "you're going to have to sit with her till she settles down."

Behind her now, Joe laughed. "You must have been talking to my sisters," he said. "They're always saying that to me."

"Uncles are notorious for that kind of behavior," Allison informed him dryly. "I bet you play tag with your nieces and nephews right at bedtime and then go home."

"I do not. I play tiger."

Allison turned around to find the mischief in his eyes. "Tiger?" she echoed, her hands folded tightly around Maggie's clothes to keep them from reaching out to test the life that bubbled from Joe.

With Maggie still in his arms, Joe gave Allison a look as if she were very ill-informed. "Tiger," he repeated. "I am the man-eating tiger, and they are the hunters."

The life bubbled in her now, mimicking laughter, joy, pleasure, cascading in her chest and fighting for freedom. She scowled at him. "Not very ecology minded," she admonished. "You're an endangered species."

His smile was brash and unrepentant, and Allison wanted to weep with sudden longing. "That's okay," he assured her. "This is one game where the endangered species usually wins."

"Well, be a pal and don't teach Maggie just yet," she said, letting loose of the clothes so she could reach for her daughter. "I'm not sure I'm ready to see her with a gun in her hand."

"Not a gun," he countered, handing Maggie over. "Bows and arrows. They're Indians."

Allison crooked an eyebrow. "You haven't educated them about geography yet, have you?"

Joe just smiled. "From never-never land."

Allison did laugh then, Maggie's familiar warmth suffusing her with even more well-being. "Well, then, they're sure playing with the right tiger."

"What is that supposed to mean?"

Allison knew that some of her exhilaration had escaped into her eyes, but she was unable to do anything about it. "Nothing," she hedged. "I'm sure you're a perfectly wonderful tiger."

He was scowling at her now. "The fiercest one in the jungle. You can hear me roar all the way into town . . . want a demonstration?"

She chuckled as she settled Maggie into bed and covered her up. "No, really. I don't think I'm up for a game of tiger hunt tonight."

"Oh," he said behind her, his voice suddenly soft. "I don't think it's going to be the tiger that's hunted tonight."

Allison turned on him, the subtext in his words skittering across her skin like the first warning breeze before a storm. She made the mistake of looking into his eyes. Dark eyes, deep and rich and velvet-soft, smiling and hungry at once. A man-eating tiger setting sight on his prey. A man setting his sights on a woman. A woman he wanted.

Allison shivered. "Coffee?" she suggested, stepping quickly away.

She made it into the hall before he caught her.

"There's something you need to know about tigers," Joe warned her, his voice impossibly soft, languorous.

Allison shut her eyes, stopped dead by the weight of his hand on her arm. "What's that?" she asked.

"We always get what we want."

She turned, did her best not to crumble before the naked desire in Joe's eyes. "And what is it," she asked, "that you want?"

Joe didn't waste words. Turning her around to him, he simply pulled her into his arms. Frightened, intoxicated, frustrated, Allison went. Her heart skidded against her ribs, and the air in her lungs disappeared. She lifted her face to him, challenging, begging, taunting. Furious for the taste of his mouth, for the sweet communion of his touch. Terrified of wanting even that, knowing and yet still denying what she really wanted—what she suddenly needed so much that she battled a sob of frustration.

He didn't promise. He didn't explain or demand or excuse. He cupped her head with his hands and kissed her. Allison shuddered with the brush of his lips, instinctively recognizing his intent. She whimpered with the rasp of his fingers in her hair. She tasted chocolate ice cream on his tongue and smelled soap and cologne on his skin. She lifted her own hands to his chest and nestled there, her fingers discovering the uneven thud of his heartbeat.

"This," he whispered against her mouth, "is what I want. It's what you want."

Allison was sinking into the sudden cacophony of sensations. A crisp cotton shirt against her fingertips, the soft assault of Joe's mouth on hers, the hard length of his body against hers. The grip of his hands holding her to him, filling himself with her. The sigh of his breath against her cheek.

I want it too, she wanted to say. I want to feel your skin against my fingers, to winnow my hands through your hair and kiss those umber eyes closed. I want to see joy in your eyes, to hear the groans of satisfaction and know they are my gift. I want wholeness.

"No," she whimpered, her fingers curling in protest, her eyes squeezed against the tears. "I can't."

Her belly was on fire. Her legs were trembling and her head spun. Wanted and could were two different things. Yes, she wanted it. She wanted him. But it wasn't right. Not now. Not yet. Maybe not ever.

She steeled herself for Joe's protest. She could feel it in every muscle and tendon in his body, and yet he kissed her just once more, a long, gentle foray that promised and conceded at once.

"You will," he said quietly, bending his head over hers. Allison listened for bravado in his words, boast, but heard none. He sounded more resigned than anything. "And when you do, I'll be the one to be there."

From *There's a Monster in My Bathroom*
by L. Wood Dowd

*M*onsters are not supposed to be afraid of dogs. After all, monsters (at least full-grown ones) breathe fire and shatter windows with their terrible roar. They have iridescent scales (which means they shimmer all different colors in lightning), and fierce yellow eyes that are terrifying. Dogs are furry and loud (no dog knows how to properly sneak around) and often dirty. Monsters consider them silly.

But most dogs weren't this big. Unctious peeked back out the bathroom door and shuddered. VERY big, with a deep, sloppy woof and great shining teeth. (Not iridescent, of course. But impressive all the same.) And he had Wanda, who was not a monster and therefore very afraid of dogs, backed into a corner.

It seemed they wanted the same shoe. Now, anyone else might have just given the dog the shoe and waited until later when he was asleep to scare him to get even. But shoes were Wanda's job. It was like if the dog had decided that he wanted to scare little children under the bed. Unctious sim-

ply couldn't let him. Dogs were for fetching and barking at strangers and tearing up newspapers.

Unctious knew that Wanda could never let go of her half of the shoe. Nor, it seemed, did the dog want to let go of his. Unctious knew what he must do. Even so, he was really still a very small monster, and the dog's teeth were very big. Very, VERY big.

"Hold on, Wanda!" he yelled through the crack in the door.

"Who's that?" Wanda asked in her tinkly little voice, both claws firmly wrapped around the toe of a battered old sneaker.

"It's me," he called, opening the door just enough for her to see but not for the DOG to get in. "Unctious Binkley."

"Oh, hi, Unctious," she answered. "How are you?"

"Oh, I'm fine, Wanda. Hold on a minute longer. I'll chase the dog off." He hoped she couldn't see that his paws shook around the door. "After all, he's just a dog. I'm a monster."

It was his big chance to show Wanda how wonderful he was. How brave and terrible and handsome. If only he'd had time to put that fruity-smelling stuff on before he'd heard the DOG growling.

"He won't give me my shoe," Wanda explained.

Unctious nodded. "Dogs are very stupid," he informed her.

The DOG didn't seem to like that. He growled very low in his large, large throat, and his hair rose up, just like those funny scales Unctious couldn't get to lay flat.

Unctious took a deep breath. He took another one. But that just made him sneeze. Billy's mom hadn't vacuumed in a couple of days.

"Are you coming, Unctious?" Wanda asked politely. (Gremlins might not have been well thought of, but they were very polite.)

"Of course, Wanda," he answered, wiping his snout with his sleeve. "I'm just deciding the best . . . plan of attack."

"I'd think," she said, giving another small tug on the shoe, "that from the back might work nicely."

"Why, that's just what I'd decided," he assured her, then wiped his paws on his hips. His tail thumped nervously. That DOG was BIG. And ugly. But Unctious knew that Wanda couldn't hold out much longer. Gremlins were sneaky and quick, not strong. Like monsters.

He opened the door another crack, just enough to slither through. None of the other monsters were about, and since it was too early in the morning even for sunlight, the humans were all asleep. It was going to be up to Unctious to save Wanda. He tip-toed right up to the dog's tail. The dog never saw him.

"Aaaaaaaaaaaargh!" Unctious yelled, running right under the DOG's belly.

The dog never had anything run under his belly before, so it jumped straight up, barked a high, frightened bark and ran. He was probably surprised, but the ridge of scales on Unctious' back that scraped his tummy probably convinced him that he didn't want to hang around. Of course, being a stupid dog, he forgot to take the shoe with him when he ran off. He did remember his tail, because he kept tripping over it where it was tucked between his legs.

Wanda wrapped her arms around the shoe and smiled. Suddenly shy, his little heart still pumping wildly, Unctious smiled back.

"Thank you, Unctious," she said, her head bent low. "This is a very special shoe. I'm going to make it into a hot tub."

Unctious' eyes opened very wide. "Oh," was all he could say.

"Nobody else came to help me," she said. "I think they were afraid of the dog."

Unctious straightened up tall and stuck out his chest just a little. "Oh, pooh," he scoffed. "Who's afraid of a stupid old dog?"

And then it happened. The miracle Unctious had prayed for every night that he'd walked by Wanda's nest. The most wonderful thing in the world. Wanda smiled at him. Not her usual friendly smile that she gave to everybody. This was a *special smile, just for Unctious. This was a smile that made the wart on the end of her nose wiggle.*

Unctious thought he was going to die of happiness.

And then, she did it. "Unctious," she said, dipping her head again. "Would you like to come sit in my hot tub when it's finished?"

"Oh, yes," Unctious agreed. It didn't even matter that monsters didn't fit into hot tubs made from tennis shoes. It didn't matter that his mama and his papa were going to be really, REALLY mad. Unctious was happy.

Chapter 10

J oe read over what he'd just written and crumpled it into a ball. Don't be ridiculous, he thought sourly. Unctious didn't get the girl. What really happened was that he saved Wanda's life and she ran off with the dog and Unctious discovered baseball, which was much more fun.

Joe's smile was wry and dark. Well, maybe not the running off with the dog part.

Scraping back the stool, Joe got to his feet and stretched. He'd been stuck on the book ever since the day he'd helped take Maggie to the hospital. There wasn't any deep secret about what was wrong. He was beginning to project his problems and dreams into his work, just like his music. Well, for jazz it worked fine. For children's literature, he wasn't sure.

The river was gunmetal gray today beneath a lowering sky. Out beyond Joe's window, the world had faded into grays and browns. Rain had been threatening all afternoon, and Joe had to say his mood matched the weather. He should have been over at Allison's having the most important discussion of his life, and here he sat, with a monster and a gremlin acting out his fantasies for him. He should be sitting in his den finishing that stack of books he'd bought on Down syndrome. He couldn't.

He was too restless, too unsettled. He was too frustrated. There on his drawing board Unctious was crouched within inches of the DOG's backside, eyes shut and fingers crossed, knowing he was about to end up in pieces. Joe sympathized with him. Some things were just too scary to face.

"Joe? You up there?"

Startled by the intrusion, Joe looked up. "Yeah, Tony. Whatchya want?"

Older than Joe by three years, Tony had a sturdier, handsomer version of the Burgett looks. Married for eight years, divorced four, home from the marines where he'd spent his formative years in combat and covert action, he was Joe's lawyer, agent and the other instigator of nieces-and-nephews night with two kids of his own.

He topped the steps with the same light tread that had allegedly surprised more than one counterintelligence foe and leaned in the workroom door.

"So it's true," he said in greeting. "You do still live in town. Some of us were wondering."

Joe scowled and walked over to him. "I miss one dinner and the police have an A.P.B. out on me. Don't you think this family is just a little too intense?"

Tony's grin was bright and sly as he leaned against the door frame in jeans and rugby shirt. "I'm not sure whether it's intense or just dying of curiosity. The last we heard, you were heading out with a bottle of wine under your arm and a bouquet of flowers in your hand. And then *I* hear that all this is for your editor? The same editor we've been corresponding with via post-office box? I wonder to myself. Self, I wonder, what did I miss in all those conversations about print runs and advances?"

Tony was expecting a flip answer in return. Joe couldn't quite give him one. He smiled at the open curiosity and tolerated the family's notorious nosiness. But he couldn't exactly joke about something that was consuming his sleep.

"Surprised me, too," was all he would admit.

Evidently, he didn't need to say any more. Tony's eyebrows rose and he straightened, quietly on alert. "My God," he said softly. "You *did* have flowers in your hand."

For a moment, Joe didn't move. "How 'bout a beer?"

Tony nodded and preceded him back down the stairs.

"Shouldn't dad be the one to tell you about the birds and the bees?" Tony asked once he'd popped the can and pulled out a chair.

Already draped backward over his chair, Joe took a good slug of his beer before answering. "He'd be about fifteen years too late. We got bigger problems than the birds and the bees."

Tony shook his head. "There are no bigger problems. Take it from a man with an eleven-year-old daughter."

Joe didn't even answer. The rain had decided to make an appearance, after all. He could see it shimmering out beyond the garage, dimming the early summer grass into gray. Perfect scene; perfect dull, dismal feeling.

"This all has to do with Ms. Henley?" Tony finally asked.

Joe didn't bother to look over at his brother. "What kind of problems do you think are big enough to sabotage a relationship?" he asked.

Tony quirked an eyebrow, but answered the question all the same. "Considering the history of mine, I feel I can speak as an expert," he assured Joe. "Infidelity, the commitment of one or more major felonies, the interference of scheming in-laws. Money, too much of or not enough of, in that order."

Joe ran a finger down the side of his can. "What about existing children?"

"I certainly hope not or Sylvia will never be off my payroll." There was a pause, a reconsidering. "Since I haven't heard that you've been blessed with any offspring, can I assume that your editor has?"

"Yeah. A baby girl named Maggie. She's six months old."

Another tactful silence. "You're not saying that there's already somebody sleeping in her husband's bed, are you?"

Surprised, Joe looked up. He had to grin. There was so much already on his mind, he hadn't even considered that he'd give that impression. "No," he allowed easily. "Her husband walked out on her when Maggie was four days old."

Tony grimaced. "Nice guy. What was the matter, he wanted a boy?"

Joe shook his head. "He wanted a healthy child. Maggie has Down syndrome."

Tony never flinched from the news. His eyes, as dark brown as his brother's, seemed to melt with the news, and Joe knew he'd never have to ask for his brother's support.

"And you're serious about her mother?"

Joe smiled. "Serious enough that I talked a blue streak to convince her that she could trust me."

"Can she?"

Joe looked down at his hands. It had all been so simple when he'd sat up in his room daydreaming about what his family would be like. Allison to come home to, children to tuck into bed, baseball games and Boy Scout campouts. Waking up each morning looking forward to the next fifty years, planning his children's futures and knowing that he could grow old surrounded by the generations he'd helped create and mold.

"I love her," he admitted softly, facing his brother with the truths he battled. "She's so fragile right now, trying to deal with Maggie all alone after that son of a bitch walked out on her. I can't stand to see her hurt."

"She's going to hurt," Tony said. "There's no way she's not. Is the baby bad?"

Joe laughed, a short bark of frustration. "Well, I guess 'bad' is relative. She's sweet and stubborn, and nobody can say yet just how affected she'll be by the extra chromosome she's carting around. The worst part is, she might not even live. She's going in for open heart surgery in four weeks." He faced his brother, the torment of the past few weeks in his eyes, his voice. "I don't know if I can carry them both."

"What about her family?"

Joe shrugged, bitter. "She doesn't talk about them much. From what I gather, they're not really close. Especially the last six months or so."

Tony was no more pleased about it than Joe. "Well, you know you don't have that problem."

Joe nodded. "It's not you guys I'm worried about. It's me."

Tony watched him. "It's not the kind of future you'd always anticipated."

Joe's answering smile was humorless. "That," he said, "is an excellent example of understatement."

"I don't know what I'd do, Joe."

Joe shook his head, the frustrations bubbling close, the ambivalence heavy. "I found out about Maggie when she suddenly went into heart failure and ended up in the hospital. And you know how I am in hospitals."

Tony knew. He'd picked Joe up off the floor once when a doctor had asked for help putting stitches in Tony's little girl.

"I dread going back in there like I dread taxes. But that's part of Maggie's life. She's going to need special schooling and tutoring, and enough patience to solve world conflict. I just don't know if I have the patience or the perseverance. I don't know if I've got the guts to face what she's going to face as she grows." He paused, angry, ashamed, his gaze on his hands where they rested over the back of the chair, those hands he'd always counted on. His life had been too damn simple. Too uncomplicated. And life just wasn't like that. "After calling her husband a son of a bitch," he admitted in a tight, hollow voice, "all I can think of is the fact that if I marry Allison, I'll never have the family I wanted. So, what kind of a selfish bastard does that make me?"

Joe looked up at his brother, not sure what he expected to see. Not sure what he wanted to see. Recrimination, agreement, understanding.

But Tony didn't have the answer, either. "Is that what's going to sabotage the relationship?"

Joe sighed, the pain and comfort of the past weeks warring in him. "Allison said something the other day. She said that if I'm not careful, I'm going to compare every little girl to Maggie and find her wanting. I'm already doing that. I look at Betsy or Ellen and all I see is the child Maggie will never be.''

"Then leave. Take off now before anyone gets hurt.''

Joe instinctively straightened. "No. I can't leave them.''

Tony's smile bore just a hint of satisfaction. "Because you owe them something?''

"Because I love them.''

For a moment Tony did no more than consult his can of beer, as if waiting for inspiration. Finally, he lifted knowing eyes to his little brother. "I'm certainly no shining example of marital success,'' he allowed. "But I have learned that it's no sin to try your best, even if you don't make it.''

Joe faced his brother without flinching. "And who's giving Allison that option?'' he demanded.

"What would you do,'' Tony asked, "if you'd married Allison, and Maggie had been yours?''

That made Joe smile. His own argument turned on him. "I wouldn't have the luxury of grinding my teeth over it.''

"Invite them over Sunday,'' Tony suggested. "Broaden the base of support a little. Maybe the burden won't seem quite so great to either of you.''

"Maybe I will,'' Joe mused.

Grinning, Tony got to his feet. "And tell her how you feel. Everything. I have the feeling she's way ahead of you.''

"Tomorrow, maybe,'' Joe suggested, downing the rest of his beer. "Tonight I promised to take her out and just show her a good time. I have a feeling those have been in short enough supply as it is.''

Tony's answering grin was wry. "Well, you'd better stop looking like Joan of Arc at the stake before you get there, or you'll have just about as much fun.''

Joe laughed and followed his brother to his feet. "You didn't help at all.''

"Of course I did. I let you come to your own conclusions.''

Joe scowled. "And just what were they?''

Tony clapped him on the shoulder. "You're the one in the family with all the guts, boy. Have a good time tonight. And give your editor a kiss from your lawyer."

"You changed again."

Fluffing one of the couch pillows, Allison refused to turn at the taunt. "Shut up, Lucille."

Lucille clucked in admonition. "Seems to me you're making an awful lot of fuss over a man you keep sayin' won't show up."

"He won't," Allison assured her, picking up another pillow and holding it to the ache in her chest. "Not for much longer. I can spot the signs."

Lucille harrumphed. "Oh, yeah. Attending class with you. Helping with exercises. Buying books on Down syndrome so he can talk about the things you don't discuss. You're right. He ain't planning to hang around at all."

Allison sighed. "Shut up, Lucille."

"You gonna 'shut up, Lucille' me one too many times, girl," Lucille warned casually. "And I'm gonna take that little girl and go home."

Allison looked over to see her friend standing with hands on hips, a very wry smile on her broad features.

"Just don't do it until after I get home, all right?"

She was jumpy as a cat. Breathless and frightened and anxious, certain that Joe would think of some reason to cancel their evening out, even more certain that he was taking her out to politely back out of his bargain. Lucille had said he could just as easily have called for that, but the way things had gone in Allison's life lately, she figured she'd just about get to the entrée when he'd break the news. Her husband had done it over breakfast. Scrambled eggs, the *Alton Telegraph* and a quiet sigh. At least Joe was planning to take her to a blues club. It would be appropriate, if nothing else.

The doorbell rang, jerking her back to the present. Startling her into dropping the pillow. She picked it up, and Lucille got the door.

"Get her out of here," she said without preamble as she whipped the door open to reveal Joe standing on the porch in regulation blues attire—black suit and dark blue shirt and string tie. "She's just gonna explode, she waits any longer."

His grin was conspiratorial. "She is a little high strung, isn't she?"

"She is not," Allison snapped, smoothing down the cream jacket over her culottes yet again. "She does think that if you two are having this much fun, you should go out."

Lucille actually took an assessing look at Joe. "He's too skinny for me."

Joe laughed. "I'd never go out with somebody that had a bigger degree than me." Turning to Allison, he proceeded to whip out a fresh bouquet of garden flowers, still glistening with the rain that had only just stopped.

Allison scowled, hiding the silly delight the bouquet produced in her. "Maggie's already asleep."

Joe shrugged. "Since these aren't for her anyway, that's probably just as well."

The exhilaration swelled in her, tickling her, tempting her. "Well, Lucille's just behind me."

"I see her. They're not for her, either."

Lucille snorted unkindly.

"Not that I don't think she deserves them," Joe corrected, then shot a look Lucille's way. "How many times did she change this time?"

"Four."

Allison scowled again, hands on hips. "Knock it off, you two."

Joe's grin was brash and broad. "I just wanted to make sure you were looking forward to the date. Then I wouldn't mind stripping my garden for you so much."

Allison lay a hand on her chest. "For me? You're sure?"

Joe nodded grandly. "Positive. I figure a first official date deserves some kind of recognition."

Allison had had her hand out ready to take the flowers. At Joe's words, she pulled it back in. "It's not a date."

Joe made a show of considering that. "Well, I thought of calling it a conference, but that didn't sound like as much fun. *Debate* and *rodeo* didn't really fit, so I was stuck with *date*." Reaching out, he grabbed her hand and placed the bouquet squarely inside. "So, yes, it's a date," he informed her, his eyes sparkling. "The first, which means I intend there to be more. Get used to it."

Allison stood there before him, the bouquet in her hands a riot of color, reds, blues, yellows, greens, whites. The soft, seductive scent of spring, promise and fulfillment. Rainwater slid down the stems over her wrist, cold and sweet, and all Allison could feel was the sweet heat in Joe's eyes. All she could see was the determination there, the invitation. All she could feel was the thunder of her heart, so long steeled to endings and disappointments. And she didn't know what to do.

Joe nudged her with a gentle, callused hand. "Water," he suggested. "They last longer that way."

"I'm putting them in Maggie's room," she announced.

He grinned. "You can put them in the bathroom, if you want. Just put them in water."

Allison had promised herself she wouldn't have fun. She'd sworn that she wasn't going to count on expecting to go out. Not tonight, and not again. And yet, every time she let her gaze stray to Joe's, she was struck by the anticipation that seethed in his eyes, the delight that crinkled them at the corners into crow's feet. She couldn't quell her own anxiety, because even though she refused to believe in Joe, she couldn't help wanting to. She couldn't control her rebellious body or tamp down that deadly exhilaration.

It grew worse as the evening progressed. Joe found one of the only Thai restaurants in the metro area, a cuisine Allison hadn't tasted, and to Allison's amazement, she loved it. She ate more at dinner than she had in days. They talked about the other people in the restaurant, other restaurants and other people. Joe guided the conversation and kept it strictly light and impersonal. Allison knew exactly what he was doing and was grateful. For once, she didn't have to wrestle with the ramifications of Maggie in her life or their relationship or the meaning of life and death and imperfection in general. She was just a girl out on a date. Just like high school, except she had fewer pimples and more wrinkles. Less optimism and more composure.

By the time they reached the club, she was actually relaxed and enjoying herself.

"Do you mind if I desert you for a while?" Joe asked as he settled her at one of the high tables near the front of the room.

Allison took a look at the sax case he'd hauled out of the back seat of his Jeep. "If I say yes, you'll pout all night long."

Joe had the good grace to grin. "And I can be really annoying when I do, too."

Allison chuckled and waved at the case. "Go on. If I hadn't wanted to listen to a little jazz, I would have had you take me to the ballgame instead."

The members of the band were setting up and testing instruments, doing little runs and snatches of tunes in a comfortable discord up on the stage. Allison watched Joe slip on his neckpiece and then attach his sax. He looked so sexy in his bluesman persona. Not like his carpenter mode, all earthy and wholesome, with muscles rippling and the sweat gleaming on his skin. Not even the hot intensity he gave off when he was discussing his books, as if the gears of his imagination were working so fast they actually gave off a kind of glow that made a woman want to reach out and test the air around him.

This was a more sinewy, darker attraction. Smoke and fire, the intoxication of raw pleasure, the seduction of soul-deep, throbbing life. Joe was alive in a more primal way up on that stage where his music existed, and Allison couldn't take her eyes off him.

Desire again. Stunning, surprising, rising inexorably to snake along her limbs and settle into fingers and toes. Sucking the air out of her lungs and sinking into her belly.

Allison couldn't seem to breathe in the suddenly close air, couldn't hold still or command language to describe what she felt.

And he was still standing close enough that she could smell his cologne, the dusky scent of night. The perfect aroma of jazz, mixing with cigarette smoke and the tang of bourbon. His eyes closed as he ran his fingers over the keys, loosening up, freeing the first notes from the cold instrument. Low notes, growling moans of pure pleasure. Allison wondered how he could get that sax to sound the exact way she felt, unsettled and alive. Hungry and afraid. And he wasn't even doing the music yet.

Abruptly, he opened his eyes and turned them on her, and Allison felt herself slip right in.

"Are you sure you'll be all right?" he asked sincerely, although she could see that he'd already moved beyond her to wherever his music was.

She smiled, mesmerized by the smoke in his eyes. "You like playing and I like listening," she assured him. "A perfect combination, if you ask me."

Joe grinned back, not realizing that his fingers still stroked the chrome. "That's what I've been trying to tell you."

"That's what you've been trying to tell Lucille," Allison retorted, wishing she could properly catch her breath. "Now, go on and get up there before they take off without you."

He went up. A waitress stopped by to drop off Allison's coffee, and a couple commandeered two of the other chairs at the table. Allison barely noticed. She watched Joe interacting with his friends on the stage and thought of how happy he looked. How open and carefree. She ached to feel like that again, to know what it was like to wake up without a burden sitting foursquare on her chest. She wanted to remember what it had been like to savor the day like a good wine and see nothing in the years ahead but possibility and potential.

"Good evening, and welcome to B.B.'s," the singer, a rake-thin black woman with the most unbelievable smoky voice announced. "Tonight we'd like to start out with a little of the Duke."

They started with "Take the A Train," then "Sophisticated Lady," and "Caravan," with its seductive minor progressions and throbbing drumbeat. Allison let the music wash over her, shutting out the rest of the world, nestling her right into the wail and shudder of jazz. She sipped her coffee and watched Joe, his eyes closed, his fingers strong and supple, his body swaying with the music. She listened to the music that came out of his sax, and was struck by the difference.

What was it? she wondered. Something she heard tonight she hadn't heard the last time she'd been here. Something that pulled her deeper into the melodies he stroked out of his instrument, sent her soaring and plummeting right along with the notes. Something darker, deeper, richer.

Joe had been very good before. He'd coaxed the most difficult songs from his sax with a velvet touch. But tonight... tonight he was magic, and she couldn't quite decide why.

It was Ellington again, later in the evening, when she realized what she'd been listening to. "Lush Life," a poignant song of waste and loss, of emptiness, that Joe was bending into. Allison saw the other sax player watching him, saw that the singer had closed her eyes. Heard that the audience, usually so loud, often indifferent to the magic being spun before their eyes, grew almost quiet. Allison turned back to Joe and really listened.

And suddenly, she heard Lucille's voice. "He's good," she'd said about his writing. "But one of these days, he's gonna know trouble. And then he'll know how to write."

One of these days, he's gonna know trouble. It was what Allison heard. The real soul of jazz, of blues. The roots of every one of those notes. Pain, longing, confusion. It was all there in Joe's music tonight, when it hadn't been there only a few weeks earlier.

Joe had been good. Now he was magic because he knew trouble. And Allison knew exactly what that trouble was. She sat very still on her chair and listened to Joe tell her just how he felt about meeting up with her, and she thought her heart would break.

Chapter 11

"I don't want the evening to be over with yet," Allison admitted as the lights came up.

Fitting his sax back into its case, Joe looked up in some surprise. "You mean it worked? I actually got you to have some fun?"

Allison smiled. "Don't go spreading that around. Lucille would never let me hear the end of it."

He closed the lid and flipped the latches. "Well, I have an idea. I know a little place that stays open all night, and all the coffee you want is free."

Allison immediately shook her head. "I shouldn't. Lucille's going to want to get home."

"She told me that if she saw you before dawn, she'd never speak to me again."

Allison scowled. "The last thing I need is you two ganging up on me."

"Not the last thing," he disagreed with a gentle smile. "The first thing. You look younger tonight than you have since I met you."

Allison fought down a tumble of emotions unleashed by his words, by the soft reproach in his eyes. She knew now what was creasing his forehead, what fueled his music and his manic humor. She knew that he was defraying his own pain to give her an evening off, and it hurt worse than her own burdens.

All the same, she scowled playfully at him. "You met me a month ago, Joe. Don't make it sound like we've been through the Civil War together."

His answering grin was broad. Before tonight, Allison wouldn't have caught the shadows in it. "We'll call Lucille when we get there," he bargained. "If she has to get home, we'll just go on to your place. It's close."

"How close?"

He shook his head. "I'm in charge of this evening. Your job is just to ride along and laugh at my jokes."

"Only if they're funny."

Leaning across the table, he dropped a quick kiss on her lips. "They're all funny," he assured her. "Let's go."

"Great gig, tonight, man," the drummer praised him on the way by.

"You almost good enough to be black," Little William teased.

"Does this mean I can come back?" Joe asked, the picture of sincerity.

"Only if you still hangin' with that fine lady, here," the man retorted with a wide grin. "She's been awful easy on the eyes tonight."

Joe took an assessing look at Allison, who was flushing again. "Yeah, she does clean up nice, doesn't she?"

Allison made the mistake of crossing glances with Joe and stumbled over the frank desire in the depths of that chocolate brown. The flush deepened. Her heartbeat faltered. She ducked her head a little and made it a point to pick up her purse.

"I'm breathless with the flattery," she teased darkly. Except, of course, that she was. Not with the words, with the sensations. The brush of Joe's hand against her arm, the whisper of his breath against her cheek, the sense that his gaze swept her like a morning sun, glowing against her skin.

''Hey, we're goin' down to the Landing for a while,'' Little William offered, referring to Laclede's Landing on the riverfront, where the action lasted longer in the evening among bars and clubs that had once been fur warehouses.

''Thanks,'' Joe answered, his voice crackling with sudden tension, ''but Allison and I have another appointment.''

Allison lifted her eyes to find purpose in his. Little William didn't seem to see it. He hadn't seemed to have heard the sudden charge in Joe's words. Allison wondered how he could miss it, could stand so close to the two of them and not flinch from the electricity.

''The Landing?'' she asked, suddenly seeking haven.

Joe didn't bother to look away. He smiled, though, and it was full with every promise he'd made that evening. Every promise he'd made since he'd met Allison. ''Too crowded. The place I'm thinking of is a little more low key.''

Allison nodded. She fought the slow, sensuous curl of lightning Joe's smile was setting off in her—down her arms, up her chest, the back of her neck, tightening, tensing, aching with the sweetest of pains.

Pain. She saw it still, there deep in his eyes, the reflection of hers, metamorphosed by his strength and vulnerability. Deepening his eyes, darkening his music, sharpening his attraction. Battened down to allow Allison the room, at least tonight, to skirt her own problems. Channeled into performance and concern.

It pulled at Allison because she'd never seen pain that color in her husband's eyes. She'd never expected it in another man's. She wasn't sure, seeing it, whether it was something that would cement or shatter their relationship.

She just knew that it reflected the kind of man Joe was. And that made walking out of that club with him easier— and much, much harder.

''This wasn't what I had in mind,'' Allison informed Joe as they stepped into his kitchen.

"It's quiet, it's small, it's open late," he protested as he unpeeled a sticky note from his back door window on his way in.

"And it has a great view of the Mississippi," she retorted dryly, dropping her purse on the kitchen table. "I know. What's the note?"

Joe's grin was a bit sheepish. "It's from my mother. She says to make sure I invite you to dinner on Sunday."

Allison overcame the urge to look over her shoulder. "How'd she know I was coming over?"

Crumpling the note, he scored two points with it in a corner trash can before setting his sax case carefully in the hallway. "Considering the fact that *I* didn't know you were coming until forty-five minutes ago, I have no idea. Are you going to be at dinner Sunday?"

Allison waited to answer until she'd pulled out a chair and sat down. "I'm not sure if I dare turn her down. She probably left a note on my door, too." She was fighting anticipation again, and that unnerved her. She didn't want to meet Joe's family, to like them and count on them liking her. She was too unused to families to know how they'd feel about her.

Shucking his jacket and tossing it over one of the chairs, Joe headed for the refrigerator. "She's not very good at taking no for an answer."

Allison had to laugh. "So you come by it naturally, huh?"

She caught him loosening his tie. He stopped and turned on her, his grin challenging, his fingers still caught in the slide. "She's an amateur compared to me."

Allison challenged right back, her eyebrows raised in dry amusement, her mind set for a pithy comeback. Comeback and amusement died when she locked onto his gaze.

Again, lightning. Searing contact, the crackle of intoxication. Surprised into silence, stunned to stillness. Too long, Allison thought disjointedly. It's just been too long since I've acknowledged that a man was attracted to me. Since I've believed it. Looking at Joe, at the sudden, searing heat in his eyes, she could hardly deny the fact that he was attracted. He was aroused. He was deadly as the snake nudging an apple across the ground.

Allison faltered first. "Does she know about...umm, Maggie?"

She simply couldn't hold his gaze. It was too hot, too intimate. She had to retreat to the sight of scarred Formica beneath her cold hands. She listened to the staccato of her heart and the rasp of her own breathing and thought that she should be anyplace but here. She should be with anyone but Joe, because he could crumble her defenses with no more than a glance.

"By now, she probably knows your social-security number and the name of the minister who baptized you," Joe countered, finally pulling a beer out of the fridge. "What would you like to drink, Allison?"

Allison took a breath. "I should call Lucille," she objected, still looking at her hands.

Joe didn't answer. Instead he reached over and picked up the phone and made the call himself. "Hi there, gorgeous," Allison heard him greet her friend. Couldn't Lucille hear the tension in his voice? she wondered. "We've found this great little all-night place. Thought we'd stop in for a bit...yeah, it is. How'd you know?"

"Tell her I'll be home soon," Allison asked, preoccupied with the struggle to get her body under control.

"She'll be home after a while," he said instead.

That made her turn around. He was smiling at her, his eyes sharp and perceptive. Just the sight of him sent her heart off again, and Allison had to turn away.

This was stupid. She'd known Joe for almost three months. Known him face-to-face for over a month, spent time in the hospital with him, perpetrated hoaxes on her company with him. So why, suddenly, should she itch to get her hands on his skin? Why should his eyes suddenly speak to her in a language that sounded suspiciously like the growl of an alto sax. Why should she suddenly be nervous to be alone in his house with him?

"She said be home anytime before her kids get up tomorrow," he said, suddenly at Allison's elbow. "Now, what do you want to drink?"

Allison started, fought for control. "Nothing," she demurred. "Really."

Joe eased down in the chair next to hers and took hold of her hand. "Allison," he soothed. "I'm not trying to coerce you. I just didn't want the evening to end yet, and I didn't want to share you anymore. Okay?"

She looked up to see the concern in his eyes, soft eyes, soulful, deep eyes that she couldn't pull away from. They suddenly frightened her because she realized how much she'd come to love them.

"Anything," she finally conceded, surprised that her voice didn't shake. "Soda, coffee, tea, whatever you have."

She expected Joe to immediately brighten. He didn't. For a moment he didn't even move, his hand still calming her, his eyes embracing her. "Give yourself a chance."

Allison wanted to pull away from him. She wanted to protest, to shrink back into her cold, comfortable shell where she never expected too much or looked too high. Where the sky was only something you looked at out windows. Joe kept lifting her head so she could see what was above her, and that was dangerous. It was foolish. Because no matter how much she looked up, she was never going to fly, and she knew it.

But oh, how good it felt, just for now. At least until she tumbled back to earth.

Her smile was tremulous, but it was the best she could do. "I thought you promised me jokes."

Joe brightened then, by careful degrees. He squeezed her hand before letting it go and returned to the fridge for a can of soda. "All right, how's this one? What do you get when you cross a gremlin and a monster?"

"I'll bite."

Adding glass and ice to the soda, Joe returned it to Allison with a wry grin. "A book that doesn't go anywhere."

Allison immediately scowled. "You mean the bathroom book?"

He threw a leg over the back of the chair and settled in, rolling up shirtsleeves to reveal the muscles Allison had seen coax a sax and plane a door. Allison was hard-pressed to take her eyes from them.

"The bathroom book," he allowed, reaching over for his beer and taking a long pull from it. "I have come to the conclusion that Unctious is simply not meant to fall in love."

"He's only seven," Allison protested. "How can he fall in love?"

"Precisely the point."

Allison felt her shoulders relaxing, felt the electricity dim to more manageable friendship, and was grateful.

"Does this mean you're going back to the jungle expedition?"

He shook his head. "No. I think I'm going to settle for the lesson about how things change. No matter how badly you may want something, if you lose it, it's not the end of the world. Something else comes along."

"What something else?"

"For Unctious, it's going to be baseball. He survives."

Allison took a second to consider the state of her drink before facing Joe again. Suddenly, the conversation had taken on more meanings than they had intended. Allison fought against asking, against discovering the truth about the book Joe and Lucille had been talking about in such cryptic terms.

"So, he does fall in love," Allison countered quietly, her eyes still down. "But it doesn't work out."

"At seven years old, it rarely does."

Allison looked up then, to see the wry humor in Joe's eyes. He knew exactly what she'd been thinking.

"That was the problem with the book," he admitted. "I think I ended up transferring a little too much. It wasn't healthy for Unctious."

"Was it healthy for you?"

He shrugged with a self-effacing grin. "I came up with a couple of great sketches and a dog that will probably show up again."

"Are you still going to make deadline?"

"The only thing that's going to change is the last two or three pages," he said, finishing the beer. "Instead of walking off claw-in-claw, Wanda thanks Unctious for saving her life and heads back to the nest, and Unctious realizes there's something to live for the day he discovers baseball."

Allison rolled the sound of that around for a minute and nodded. "I think it's going to be perfect. I'd love to see that dog."

Joe motioned with his can. "He's right upstairs."

He was already getting to his feet. Allison faltered.

"Inviting me to see your etchings?" she teased, except that the air had somehow seeped out of her lungs again. Somehow, it affected her knees.

Joe's grin was wicked and bright. His hand was out to her. "What's the good of having them if you can't lure unsuspecting females up to see them?"

She hesitated a moment, suspended on the invitation of Joe's outstretched hand, frozen by the desires underlying the teasing. Allison looked from callused hand to laughing eyes, from offer to promise, and found herself held immobile by fear. By an unspeakable longing to be able to follow him without question.

Joe didn't say another word. He reached over, took hold of Allison's hand and gently pulled her to her feet. And Allison went.

"Come to think of it," he offered, about a flight later, as if simply continuing a conversation, "you haven't seen the house at all, have you?"

"The living room," Allison managed, her attention more on the grasp of his hard hand around her suddenly cold one than the faded cabbage rose paper that lined the stairwell. "The kitchen."

Joe nodded. "The garage. Yeah. Well, you're about to get the grand tour."

"Joe," she protested halfheartedly, her heart skidding uncomfortably. "It's late."

"That just means we won't have to battle our way through the crowds," he retorted, his voice echoing in a rumbling baritone back down to the ground floor.

They passed the second floor, more peeling wallpaper with pristine oak woodworking and several closed doors leading off the hallway, and continued straight on up to the third floor.

"This," he acknowledged, flipping on a light, "is where the Binkley Brothers really live."

Allison was amazed. Joe had turned the attic into one great workroom, with hardwood floors and high white walls and gleaming woodwork. And windows everywhere. He must have enlarged the existing ones, and most of them faced the river. His drawing board was in front of one, and his desk in front of another, both spotlighted by track lighting. A framed sketch Allison recognized as one of the very first Binkley representations hung on one wall, and posters of jazz and blues concerts decorated the rest. There was a state-of-the-art stereo system, a computer, and a rolltop with an inkwell. And in front of another window, a rocking chair.

Scattered in the far corner were the remnants of a child's army. Allison pointed. "Educational toys for the illustrator?" she asked with a grin.

"I baby-sit sometimes," he allowed. "I find they're much easier to control if you give them an outlet for all that aggression."

"Surely not the girls."

"Especially the girls. Don't be so sexist."

Allison laughed, then. "I just can't imagine Maggie marshalling her forces to annihilate the enemy."

"That's just because she doesn't have a bunch of brothers to want to knock off."

Allison walked on in, fascinated by Joe's spare taste, impressed with his work. Compelled by the place where he let his imagination take charge.

"This is the dog?" she asked, spotting the sketch still on the drawing board. She recognized Unctious crouched behind the massive hindquarters of the hairy beast and chuckled. It was a great scene. The kids would love it.

"That's him."

She hadn't heard Joe follow her over. Suddenly, he stood right beside her, examining his own work over her shoulder. The air seemed to shimmer here, to swell with his proximity. Allison could feel it like a current skimming her fingertips.

It wasn't going to ease. It wasn't going to magically disappear, as if it had never happened. Allison would not wake suddenly tomorrow and find that Joe no longer set her off like fireworks on the Fourth, and she wasn't sure what she could do about it.

She knew what she wanted to do, suddenly, as she stood there, her hands out to stabilize herself against his drawing board. She wanted to give in. She wanted to dive headfirst into that current, to let it swallow her whole. Just once, she wanted to abdicate responsibility and ignore consequence. She wanted to act as if Maggie didn't wait at home for her. Instead, she turned abruptly on her heel.

"The rest of the house—" And bumped right into Joe.

He reached out to catch her, and Allison came to a shuddering halt. She could smell the soap on him, the smoke from the club and the cologne that eddied around him like a dark mist. She could feel the power in those hands that grasped her shoulders. She could see the fire leaping in those dark, dark eyes.

He managed a crooked smile. "The only other room I've finished is my bedroom."

Allison couldn't pull her gaze from his. Couldn't seem to stiffen in protest or melt into submission. The air in the high, cool room crackled, and the night seemed suddenly warmer. Joe began to knead her shoulders, his fingers gentle, his eyes darkening even more.

"What about...the den?" Allison asked, rigid and afraid. Compelled.

Somehow, his face seemed closer. "I'm still working on the shelves."

Allison stopped breathing altogether. She couldn't feel anything but Joe's fingers and the crawl of desire they ignited. Her belly ached. Her knees shook. She tried her best to pull her whirling thoughts into some kind of order and couldn't.

And then she realized that Joe was closer. He was bending to her, his hands tightening on her, his eyes closing. Somehow, her eyes closed, too. She raised her face to him, sighed with futile protest. His breath stirred the fine hairs at her temple. Somewhere deep in her subconscious, a barrier wobbled dangerously, and she didn't even notice.

His kiss wasn't gentle. Wrapping her into his arms, he commanded her, his mouth at once hungry and lazy. Allison lifted her hands in uncertain protest and left them to rest on his chest. She could feel his heart thunder beneath her fingers. She could hear the ragged cant of his breathing and tasted his sharp sigh.

His lips were so soft, like his eyes. So fierce, like his mind, so delicious, like his body. Allison tasted them and wanted more. She drank the music of his groan and offered her own. The lambent heat that had seeped into her limbs ignited, flared, centered. It had been too long since Allison had allowed a fire to be out of control. She had been too long silent, and now the cacophony of desire deafened her.

"I...like shelves," she managed to say when he lifted his mouth.

He kissed her cheek, her ear, her throat. She arched to his touch, to the moist invitation of his kisses. She clung to him, afraid of falling. Knowing that it was too late already to save herself.

"All shelves look alike," Joe assured her, wrapping his fingers into her hair and pulling her close.

Allison was on tiptoe, caught tight in Joe's arms, intoxicated by his feverish assault, surprised by his arousal. She knew she should let go, should push away and demand a drive home. Better yet, a cold shower. It was already too late.

"Allison," he moaned into her throat, and she shuddered. He swept a hand along her throat and she whimpered, the heat stifling her, only the hard angles of his body real in the wash of light and the throbbing silence.

She felt him ease his fingers toward her buttons and couldn't stop him. She felt his mouth trace her jaw and curled her fingers into the fabric of his shirt. She shouldn't allow this. She should back away, should run away. She should escape to safety before she couldn't.

She couldn't.

"Do you . . . like antiques?" he asked, his voice dark and taut.

Allison's eyes were closed against the light, against the torment his fingers were unleashing as they worked one button after another, brushing against the hesitant skin of her breasts. Her mind whirled and swooped. Her throat seemed to close in on her words, so that her "yes" sounded like a groan.

He dipped to trail kisses along the path of his fingers. "Good. You'll . . . like my bed."

Allison tried to say no. She gasped for air, for control. She tried to pull away against him. Her body wouldn't cooperate. It arched closer, seeking his lips, his tongue, his touch. It trembled in anticipation instead of outrage. It welcomed instead of repelled.

In answer, Joe slid an arm beneath Allison's knees and lifted her into his arms. "You'll like it a lot," he promised, his eyes like smoke, like night.

Allison couldn't find words. She wrapped her arms around his neck, afraid of falling, afraid of letting go, and greeted his mouth with her own. He carried her back down the steps as easily as if she'd been a child, his attention all hers, his arms a haven, his eyes and lips a promise.

Allison had lived without promises for too long. She had lived without hope or anticipation or exhilaration. In one evening, Joe had bestowed them on her again like a gift. Like a precious trust that filled her with heady wine.

He kicked in the door with his foot and carried her into the darkness. Allison felt herself sinking into a cloud of down, Joe falling with her. Shadows danced in the room. The fragrance of a thousand flowers drifted in through an open window. A chorus of insects throbbed in the night. Allison soared on Joe's touch, sank into his eyes, died a little in his arms. His kisses were hungry, his callused hands tender.

Allison felt his fingers sweep her skin, felt his lips follow. Whimpering, she scrabbled for him, his clothing too thick, too stubborn for anxious fingers. She laughed when he groaned in frustration at her zipper. Clothing rustled in the darkness, and fragile moonlight illuminated the gleam of sweat on his skin. She reached for it, savored it, so sleek and strong against her hands. She curled her fingers into the hair that swirled on his chest and tested the calluses on his thumbs with her tongue. She danced with him, sang with him, begged for him. His hands were like life against her skin, against her too-cold body so long enured to emptiness.

His mouth was intoxication, praising her with lavish attention, shoulder and wrist and throat. Lightning sparked and splintered, sluicing along her limbs and coiling in her belly. Her heart stumbled before his approach. Her breath faltered. Her mind tumbled headlong.

And then, just shy of oblivion, caution caught hold.

"Joe," she gasped, suddenly chilled with the fear of having forgotten, even for so short a time. "I'm not . . . I can't . . ."

She could see the cost of control. Even in the darkness his jaw looked like steel. His hands stilled where they were as he lifted his head to face her fears.

"You're not what, honey?" he asked, those dark, deep eyes lost to the night.

Allison flushed a hot red, not used to being frank. Never having needed it before. Not knowing how to avoid it. Stunned at how the pleasure had suddenly died with this one thought.

"Protected," she whispered, apologizing and begging at once. "I can't believe . . ."

Joe lifted a finger and laid it gently against her lips. "It's okay," he soothed with a smile. "That's a gentleman's responsibility, anyway. At least, that's what my father always taught me."

Allison couldn't help a small giggle. "Your father was that open?"

Joe's smile grew even as he let his hand begin to wander again, spreading chills in its wake. "A very practical man. He never believed in taking chances."

Allison tried to keep her mind on Joe's words when his hands were distracting her. "A wise man."

Joe dropped a line of kisses along Allison's throat. "I figured you might not want to take chances either."

Allison closed her eyes, tears stinging them. "I *can't* take any chances anymore, Joe."

Joe stilled against her. Allison couldn't open her eyes again, couldn't face him. She ached with wanting him. She shuddered with loss, even though she still lay in his arms, even though she could feel his body warm and alive against hers. An ending even before a beginning, and she didn't know how to deal with it.

He kissed her closed eyes. "Then we won't take chances."

But she heard the sorrow in his voice, the death of his dreams, and it shattered her. She wondered if Joe knew when he entered her that she wept because she already knew he was going to leave.

Chapter 12

Joe had felt Allison withdraw long before they fell into stillness. He lay now in the darkness, her head cradled on his chest, his arms around her, furious and frightened.

What was he going to do? How was he going to convince her to stay, to give them both the chance they needed? He'd known what was going to happen the minute she'd felt the need to discuss birth control. He'd been ignoring it for the past month, even after reading the information on Down's, because he simply couldn't come to grips with it. Now, he had no choice.

"We need to talk," he said, stroking her hair, his body still humming with the residue of passion, his skin still cooling from her touch.

For a moment, Allison didn't answer. Joe knew she was awake. He could tell by her shallow breathing. She had been the sweetest of songs in his arms, hungry and generous at once, with a vitality that suffused him. She had been magic and then loss. He could still feel her delicate hands against his skin, and his body ached for more. He felt her drawing away, even in his arms, and couldn't accept it.

"Allison."

"I have to get home," she hedged, her voice small and quiet. Defeated.

"Not yet." He held tighter, instinct rather than control, needing to feel her safely in his embrace, needing just as much the nourishment of her presence. "Lucille only baby-sat because she thought we were going to get someplace in this relationship tonight. I don't think we've done that yet."

Allison's laugh was dry and sore. "We've been pretty busy for not doing anything."

"You're treating me like Maggie," he accused, struggling to keep his voice gentle. "Distancing yourself so that it won't hurt so much when I'm gone."

She didn't move. Didn't breathe. "Shouldn't I?"

"Because of what you said tonight?" he asked. "I don't know."

That got her to move. Pulling out of his embrace, she sat straight up and faced him, her eyes bleak. Her skin glowed in the darkness. Her hair tumbled like smoke about her face. Her areolas, like dark flowers against the ivory of her breasts, beckoned even yet to him. Joe had held those breasts in his hands, had tasted them and taunted them. He'd come home in her arms and couldn't imagine leaving again.

"I can't afford to have any more children, Joe," she said baldly. Challenging, just as she had with all the other truths about her life. Daring him to leave her for it, demanding his outrage.

Joe pulled himself up alongside her. "That's more like it," he allowed quietly.

She bristled. "What do you mean, 'That's more like it'? Don't you understand what I'm trying to tell you?"

Joe lifted a hand to her cheek, wishing she weren't so right. "It's not just Maggie that's the problem between us," he retorted. "It's the possibility of more Maggies."

"Yes. Don't you see? You ache for a family, for a bunch of kids like your nieces and nephews. And you should have them, damn it. You should be able to fill every one of those damn rooms with a little Joe Burgett, and teach each of them to build birdhouses and play the sax. You should be able to anticipate your wife's pregnancy, not dread it.''

How did he fight the truth? How did he accept a compromise that ate at him? She was right. He couldn't imagine his life without children. And if he married Allison, that was just what he might be getting.

Maybe he'd been wrong about his book, he thought. Maybe you couldn't find something to replace what you lost.

"You don't know you'd have another child with Down's,'' he argued, reaching to pull her back into his arms.

She pulled away. Not even thinking to find her clothes, she climbed out of bed and walked to the window where she stood facing the moon like a wraith in the night, fragile and soft and torn, her arms crossed over her stomach and her face up to the sky.

"I have a one-in-a-hundred chance of having another child with Down's."

"Only if it was the egg that was the problem."

She turned on him, her eyes glittering with unshed tears. "You *have* been doing your reading,'' she said. "You're right. It could have been my husband. The new research says that thirty percent of the time it's the husband who had the problem. But, you see, Joe, we just don't know. He won't be having any more children, and that seems the only way right now they can tell."

"And if he is the problem, you're sentencing yourself instead."

Joe thought he heard a sob, a small, lonely sound. Still, he didn't move, knowing she would shy away if he came closer.

"And if I'm the problem," she countered, "I'd be sentencing another child to Down's."

"You don't know that."

"And that's just the problem," she argued, the ground too obviously familiar. "I don't know. I'd have to get pregnant to find out. And I'm just not one of those people who'd play Russian roulette with a baby and then just get rid of it if the chromosome pattern wasn't what I wanted."

"I wouldn't want you to."

"But would you want the responsibility of another child with Down's? Would you want to live with that kind of guilt? Once is an accident, Joe. Twice is choice."

Joe swung out of bed then, standing carefully away, his eyes locked into hers. "Maggie is a beautiful little girl, Allison."

She laughed again, a painful sound. "You're wasting your time convincing me. I'm the one who's been there all along, remember?"

"Do you think if you'd done something different she could have been normal?"

He saw the tears fall, old tears, familiar enough tears that Allison didn't even reach up to wipe them away. "Maybe I exposed her to something. Maybe I wanted her too selfishly. Maybe I'm the one who's tainted, and she's paying for it. She's going to pay for it her entire life."

Joe stepped closer, those tears beckoning. Her proud posture taunting. Her dark, grieving eyes compelling. "Do you think she's going to see it that way?"

Allison stiffened. "I'd never let her."

Joe stepped even closer. "Did it ever occur to you that maybe she's a luckier child than most?"

"Because she's simple?" Allison retorted hotly. "Because she'll never grow up, never be unhappy, never know what it's like to set foot in the rat race? Spare me the clichés, Joe. I've heard them all."

But Joe shook his head. "Because she has a mother who'd give up everything for her."

Allison sobbed again, her hand up to her mouth, the truth glittering from her eyes. She saw her life falling apart again, and Joe couldn't yet convince her she was wrong.

Having no words that would say enough, he crossed those last few feet and folded her back into his arms. She shuddered with the contact, at once fought his hold and sought it.

"I can't...do that...to you," she whispered, her head buried against his chest, her arms tightly around him.

"I love you," he insisted, his own head bent over hers, his eyes closed to the moonlight and the distant river. "We should be able to work something out."

"I can't see how," she admitted bleakly, still holding on, still small and tremulous in his arms. "I just can't see how."

Lifting her chin so she was forced to face him, Joe wiped her tears with gentle fingers. "Just don't consign me to the missing-persons bureau before I get there, okay?"

She managed a small smile, and Joe thought of madonnas, beautiful with their tragic knowledge. "As long as you're honest with me."

Joe crooked an eyebrow. "I'm always honest with you."

She shook her head. "I don't think you realize how much that sax speaks for you. It told me a lot tonight you haven't."

Joe couldn't pull his gaze from hers, trapped by the truth there. "I haven't sorted out a lot of it myself," he admitted.

She nodded. "Just don't pretend. Please. I couldn't take it."

Joe drew a finger along her lips. "I wasn't pretending tonight."

Her eyes, so smoky in the dusk, widened, darkened. "I know."

"Nobody's expected to fall in love without a few problems."

She scowled. "We just happen to have a few more problems than other people."

"We'll work them out," he promised, gently pulling her closer, letting his body savor the soft warmth of hers again. "I promise."

She shook her head. "I told you. No promises."

Even so, she eased back into the slow dance Joe had begun. Fitting her belly against his hips, sliding her hands to the small of his back, nuzzling her cheek against his chest. Joe's heart quickened and his breathing stilled.

"One promise," he amended, his eyes on her lips, so full and bruised from his kisses, so beguiling in their trembling uncertainty. "This time, you're not getting away from me before I thoroughly love you."

And much to Joe's delight, she didn't.

"I have her scheduled for the fifteenth. Is that convenient for you?"

Allison looked up from her sleeping daughter to the cardiac surgeon. "I guess 'convenient' is a good enough term," she conceded in a small voice.

A small, bald gnome of a man who looked as though he'd be more comfortable in one of Joe's books than a surgical suite, Dr. Goldman lifted his attention from his schedule book with a tight little frown.

"I expect you to take the best care of her between now and then," he commanded.

Allison fought the urge to set him straight. Goldman was the best in the business; he just needed a little work in the area of bedside manner. Parents respected, resented and feared him in equal parts.

"I was thinking of leaving her out for the wolves to get her," Allison retorted dryly.

Another doctor would have caught the humor. Goldman was the one who bristled.

"She's not going to make it through this surgery without good care," he informed Allison archly. "And you're just as important for that as I am."

"Well, not quite. I'm all thumbs with a scalpel."

Lord, she'd been hanging around with Joe too long. Three months ago, she never would have thought of talking to the great and exalted Dr. Goldman like this.

"You're her mother," the good doctor accused.

"And her father, right now," Allison allowed. "Don't worry. Both of us will be right there on the job."

"She's taking her digoxin and Aldactazide properly?"

Allison did smile then. She was going to be in hock to the pharmacist if Maggie didn't straighten up. She could spit medicine farther than ice cream.

"No problem."

He nodded briskly, as if giving Allison a passing grade.

"Well, if we can keep her from getting congested or overtaxed in the next two weeks, she'll be right on schedule."

Allison checked her watch, already late for another appointment, and still forty-five minutes away. "We'll do our best."

"See to it, Mrs. Henley," he commanded. "See to it."

Allison looked up to see a hint of censure in the doctor's eyes. A sharp assumption born of dealing with other Down's parents. He can see my doubts, she thought with a catch. He's heard me wonder in the early-morning hours and doesn't understand. Well, Maggie isn't his. He only has to cure her. He doesn't have to always worry about what's best for her. He doesn't have to forever strike that perfect, treacherous balance between what will help and hurt her.

Three months earlier, Allison would have left without another word. Today, though, she shot the doctor a stiff smile. "I will if you will." Then she picked up her daughter and left.

Allison spent Sunday afternoon line editing a book of oral history of the Ozarks. Tired out after church and an exercise session, Maggie slept. Thick, white clouds danced before the sun and a cool breeze winnowed the trees. Allison opened the sliding door to the patio and listened to the birds and distant traffic as she worked.

As she *tried* to work.

Instead of descriptions of folk cures, she saw Joe's eyes. Instead of the hush of the trees, she heard his words, both of passion and promise.

She'd been so alive in his arms. So cherished and protected. His hands, those craftsman's hands that made music and created works of art, had made her body sing. They had cupped her and cradled her and opened her, their clever dance igniting a fire that refused to die. His mouth, that quirky sweet mouth that so delighted her, had tasted her like a feast. Had awakened and tormented her, seducing her, savoring her, singing to her with his hoarse groans and whispers.

He had loved her so intimately, so preciously that she could never again doubt him. He had held her as she'd settled back into sleep, cushioning her fall from the heights, protecting her from the uncertainties they both still faced. No matter what else happened, she would know that Joe loved her more than any man had. No matter what he could or couldn't give her, he had given her back her sense of worth.

Allison shook her head and bent again over the pages. And heard the grief in Joe's voice in that silent, darkened room when she'd faced him with the truth. She had heard all the plans he'd made, all the fantasies he'd entertained in that big, old house that had been made for children.

She hadn't thought she could hurt any worse after what she'd been through with Maggie. She'd been wrong. It was one thing to give up your own dreams because you don't have the choice, to watch them wither from want and finally blow away like dust in a dry wind. It was another to demand that someone else sacrifice his dreams just because you can't accommodate them.

She couldn't bear the thought that Joe would walk his house and hear the echoing emptiness. She couldn't condemn him even before he got the chance to have his children, to never see those sly eyes on a child, to never nurture another imagination like his. She wouldn't be marrying him, she'd be sentencing him, and she simply couldn't do it. She couldn't face that kind of regret in his eyes for the rest of her life.

She tried once more to focus on the words, this time beyond too familiar tears. The doorbell interrupted her. Climbing to her feet, Allison wiped a quick hand across her eyes and padded across her floor in bare feet. Any interruption was better than none.

She was wrong again. When she opened the door, it was to find Joe standing there in oxford shirt and jeans. With flowers.

The minute he caught sight of the shorts and T-shirt, he scowled. "Maybe you're right. What good would it do trying to impress my family?"

Beset by the suspicion that Joe had heard her and come to argue, Allison couldn't even marshall her thoughts enough to invite him in or throw him out. "What?"

He flashed her a tolerant grin. "It's Sunday. Dinner at the Burgett's, remember?"

It took Allison a moment to connect. "Oh, God," she breathed, casting a revolted look down at her attire. "Joe, I can't go. I really can't. I have work to do, and Maggie—"

She didn't stand a chance. Without a word, he walked right in, pushing her back and shutting the door behind him. Allison tried to protest. Joe shoved the flowers into her hands.

"These are for Maggie," he claimed. "I'll get her ready while you get yourself ready."

"You can't—"

"Do you dress a baby with Down's any differently than any other?"

"Of course not."

"In that case, I have plenty of experience. Now, get dressed."

"Joe, really," she tried again, waving the flowers at him in limp protest. "I don't think it's a good idea."

"It's a great idea," he assured her, heading right past. "After all, Maggie should start getting used to me."

"No, Joe, please." She grabbed ahold of his arm and turned him toward her. The flowers hung from her other hand. "Listen to me."

He kissed her instead. "Okay."

She flinched away. "Stop that. You're not going to change things by bulldozing your way through my life."

That stopped him. His smile eased a little and his eyes darkened. "There aren't many things I want to change. I love you, I'm getting pretty damn fond of Maggie, and I want to get to dinner before my brothers and sisters get all the steaks."

Tears threatened again, harsh, stinging tears. Allison fought them back. "I can't ask you to marry me and give up everything you've hoped for."

That brought Joe's hands up to her shoulders. "I've made a decision myself," he admitted, his hands sure and gentle against her. "No decisions until after Maggie's made it through surgery okay."

Allison stiffened. "Why?" she demanded. "Do you think things might just clear up then?"

"No. But I think you have too much to handle right now just dealing with her. I'm going to be here for you till then. No questions, no demands, no expectations. Absolutely no decisions. We'll have plenty of time for that when she's healthy."

Allison tried to shake her head, tried to pull away from him. He couldn't do this to her; not after she'd just worked up the resolve to let him go. She couldn't allow herself to retreat to his arms only to have to leave them again. She couldn't face his family, waiting for their censure and knowing that she wasn't what they wanted for him.

"This isn't a game," she grated out, her gaze on the floor, her posture rigid. "I'm not going to change my mind just because you give me the bum's rush."

"I don't think I asked you to change your mind," he retorted evenly to the top of her head. "I think all I asked was that you don't wear those shorts to dinner at my mother's house."

Allison's head snapped up. Her eyes crackled with sudden fury. "You just don't get it, do you? This isn't a book, Joe. Maggie isn't going to wake up from her nap with a whole heart or one less chromosome. I'm not going to risk having another baby, no matter if I love you or not, and nothing you say or do is going to make any difference."

His eyes were dark and serious. His jaw worked with patience. "And I'm not going anywhere until Maggie has her surgery. Consider me a male Lucille, if you want. I don't care. I'm not leaving just to prove you right."

"Joe," she begged. "I can't risk having children. There's nothing you want more. How are we supposed to compromise on that?"

"We're not," he assured her. "Not until Maggie's healthy. Then we can talk all we want. Right now, unless you were lying through your teeth the other night, we love each other. Let's just spend some quality time together. Okay?"

Allison grimaced. "Quality time? Where did that come from?"

Joe grinned. "One of the educational houses has been courting me."

She was outraged. She was terrified and giddy at once. Damn him for tossing her over on her head just when she thought she'd made sense of everything. Damn him for not giving her so much as a chance to get a breath. Damn him for being so good to her.

"In that case," she relented stiffly, finally pulling free of his arms. "I think you and I need to meet with your lawyer."

"And his kids."

"And his mother."

Joe gave her a push. "Get going. The grill's already fired up."

Joe had done his best to ease the meeting for Allison. He'd sat over at his family's that morning explaining Maggie's situation and Allison's, and his. He hadn't wanted to even mention Maggie's condition, hoping he could just let his family fall in love with her—and her mother—without prejudice. But it wouldn't have been fair to anyone.

He needn't have worried.

Maggie was tired and a little crabby, but she didn't know a stranger, and her smile was like sunshine when the kids popped around adult backs to play hide and seek with her.

Allison took a few minutes longer to ease up, standing out in the Burgett backyard with a glass of iced tea in her hand, her white cotton sundress drifting lazily around her legs, Maggie snuggled against her chest.

Joe could see the taut hesitation in her stance, the darker shadows in those green eyes as sibling after sibling came over to meet her and discuss her work and her daughter. It helped, of course, that Tony was first.

"I should have insisted on face-to-face meetings," he said, greeting her with a smile. If Allison had had a free hand, Joe was convinced Tony would have bent over it.

Allison's smile was shy and tight. "So, you're the famous Burgett Barracuda that's had the office quaking in its boots. I thought the threat of injunction against publishing if Joe's real identity was revealed was especially inventive."

Tony's grin grew geometrically. "You have to know how to deal with those publishing types. By the way, madame editor, the kids around here don't know, either."

Joe saw Allison look around at all the tumbling, shrieking little bodies on the long, sloping lawn. "Sorry," he apologized. "I forgot to tell you."

She turned on him. "But, why? They'd be so tickled to know."

His grimace was dry. "Exactly. If they did, I wouldn't have to worry about River Roads blowing my cover."

Her answering smile was understanding. "Tough being a masked man, isn't it?"

"You gotta be on your toes all the time."

Joe's mom, Theresa, approached, wiping her hands on an apron, her eyes taking in all the activity in her yard. "Joseph, are you taking care of your guest?"

He turned to slip an arm around the petite shoulders and thought again that his mother shouldn't be so gray. She was too bright, too alive. "Nice to see you out of the kitchen for a change." He gave her a quick kiss on the top of her head.

She waved him off with an impatient hand and reached out for Maggie. "I came to play with the baby."

Allison surrendered her daughter with good grace. Maggie, by now sleepy, took one look into Theresa Burgett's laughing black eyes and settled right in on her chest.

"She's beautiful, aren't you, baby?" Theresa crooned, rocking back and forth. "A beautiful little girl."

Joe saw the melting continue in Allison's eyes, saw the defenses ease just a little more. She still had to get through a lot of people, but she was doing well.

"'Scuse me."

They all looked down to find Ellen looking up at Allison, with Marcy and Mike standing backup. Allison smiled and crouched down to speak to the naturally grave little four-year-old.

"Is that your baby?" Ellen asked, pointing to Maggie.

Allison nodded. "Yes. Her name's Maggie."

Ellen nodded solemnly. "Can she play?"

"I think she'd probably like to after she takes a little nap," Allison allowed.

Ellen took a look back at her cousins and then back at Allison. "Okay. My mom said that baby was down, and we thought we should make it happy."

Joe's heart stopped. The little group shuddered to sudden silence. He was moving to answer when he realized that Allison was already smiling at the little girl. A genuine smile.

"Oh, I see," she answered with a considered nod. "Well, the truth is, Maggie's not sad at all. What your mommy meant was that she has something called Down syndrome. All that means is that she takes a little longer to learn things than you do."

Ellen digested the information with solemn brown eyes. "It doesn't make her sad?"

Allison shook her head, perfectly still before the little girl. "No. In fact, she's usually very happy when she's not tired."

Ellen smiled then, content with the explanation. "Okay. We'll play when she's awake."

Ellen and the boys headed off for the swings, and Allison regained her feet.

"I'm so sorry," Theresa apologized, holding on even more tightly to the baby in her arms, as if able to physically protect her from the group's discomfort.

Joe's first inclination to reach out to Allison died when he saw that she was more composed than his family.

"I have to admit, that's a new one," Allison said with a smile. "It was so sweet that they wanted to make her feel better."

"Ellen's going to save the world someday," Joe admitted, the residue of shame still eddying through him.

He could see that Tony and his mom were still mortally embarrassed at Ellen's approach, but Allison was touched. He hadn't needed to worry about her at all. She wouldn't have any problems with his family. They certainly wouldn't have any problems with her. Everything was going to be all right after all.

Tony had been right. With his family behind him, the support base would be strong enough to deal with whatever Joe had to do to keep Allison and Maggie in his life.

"Joe," Maria said, pulling him aside an hour later when everybody was inside dishing up dinner. "What are you doing?"

Joe turned to his little sister, saw the pain and frustration in her soft brown eyes, the eyes he'd just seen on her little, care-giving daughter, and came to a halt. His heart slid. Maria was too close to him to be saying that.

"What's the matter, Maria?" he asked, turning to her.

She was a small woman, like her mother, with eyes straight out of a Raphael painting and a great, giving heart. She'd been the one who'd patched up dolls as a kid and who still worked part-time as a nurse in the pediatrics wing at the local hospital. If anyone should have greeted Allison with enthusiasm, it should have been Maria.

She looked briefly at her feet. Around them, the early summer whispered and hummed. The air was still, the sky high with cirrus clouds that the sun had begun to gild.

Laughter and the mumble of conversation drifted out from inside the house.

"If there's one thing I've wished for you ever since I've been a girl," Maria said, still not facing him, her voice low and tortured. "It's that you could be a father. You are the most natural father I've ever seen."

Joe's chest tightened. His breathing slowed. "And?"

She lifted tormented eyes to him. Sincere eyes, loving eyes. Maria had been his shadow since she could walk.

"Allison is lovely," she protested, her hand to Joe's arm. "Maggie's a sweetheart."

"But?"

"But if you marry Allison, you'll never have the chance to be a father. You'll never have those kids you want so badly."

He didn't know what to say, how to convince the last person he should have had to convince. "Being a father to Maggie isn't enough?"

She shuddered with frustration. "You have so much more to give."

He couldn't be angry at her. She loved him. She wanted what was best for him. But in those few words, she fractured years of trust.

Joe wanted to hold his little sister. He wanted to shake her. Instead, all he could do was turn away and walk back into the house, knowing that he would never be the same.

Chapter 13

Allison saw the change in Joe the minute he came in the door. A light had gone out. A new weight settled on his shoulders, and it hurt her. She wanted to take him aside, to take him home and talk to him. She wanted to find out what had happened, because she knew it had something to do with her. With her and Maggie.

One look told her he wouldn't accept her words right now. He wouldn't share that burden. She saw his sister follow him in, saw his surreptitious look her way, and knew without hesitation that Maria had been the one who had taken the light out of Joe's eyes. She knew, too, that Maria hurt for it even more than Joe.

"Have some more of Theresa's mostaccioli," Joe's father, a tall, broad-shouldered man demanded, his startling blue eyes laughing. "You're too skinny."

Allison managed a smile and held out her plate. "This is all delicious," she admitted, her easy tone at odds with the sudden tension in her chest. "My cooking talents are limited to eggs and hot dogs."

"Hear that, Joe?" one of his brothers demanded. "You're gonna have to do the cooking in that household."

"Vincent," his mother admonished. "Mind your manners."

Vincent didn't seem to notice. The kitchen was a madhouse, with all the siblings, mates and grandchildren milling for food and then perching at the long trestle table or the ancillary card tables to eat. The sound level rivaled B.B.'s on a good night, and everything seemed to warrant laughter. For everybody but Maria and Joe. They picked at the food listlessly and settled at their places in silence.

Joe slid in next to Allison and considered his food as if he were recovering from the flu. Avoiding her, avoiding the question in her eyes about the difference in him. His mother saw, too. Her dark eyes grew even darker and darted between her children with precise attention. Whatever she surmised didn't make her happy. It made Allison even less so.

A rift in the family. An argument, and over her. The worst part was that nothing could be resolved until the afternoon was over. Allison sighed, the weight of his silence settling even more heavily on her, and turned back to her food. But before she could escape, she was caught by Theresa's glance. Sharp, certain, judgmental. Telling Allison in no uncertain terms that she was welcome in Theresa's home, no matter what. That whatever was wrong was insignificant as far as Theresa was concerned. Which, of course, Allison knew, it wasn't.

The evening continued. Allison did her best to enjoy the company, helped with dishes over Theresa's protests and held Maggie while the children played peek-a-boo with her. She laughed and talked and visited, and found a home with Joe's family she'd never known with her own.

Where her parents' house had been silent and auspicious, this household rocked with opinion and laughter. Where hers was a collection of separate dens of privacy, his was a jumble of sharing and interference. Her own mother might not have known she was there. Joe's mother took Maggie and shooed Allison out the back door so she could spend time alone with Joe away from the prying eyes of his sisters and brothers.

"You have a terrific family," Allison allowed as she settled onto an old wood swing out in the front yard.

Hands shoved in his pockets, Joe looked up to where the moon was playing hide-and-seek behind scudding clouds. "They like you."

Allison's smile in the darkness was soft and sad because she knew that not all of them liked her. "I like them. You were lucky to grow up in a household like that. Everybody concerned about everybody else."

"You never talk about your family," Joe offered, the moon glinting on his dark hair as he moved. "Aren't you close?"

Allison pushed off on the swing, gliding back and forth in the darkness, her skirt skimming within inches of Joe's slacks. "No," she admitted softly, knowing that the yearning no longer reached her voice. "We're not close."

"Do you have any brothers or sisters?"

"An older brother. A full professor of ancient Greek studies at Yale. My parents are both professors, too. Very intelligent family."

She closed her eyes, letting the moist breeze kiss her cheeks and dance in her hair. Joe's voice and the moon were all that made up the night. Silence, solitude, a bubble of peace.

"You decided not to go that route?" he asked.

"I didn't have the talent or the inclination. I couldn't care less how the Greeks viewed the model human, or what weaponry they used to settle their disputes."

Again, silence. The smell of iris and honeysuckle on the night air. "I guess that wouldn't leave much for conversation around your house."

Allison smiled wryly to herself as she thought of the last stilted phone call she'd made home. A shock met with clinical medical opinion that never somehow betrayed the slightest understanding or pain. Disappointment instead of concern.

"I guess it's why I live so well by myself. I'm not sure how I'd do with all that noise in there all the time."

She'd love it, Allison admitted silently, like well water on a dry, hot August day. Suddenly, her carefully insulated life with Maggie seemed too sterile, even for her. A sentence for her daughter.

"What did Maria say?" she asked suddenly, knowing that it had to come out for Joe to be able to deal with it.

He went very still, his head down, his eyes lost in the night. "What do you mean?"

"She said something to you before dinner," Allison said, still swinging, trying her best to defuse the importance of her question. "It really upset you."

He shook his head. "It wasn't anything."

Allison planted her feet in the dirt and came to a stop. "No, Joe," she disagreed. "It wasn't 'nothing.' It's been bothering both of you since dinner, and I have a feeling it's about me."

He stood before her, the moon silhouetting him, the breeze picking at his hair, his hands still in his pockets. Allison couldn't see his eyes, couldn't even see the set of his jaw in the darkness. Still, she could feel his tension, shimmering off him like a glow in the vibrating darkness.

Suddenly, a pair of headlights stabbed at them. Swinging over Joe's face, exposing just what Allison had imagined. Stark eyes and clenched jaw, pain and frustration and disillusionment. Just as quickly the light was gone, but the car had swung to a halt and a door slammed.

"Joey? Is that you?"

Joe turned and straightened, as if warding something off. Allison followed his attention to discover a long-legged woman striding up the lawn in a flowing pale dress and high heels.

"Hello, Syl," Joe greeted her.

Allison heard the undertone of distaste in his voice and couldn't help paying closer attention. The woman sidled up to them, a lot of blond hair and a great figure was all Allison could make out in the darkness. Enough to make her even more intrigued, especially since Joe was standing there as if he'd been planted.

"I'm surprised you're still here," the woman allowed in a sultry voice. "I thought you were headed off for a date this afternoon."

"I was. Sylvia, I'd like you to meet Allison Henley. Allison, this is Sylvia Burgett, Tony's ex. She's here to pick up the kids."

Allison hoped that Sylvia couldn't see her smile. It wasn't as friendly as it could have been. "Nice to meet you," she said.

Sylvia came to a kind of attention. "Oh, I'm sorry. I didn't see you over there. So, you did show up."

"Pardon?"

"I was betting you wouldn't. Not with this bunch. I'd be leery of them without any strikes against me. You must be petrified."

"Sylvia," Joe growled in warning.

Allison began to swing again, just a little, back and forth as the woman stood her ground.

"I like Joe's family a lot. You didn't?"

Sylvia's laugh was at once delighted and just a little nasty. "A mutual admiration society, wasn't it, Joe?"

Joe didn't answer.

"Allison, why don't we go on in?"

"I'll come in with you," Sylvia announced, hefting her purse strap higher on her shoulder. "I have to find the kids. Is your baby inside, or didn't you bring it?"

Allison couldn't see very well in the darkness, but she looked right at Sylvia. A very selfish lady with a very defensive attitude about the Burgetts. They must have given her a rough way to go.

"Joe's mom has her."

"Really. She's Mongoloid, right? Tony said something about it."

"She has Down syndrome."

A brisk nod, then a dramatic shudder. "Aren't you too young to have a Mongoloid?"

"I'm twenty-six," Allison managed to say, wincing each time Sylvia used the old epithet. "Older women can have babies with Down's, but in fact seventy-five percent of mothers who have kids with Down's are under thirty-five.''

"Wow, then you just don't stand a chance of having a normal kid. Why didn't you just have an abortion when you found out?"

Allison's heart went cold. It was all she could do to keep swinging, maintaining that even rhythm. Joe wasn't nearly as controlled. He stiffened as if he'd been shot.

"Get out of here, Sylvia."

"Well, it only makes sense," she defended herself. "After all, who'd really want a baby like that? I mean, it's tough enough raising a normal one."

"I would," Joe informed her blackly.

Sylvia's laughter was tinkly. "Which is why Maria is so mad at you. Has she told you?"

"I said it's time to go, Sylvia," he threatened, edging closer. "I mean now. Before I hurt you."

Allison brought the swing to a halt and got to her feet. She walked over to where Joe stood and laid a gentle hand on his arm. Then she turned to Sylvia. "My daughter's name is Maggie," she said, her voice even and soft with the effort to maintain control. "And I'd really appreciate it if you didn't use the word *Mongoloid* around her or the other children. It really has unpleasant connotations."

Sylvia shrugged. "Sure. That's just what we always called them. I guess they don't anymore, huh?"

"No," Allison replied, surprised at her own calm. "They don't."

The blonde nodded, sending moonlight tumbling in the curls. "No problem. And good luck with her. I still think it would be too tough for me."

Allison managed to keep the bitterness out of her voice. "I think you're probably right."

"I'd probably hope she didn't come out of that surgery they were talking about today. I guess you're maybe thinking the same thing."

"What the hell is that supposed to mean?" Joe demanded, breaking free of Allison's hold.

Sylvia started, and for the first time, Allison saw a glint of her eyes. She'd expected enmity. All she saw was stupidity.

"I didn't mean anything—"

"Would you hope that Ellen or Ted wouldn't come out of surgery?" he snapped, towering over her.

Sylvia stepped back again. Allison made another grab for Joe's arm and missed.

"Of course not . . . but they're not . . . they're . . ."

"They're what?" Joe retorted. "Normal? They're healthy? Is that the only reason to keep them? What if one of them would have had Down syndrome? What if they'd had a hand missing, or a cleft lip or a heart defect? Would you have demanded a refund? What the hell am I talking about? Of course, you would."

"Joe—" Allison tried, catching hold again before Joe leapt across the yard.

Sylvia's hands were up, and she was edging toward the porch steps. "Joe, for heaven's sake, I'm sorry."

Allison heard the slam of the front door and saw a silhouette on the porch.

"Sylvia? What the hell are you up to?"

Tony. That was all she needed.

"Go on up and get your kids," Joe threatened in a voice that reminded Allison of pit bulls. "And then stay as far away from me as you can."

Sylvia turned and scuttled up the porch steps to be met by an irate Tony. Allison didn't even bother to listen to their conversation or wait for the slam of the door again. She turned to Joe, who was trembling with fury.

"How come you're so calm?" he grated out. "That was your daughter she was babbling about."

"I'm used to it," she admitted, still holding on to him.

She saw his face swing toward her, heard the sick surprise in his silence.

"Get used to it," she advised. "That's not the last time you'll hear it."

"What right does she have to say that to you?" he demanded.

Allison laughed. "People assume they have the most interesting rights when you have a baby like mine. A woman in the street demanded to know what right I had bringing a child like that into the world. The new mother's group I was in stopped inviting me back when they realized that my child had Down syndrome, as if their children could catch it. Sylvia isn't the only idiot in the world."

He wanted to pace; she could feel it in the tension in his arms. "But talking about Maggie as if she weren't even human..."

"It's the society we live in. Now that people have a choice of whether they want a defective baby or not, suddenly no one should want to bring a baby with Down syndrome into the world. It's not fair to the family, to society, to the child. Nobody seems to remember that that child hasn't forfeited any rights simply because she has faulty chromosomes."

"But she actually accused you of wanting your baby to die."

That brought Allison to a standstill. She turned her face to the sky, wishing desperately for a place to hide. For sanctuary.

Joe moved closer. "You're not surprised."

"It's another favorite theme," Allison admitted in a small voice, still not facing him. "I'm telling you, people like Sylvia just don't count. The only thing you can try to do is gently educate them and hope for the best. It's the Marias that have the capability of really hurting."

She'd succeeded in turning the conversation the way she wanted it, away from her and toward Joe. He didn't answer, but she felt his reaction as surely as if he'd cried out. He stiffened next to her, stilled. Pulled away.

"Tell me about it, Joe," she demanded.

He shook his head. "It's nothing, really. Sylvia was just doing her best to drive a wedge in the family. It's her favorite sport since the divorce."

"Not good enough," Allison argued. "Maria is upset that you're serious about me, isn't she?"

He took Allison by the arms. "I told you," he argued. "No problems to deal with until after Maggie's well."

This time Allison shook her head, looked up at him and caught the torment that glinted briefly in the moonlight. "No, Joe. That won't work. You've been there to support me and to entertain me. You've made love to me and never once really talked to me about how you feel about all this."

"When Maggie's better."

"Now. When it hurts, or it'll be too late and any chance we might have will be gone."

"I have no problems."

She laughed, and it was a sad sound. "If you had no problems, you wouldn't be playing world-class blues down at B.B.'s." Lifting a hand, she turned his face to her, demanding his attention, his concession. "You keep forgetting that your sax is much more honest than you are."

Joe cupped her hand against his cheek and gazed down at her. "I love you," he insisted.

Allison didn't answer. She didn't need to. The moonlight betrayed every emotion in her eyes to him, and he held her still against him.

"I love Maggie," he said.

Allison felt the tears swell behind her eyes. "I know," she admitted.

Behind them, a door slammed open. Footsteps echoed on the porch.

"Joe? Allison?"

Allison wanted to scream at the intruder to go away, to leave the two of them in peace. They were so close to the truth, to sharing between them what a marriage involving Maggie would really mean. There, caught in the frail moonfall, they had almost gathered the courage to face their fears and name them.

"Yeah, Mom," Joe answered, not looking away.

"I'm sorry, really, but the baby's not looking well."

No, Allison wanted to cry out. Don't interrupt. Don't let reality intrude. Don't let Maggie intrude. Let Joe and I have just a little time together, distanced. Let us escape while we have the chance.

But Joe was already turning toward the house. "Sylvia had better not have—"

"Sylvia didn't do anything. I think the little thing's just tired."

Allison fought tears all the way back to the house. For the chances lost, for the frustration of knowing that no matter what happened, Maggie would always interrupt.

Hope. She'd dreaded it all along, and now she knew why. It made a person selfish, wanting just a little more, and then a little more after that. Demanding choices, sacrificing complacency. It had been so much easier when there'd been nothing to want. When living meant getting through twelve hours, and then twenty-four. Suddenly, she caught herself just shy of planning. Wanting. Expecting. And then, just as she began to really believe that it could all actually come true, reality came crashing back down.

Maggie intruded. Beautiful, fragile flower. Cherished burden. Allison wanted to laugh at Joe's outrage. She wanted to cry because she was going to have to tell him the truth, and she just didn't know how she was going to have the courage. Because when she did, he'd know what kind of mother she really was.

"You're going to have to be off for at least a week," Bill Frazier objected in his office overlooking the city. "And we're running out of time on Dowd. Now, what do you have for me, Allison?"

Allison didn't even settle into the leather wing chair. Perched on the edge of the seat, she clasped her hands together and faced Bill dead-on. "Nothing," she told him without apology. "Dowd will continue to write for us only as long as we abide by his contract. He's said it, his lawyer's said it, and if we press real hard, I imagine a judge will say it. And to be frank with you, Bill, I'm on his side."

Bill stiffened as if she'd just declared herself an enemy agent. "I don't believe Dowd's name is on your paycheck, young lady."

"I'm hardly a young lady," she countered, Bill's chronic patronization more than she could take just six days away from Maggie's surgery. "And Dowd's name is on our giant first-quarter profits, so I'd have to think he does have a choice of how he wants to handle his own career."

"But you don't. Take care of him, or I can see to it that you lose that very agreeable arrangement you have with this company. And I could probably remind you that there aren't just a whole lot of other publishing companies in town to prepare a résumé for."

Allison thought of Maggie's insurance. Exorbitant now, impossible without a job. She thought of the job market right now and fought down a clutch of blind fear. Then rage. Life was tough enough without getting squeezed in by thoughtless businessmen who couldn't care less for integrity or privacy. Life was unfair enough without having to choose between the daughter who depended on you and the man who loved you.

Her stomach churned. The band that had been tightening inexorably around her chest for the week shortened a notch or two. Unclasping her hands, she carefully pushed herself to her feet.

"I guess you'll have to do what you have to do," she allowed, surprised at how calm her voice sounded. "I can't compromise Mr. Dowd."

And without waiting for an answer, she turned and walked from the office.

Staring out the attic windows, Joe fought a growing sense of desperation. Maggie was scheduled for surgery in less than a week. Allison had been avoiding him ever since the Sunday dinner.

They had come so close that night, fingertip-to-fingertip in the darkness where pain could be masked and truth allowed. He had almost admitted his fears, shared with her the sense of betrayal his sister had left him with. He'd almost coaxed the truth from Allison about her daughter, about him, about their future. A heartbeat away, and the moment had evaporated. And now, he wasn't sure she was going to let him close again.

His house was so empty now. The wind whined, and the tugs down on the river moaned. The house echoed with frustration, shuddered with silence. The ghosts of old families haunted him. His family irritated him. New dreams shimmered in the early-morning hours, dreams that flickered with uncertainty, dimmed with distance.

He wanted Allison there with him. He wanted Maggie.

He wanted more.

It was something he could never admit to Allison. Something he would forfeit for her without hesitation. But not without regret. Those old dreams still survived, tenaciously battling eviction. They still bubbled up at odd moments when he stared out over the river, when he walked his land or polished the wood he'd crafted. Things to pass on, to share, to bestow like treasures on children.

When he saw the river, he saw himself pointing out the sandbars to a little girl, tiny hand in his. He saw them naming the hawks that skimmed the currents and making up stories of the Indians and trappers who had first navigated the great, silver waters. When he ran his hands over the smooth edge of wild cherry, he saw a smaller hand following. A son who lifted the planer in unsteady hands, who felt the power of a hammer and the magic of a lathe.

They would not surrender, those familiar eyes. They would not concede. But Allison's eyes were the most powerful. They were the eyes that followed Joe no matter where he went, haunting him as relentlessly as mortality, as seductively as morning. It was those eyes he needed, those eyes he wanted. And sitting in his silent, empty house, he knew that it was those eyes he wanted to share his world.

If only the other eyes would dim.

He looked over at his drawing table to the sketches that had begun to appear since Sunday. The new story line that kept interrupting the work even on the bathroom book. He hated the story, hated the impetus for it because he had seen its spark in the sadness in his sister's eyes.

He didn't know whether River Roads would like it. It was a little darker, a little sadder. Just another lesson in life most people never had to face.

The phone interrupted his reverie.

"Yes?"

"Joe? It's Tony. Have you talked to Allison?"

Joe frowned. "No, why?"

"Because I just got a call from her boss. Gal named Brook?"

Joe stiffened, suddenly anxious. "What?"

"It seems that the word has come down at the publishing house that if Allison doesn't deliver you up for the marketing department, she kisses her job goodbye."

That brought Joe to his feet. "What are you talking about? They can't do that to her."

"Of course they can. She's not in a union like some people."

Joe raked a hand through his hair. It was less than a week to Maggie's surgery. He'd caught the increasing tension in Allison's voice every time he called. She had all she could handle to just get through this without having to worry about some jerk with a control complex going after her paycheck.

"What do we want to do?" Tony asked.

"We aren't going to do anything," Joe assured him. "I'm going down to River Roads right now."

There was a considered pause. "Joe, I don't think—"

"Legal threats are one thing," Joe informed his brother. "The size of my fist is another. I'll be damned if they're going to screw Allison when she can least afford it."

"You're not giving yourself up."

"What's this guy's name?"

"Frazier."

He didn't even tell his brother goodbye.

Allison wasn't sure how much more she could take. The apartment was quiet, Maggie was napping, and Lucille was home with her children. Allison had work laid out on the card table. She had lunch laid out on the kitchen counter. She couldn't sit down to either.

It was all Joe's fault. Allison had long since steeled herself to Maggie's surgery. Struggled to build layers of protection from the bald, terrifying truth of it. She'd managed to survive in a strange city without family, without husband, without future. Maybe not happy, maybe not content, but managing.

And then Joe had come along. He'd stolen her complacency, sabotaged her isolation and breached her defenses. He'd laid her bare, helpless to face the searing pain of loss and uncertainty.

He'd enslaved her to hope and then pulled it away from her.

She didn't want to know anymore what his sister had said to hurt him. She didn't want the cost of her relationship to grow any more. She didn't want to see any more pain in his eyes and know that she was the cause. She was the cause of enough already. Let somebody else break Joe Burgett's heart. Let somebody else be responsible for him. She already had enough to handle.

The doorbell rang. She went on pacing, wiping at silent tears without noticing. The bell rang again, and then again. She didn't listen. Probably Brook. Allison was sure she'd heard about Frazier's threat by now. Allison was sure Brook had also left messages on the answering machine. She just hadn't bothered to listen to them.

Allison didn't want to hear anybody right now. She couldn't be civil. She couldn't be intelligent. She felt as if she were splintering into a million pieces, and the surgery still wasn't for another six days.

She wasn't going to make it.

Brook wasn't giving up. She rang and pounded and rang again. Then she yelled. And that was when Allison realized it wasn't Brook.

"I know you're there, Allison!"

A strangled little sob escaped. Allison simply couldn't answer.

"I'm in pretty damn good shape. If you don't answer the door, I'm just going to kick it in."

Still Allison couldn't answer. She just didn't believe he'd do it. If she just held herself still, battled the overwhelming urge to open the door and throw herself into Joe's arms and beg for comfort, he'd change his mind and go away.

He didn't.

There was a sharp explosion and the door slammed open, the frame splintering. Joe stood on the porch, dressed in plaid shirt and jeans, his hair tangled as if he'd been running his hands through it, his eyes dark and dangerous.

Allison backed up. "Are you nuts?" she demanded. "You're going to wake Maggie. And you broke my door!"

He strode in and closed the door. It hung just a little off center, daylight peeking around the edges of the frame. "Brook has been trying to get you for hours."

Allison shrugged, straightening, desperate for composure when she had none left, oblivious to the state her door was in. "I didn't feel like talking to anybody."

"Well, you'll talk to me."

He filled the room with his energy, a manic purpose that buffeted her. Allison couldn't face it, couldn't fight it. She wanted to crawl away and hide.

"I don't think so," she demurred, turning away.

He never gave her a chance to collect herself. Walking right up, he took hold of her and pulled her to a stop. "Frazier's looking for work."

Allison spun around, stunned. Silenced. Shaken.

Joe's smile was equal parts compassionate and carnivorous. "Sometimes lawyers just aren't threatening enough."

"But you—"

"Enjoyed it immensely. One thing being a bestselling author has taught me is only deal with the top. I walked right into Walt Thomspon's office and told him that I'd found out that Frazier had the bad sense to threaten your job if you didn't reveal my identity. We came to a fairly quick understanding that if Frazier won that argument, River Roads lost their contract with me. And Frazier might lose a few teeth."

"Joe—"

He shrugged, still smiling, still purposeful, his hold on her tight and secure. "Yeah, you're right. The contract might have been a little tough to manage. The teeth would have been a pleasure."

Allison laughed, a bubbling release of tension and surprise. Of amazement. "You *are* nuts," she accused without heat, stilling beneath the pressure of his sure hands. Forfeiting her distance.

"I'm furious," he countered, his features tightening. "You didn't even tell me. Just how were you going to manage Maggie without a job and insurance?"

Allison dropped her gaze, shrugged uncomfortably. "I've survived before."

Joe lifted her chin with a hand so that she had to face him again. His smile softened, his eyes deepened. Allison could smell the clean edge of soap on him, the hint of wood and leaves. She could see the late sun strike sparks in his eyes. "Don't you understand?" he demanded softly. "I would have given them my soul to prevent this."

Her eyes clouded again. She lifted her face to his, the band so tight she could hardly breathe. "I know," she told him. "That's why I couldn't tell you."

He pulled her into his arm, his hold clumsy with emotion. His eyes brimming with it. His jaw shifted and clenched. "I love you," he whispered, bending his head to hers.

Allison closed her eyes. She held her breath against the tide of tears he could provoke with only three words. She wanted to answer him so badly, wanted to share his gift, to repay him in kind. She couldn't speak. She couldn't move, tightly wrapped in him, enclosed by his strength, his warmth.

"Are you working?" he asked.

Allison tried her best to follow his shift. "What?"

He let go enough to look down on her, that crooked smile back in place. "Editing," he clarified, motioning to the papers spread out on her table. "Are you in your office?"

Allison took a blind look at the words she'd been trying to concentrate on all day and gave him a limp nod. "Yeah, I guess."

He nodded. "Good. I have a story idea I want to talk over with you."

Allison looked over again, then looked at Joe, not a little confused. "Okay."

Joe turned her attention back to him. "And then," he promised with a growl that betrayed his frustration. "We're going to talk. A lot."

From *Ralph Finds a Friend*
by L. Wood Dowd

*I*t wasn't that Ralph was ever alone. After all, he spent every night with his brothers and slept in a big bed during the day with everybody in the family. Ralph didn't have to be by himself if he didn't want to be.

But sometimes, Ralph didn't want to be with all those monsters. Monsters were always talking about monster things. IMPORTANT things, like Halloween and full moons and thunderstorms. (Every monster had a copy of the Farmer's Almanac to plan his schedule.) Monsters talked grandly and importantly about what special monster things they had to do. Who they'd scared that week, who they'd eaten. Things like that.

Sometimes, Ralph couldn't bear to talk about those things. Because Ralph sometimes wondered if he was really a monster at all.

Ralph didn't really like scaring people. He didn't really care for living under a bed or waiting to sneak out on a shadow. When Unctious scared Billy's little sister the night before last, Ralph had snuck into her room and whispered *into her ear that it was just the wind making that noise, that the nighttime was a nice, comfortable place to be.*

Ralph just couldn't understand why it was fun to hurt people.

He couldn't tell his family that. Uncle Ferocious would have thrown him out of the house, and a four-year-old monster wouldn't have anyplace else to go if he didn't have a house. Mama Binkley would have looked way down at him with those very scary yellow eyes of hers and snorted. And Papa... well, Ralph just didn't want to think about it.

So he figured that maybe Gypsies had left him at the Binkley's house. Maybe he was really a little boy like Billy who just happened to have sharp teeth and a tail. Maybe he was a puppy who would grow up to play with balls and sticks instead of chomping on small animals for lunch.

That was what Ralph pretended when he snuck away from the house while everyone else was asleep. While they were snoring and grunting and setting the occasional pillow on fire from belching in their sleep, Ralph snuck off into the Troll Woods and dreamed and wrote stories.

It was there that he met Rose. He'd been sitting under a very big oak tree one day trying to find shapes in the clouds when he heard a soft, sighing sound. Like the wind, but sadder. Ralph looked over to see a very strange little creature sitting on its haunches a few feet away.

"Hello," he greeted it, for Ralph was much friendlier when he was not having to prove what a fierce little monster he was. "M-m-my name's Ralph. What's yours?"

The creature had very big, soft eyes. Blue eyes and the palest, thinnest white skin, almost as if you could see through it. Ralph wasn't sure it had ears, for its head was perfectly rounded, except for the very big eyes and a small pink mouth. Its body was rather skinny, all in all, with no wings or even a very nice tail. It seemed a very sad-looking creature.

Again, the creature seemed to sigh. It watched him, but it didn't move, its small paws clutched together over its skinny white chest.

It really was a most unattractive creature, Ralph thought. Kind of slimy looking. Like it would leave a bad taste in your mouth after you took a big bite. Still, Ralph knew what it was like to feel different.

"I'm sorry," he apologized, tilting his sharp little head to the side. "I d-d-d-didn't hear you."

The creature tilted its head, too, just like Ralph.

"Ralph," it sighed.

"Well, I don't think that c-c-can be your n-n-name," Ralph disagreed. "Because, you see, it's mine. What k-k-kind of c-creature are you?" he asked. "Are you a ghost? Are you a tree frog? I've never seen a tree frog before. We usually only have p-p-pond ones here, and the Trolls eat them too quickly to make their acquaintance."

The creature looked down at the ground. It wrung its hands. "Waif," it said distinctly.

Ralph jumped right up. "Oh, d-d-dear," he stammered, backing away. "I c-c-can't talk t-to you." *Ralph, you see, knew all about waifs. He'd heard his mother talk about them. Uncle Ferocious spoke of them in whispers, and little monster children were threatened with turning into waifs if they weren't careful.*

Waifs were half-monsters. Sometimes, they said, baby monsters just weren't born right, without their scales and the bellows in their lungs that made fire. They crept along the edges of the woods, afraid of the sun and lost in the dark, watching, waiting to snatch little monster children and steal their scales. Waifs gave the wind its whine and taught the willows to weep.

Ralph knew this. And he really didn't want to lose his scales, even if he didn't think they were quite as lovely as everybody else did. Still, he couldn't quite turn away from the waif, who seemed so very, very sad.

"Is it true?" *Ralph whispered, his own paws clutched together just like the waif's.* "Do you have monster parents?"

The waif just looked at him. Just watched him like Ralph was the first thing he'd seen in a long time and he didn't want him to leave.

"*I heard you can't breathe fire and that you have to eat garbage other monsters throw out because you don't even know how to stalk.*"

The waif didn't move. Didn't tilt its little head again. It really was the same size as Ralph, except that it didn't have pointy ears or a nice snout. It just looked so . . . lonely. And even with all those monsters around, Ralph knew how that felt.

"*Do you have a name?*" *he asked.* "*Or do they just call you waif?*"

"*Rose,*" *the waif finally said.* "*My—m-my name is Rose. I saw you . . . dreaming. I'm good at that. Can I help?*"

Ralph took a very big breath. He didn't know whether to run or stay. He should have run right home and told his mother, so she could warn all the other monsters. So the monster patrol could run to the woods and chase the waif back to where it belonged. But he did like to dream, and other monsters simply didn't need to. Other monsters preferred singeing bushes and nibbling on ankles. Ralph really just wanted to know somebody who could find a cow in a cloud.

So he stayed where he was. "*Hello, Rose,*" *he said.* "*It's nice to meet you.*"

Chapter 14

"Please tell me you didn't give yourself away," Allison begged.

Joe grinned at her over his mug of coffee as they sat at her dining room table. "To tell you the truth, I was so mad when I walked into River Roads, I didn't even consider it. I just wanted that bastard fired for what he was trying to do to you." He shrugged. "Fate seemed to be with me. I walked in during lunch hour. Thompson's secretary hadn't been on your blues tour and didn't know me from Adam. I told her I was Tony. She didn't see fit to argue…which could have had something to do with the size of my temper when I walked in."

Allison's answering smile was still tentative. Joe didn't mind. He was inside, her job was safe, and they could deal with the rest of it as it came.

The rest of it. It was funny how decisions were made. Not in momentous flashes of insight, with shudders and cries of inspiration, but in small whispers that settle a person's world right back into place. His had come when Walt Thompson had gaped in realization that his very mysterious author was standing at his desk.

Joe really hadn't considered it. He'd known exactly what Allison would do because it was the person she was. Thinking of someone else first, never even considering what standing on principle and trust would do to her checkbook or her future. Caught solidly between Joe's rights and the hospital bills she was sure to face and still refusing to offer him up.

Well, it was time somebody else took care of her for a change. Time she realized that there might just be a man out there who didn't consider her a disappointment, a problem or a burden.

His old dreams would never completely die, but there had to be some way two people in love could come to peace with them. And that was what Joe had broken down the door to tell Allison.

"So Mr. Thompson knows who L. Wood Dowd is," she ventured.

Joe concentrated on his coffee. "He has a far greater respect for the word *injunction* than the late Mr. Frazier did. He assured me the office will continue to believe that it was Tony who delivered the blow."

Allison nodded this time, and the tension in her shoulders eased by increments. "Good. After all that, I wouldn't want you to go spilling the beans now."

"He also seemed intrigued by the fact that a man my age would have prostate problems."

That got a chuckle out of her. She was still tight as a tent rope, the strain of the job and Maggie's situation stretching her features and creasing her forehead. Joe didn't care. He loved her. He couldn't imagine any way he wouldn't, any time he wouldn't find her compelling and beautiful.

She was wary, too, though. Holding her breath, waiting for him to drop his bomb. Expecting him to leave now that he'd disagreed with Maria. She might have known everything there was to know about Down syndrome and editing, but she sure didn't know much about families.

Joe thought that maybe he should be the one to teach her.

"Allison?"

She lifted her head and Joe caught the fleeting fear. The settling of fatalism over that gentle green. His smile was apologetic.

"I was wrong the other night, wasn't I? We can't wait until Maggie's better to discuss things."

Joe knew she had courage. He certainly couldn't argue it now when she faced him without flinching, even believing that he had come to tell her goodbye.

"No," she allowed, her shoulders finally dropping. "We can't."

Joe shook his head, the frustration of the past few days escaping into his voice. "I'm sorry, Allison. I really thought that if we just shelved all business, we could concentrate on getting Maggie through this. I haven't been able to concentrate on a single thing."

Her eyes lightened just a little. "I like the idea for the new book."

He just shrugged that off. "There are more important things to consider."

Instead of answering, Allison climbed to her feet and walked over to look out the sliding glass doors. The sky was a flat, uninteresting gray today, the breeze still and the trees limp. Not much to inspire. "Do you want a new editor, Joe?"

She never turned around, so Joe stood up to join her.

"No," he said, standing just behind her so that the smell of her hair was in his nostrils. So he could protect her without touching her, since that would push her away right now. "I don't want another editor. I don't want another lover or another friend or another partner. I want you."

She stiffened, but she didn't move. "Maybe we shouldn't be having this conversation after all."

It was all Joe could do to keep his hands off her. She was so brittle, so vulnerable, a woman steeled to isolation and disappointment. He couldn't bear the thought that he'd almost disappointed her, too. He'd almost deserted her, just like everyone else she'd counted on in her life.

"I love you, Allison," he said quietly, simply. "I love Maggie, and that's all that matters. We can work out the rest."

She whipped around then, and he saw the tears. "No," she insisted sharply. "We can't. It *isn't* all that matters, don't you understand?"

Joe never faltered before the ferocity in her voice, the hot torment in her liquid eyes. "No," he countered. "I don't. I can't believe that you were meant to live your life all alone simply because you had a child with a genetic defect. Is that the way it's done, now? No one else is allowed to participate?"

The tears spilled over and slid down her cheeks. "It's not what you want, Joe," she insisted, rigid and unyielding. Betraying the torment that had been growing in her since he'd first discovered her at his garage door. "I'm not what you want."

"You're not?" he asked. "Why? Because my sister's upset? Because if I marry you, I'll have to rethink my future? Don't you think that those are problems every couple has?"

"Every couple does not have those problems," she insisted. "Do you really think Maria would have been upset if I'd been a different person? Do you think the two of you would have argued?"

Joe's smile was gentle. "We didn't argue."

Allison wasn't accepting. "I saw the two of you, Joe. Your mother saw you. Even Sylvia knew about it."

He did reach out, now, taking her by the shoulders, stilling her, capturing her before she could flee. Forcing her to listen to what he had to tell her. "You wanted me to tell you my fears," he said, capturing her glittering green gaze with his own. "To be honest with you about what marrying you would mean."

"I don't—"

"Marrying you," he repeated definitely. "That's what I said and that's what I meant. You're not the kind of person to expect a casual relationship. Neither am I. I've been thinking marriage since the first day you walked into my house, so shut up and listen to me."

If she'd been any less distraught, she would have smiled. Joe saw the impulse rise and die.

"I've learned everything I can about Down's," he went on. "You've been honest with me about what you face, what Maggie faces. And I'd be a pretty rank coward if I couldn't accept her future simply because she doesn't have my gene pool. True, it isn't what I'd dreamed of, what I'd expected. But it isn't what you expected, either. We can work through it together. Just like any married couple with a child with Down's."

"What about your family?" she asked, struggling for distance. "They never approved of Sylvia. It was one of the reasons Tony's marriage didn't work. It wouldn't be different with me."

"It would be the most profound of differences. True, nobody liked Sylvia. She was a cat when Tony married her and she's a cat today. You, on the other hand, had everybody eating out of your hand. Not to mention that little girl of yours. My mother is already demanding baby-sitting time."

"And what about Maria?"

Joe lifted a finger to wipe away a tear he couldn't prevent. "Maria's my kid sister. She's also one of those mothers who thinks that no one else can be happy unless they're married and saddled with a brood like hers. When she was a girl, she used to plan for us to live next door to each other so that our kids could play together, go to school together, all that. She's not mad, she's disappointed. It won't make any difference at all in the long run."

"How can you say that?" Allison demanded, really not understanding. "She'll never forgive me."

"Just like your parents never forgave you for not being a professor? Like your husband never forgave you for having Maggie?"

Allison shuddered, shrank into herself, her eyes stark and painful. "Yes," she insisted. "Don't you see? I can't do that to you."

Joe couldn't hold her away anymore. He pulled her into his arms, drawing her face against his chest where it belonged, where she could be safe and nurtured and loved. "No, honey. You don't see. My family isn't like that. We talk, we argue, we interfere with each other's lives shamelessly. But we stick by each other's decisions like glue. They love you. They love Maggie. Whatever we do, they'll be right there with us."

Still she shook her head. "They can't," she argued. "They don't even know me."

"I know you," he assured her. "And that's enough."

Joe heard her sob, felt her stiffen in his arms. Felt her pull away and let her. She faced him with anguished eyes.

"No," she argued. "You don't know me."

Before he could pull her back to him, she walked away. Paced, picked up her coffee cup and carried it into the kitchen.

"What don't I know about you?" he demanded, frustrated by the separation, furious with her arguments.

"I—I can't give you what you want," she insisted on a whisper, her back turned to him, her head down.

"What can't you give me?" he retorted, following. Reaching out to her. "What, Allison?" He spun her back into his arms. Caught her face in his hand so that she had to see the determination in his eyes. So she couldn't escape the truth. "This?"

He kissed her, a hungry, bruising kiss. She whimpered, bucked in his arms. He tasted her tears and shuddered with need. He felt her hands coming up, flattening against his chest. He felt the flutter of her heart against his chest. He heard a whisper of protest evaporate on a harsh groan.

Need, want, desire. She folded into his arms and lifted her mouth to his. She wrapped her arms around his neck and pulled him closer.

"I love you," he gasped against her throat, his chest on fire and his gut seared through with the feel of her. "I need you, Allison." Her lips were so soft, so pliant. Her tongue danced with his. Her body melted with invitation. Raw need. Memory. They had made love with a sweet ferocity that her body hadn't forgotten.

Joe sucked air into his tortured lungs and wrapped his hand in Allison's hair, pulled her back to him again. "You need me," he insisted. "You give me that."

Tears slid down her throat, tears Joe could no longer bear. "I love you," she whispered, the sound of confession instead of a declaration. "Joe, I love you so much."

He should have smiled. He couldn't. "What more can you give me than that?"

Caught tight in his arms, she shuddered. She sobbed, a soft mewling sound that tore at Joe. "I can't give you children."

Joe clutched her even more tightly to him. "You've given me you. You've given me Maggie. I'm a luckier man than most."

"But you want those children," she protested. "I want so much to be able to give them to you. Little boys with your eyes, little girls with your smile. Dozens of them, all...all waiting for their...daddy to...read them the Binkley Brothers...."

"Shh," he commanded, stroking her hair, wondering if she could feel the splintering pain in his heart, for her, for them both. For the little girl who had so changed both of their lives. "We'll have dozens of nieces and nephews. We can even adopt or try our hand at foster children. We'll work it out, Allison," he assured her. "I promise."

"No," she said with a fatality that Joe couldn't accept. "We won't work it out. I can't ask you to give that up. I can't ask you to give me everything and be left with nothing but struggle and disappointment."

"Disappointment," he echoed, looking down at her with a scowl. "There's that word again. How on earth could I be disappointed in you?" he demanded.

"Maybe because I am," she retorted, and Joe saw the real ghosts in her eyes. The darkest secrets he'd wanted to share. Now he wasn't so sure. He didn't want to know anything that could take her away from him. He didn't want to discover something that would unbalance his precious hold on the future.

She searched his face for some sign, some reaction, and her expression hardened. "You'd be giving up everything you want for me, Joe. Everything. And I don't think it would be a good trade."

"I told you," he insisted. "Maggie's—"

"Not Maggie," she interrupted, straightening, trying to pull away. Distancing herself, even in his arms. "Me. I don't deserve you. I don't deserve Maggie."

"Allison—"

She did pull away then, and gathered her determination about her like a cloak, her face still tear streaked, her voice raw and harsh. "It took Sylvia to make me admit it," she said.

"Sylvia?" he retorted. "Allison, don't be ridiculous. I told you, she's a cat."

"She was right. You should have listened to her."

"About what?"

"You were so angry with her for the way she talked about Maggie. It sounded pretty harsh, didn't it? Pretty unfeeling. And I told you to ignore her, because there were a lot of idiots like her. Well, say hello to one now, Joe. I've had every one of those thoughts."

Joe took a step, unable to give voice to the maelstrom she'd unleashed.

She shied away as if he'd been charged. "No," she insisted. "Listen to me. Listen to what I've never told anyone else because I don't like to admit it myself. I resent her sometimes, Joe. I get so angry, I throw things because I have to do her exercises over and over again, because I'll never go to her college graduation or hold her children in my arms. Why couldn't I have had a normal child? Why couldn't I be the one with Sylvia's children? Bright, happy, normal kids she doesn't even really want. I'd want them. I'd love them and nurture them and cheer them on. But I'm stuck with Maggie, who has to be cheered on in inches. I'm trapped by that chromosome as much as she is. I'm afraid for her every minute and I'm furious for her. And I'm—I'm so afraid that Sylvia was right about the surgery."

Joe was frozen by her anguish, battered by her anger and her self-loathing. How could she have possibly hidden all this for so long?

"But that's normal," he insisted desperately. "How can you not resent disappointments? You're only human, Allison. You don't really want anything to happen to Maggie. You know that."

"Do I?" she demanded, her movements jerky and sharp. "Joe, I lie awake at night and wonder what would be best for her. How can I sentence her to a life of toil and frustration? How can I face her every time some other little girl makes fun of the way she talks or the way she looks, or another Sylvia asks something stupid like why didn't I abort her? Maybe the surgery's her answer, Joe. Maybe it's God's way of letting her off the hook."

She stopped, a hand stifling the words, her eyes huge and defenseless. "How can I think that about my own child?" she demanded on a tortured groan.

Joe reached out to her, but she flinched away, openly sobbing at her own words. Joe wouldn't allow her. He couldn't let her go on thinking that she was flawed because she had perfectly human reactions.

"You love Maggie," he told her crisply. "You want what's best for her. Am I right?"

Allison didn't answer.

"Who gets her up every morning?" he demanded. "Who sings to her and exercises her and gives her a gift every day to remind them both how special she is? Who?"

Allison looked away from him. He took hold of her chin and drew her face back to him where she couldn't escape the truth.

"You've done it alone," he told her. "All alone. Friends help, but Maggie isn't their little girl. You're the only one here in the night when she wakes up, when she gets sick. You were the only one who stayed at the hospital with her all those times. You saw how tough all that was on her. How could you not want it to stop? Why would you possibly think that you're inhuman simply because you didn't want your little girl to hurt anymore?"

"She deserves everything any other little girl has," Allison insisted bleakly.

"And you've nearly killed yourself to make sure she's had it." She didn't believe him yet; Joe could see it in her eyes, in the defeated slump of her shoulders. He just shook his head and gathered her back into his arms. "Well, there's no question of my going anywhere now. I'm going to have to stay right here to make sure you treat yourself half as kindly as you treat your little girl, or you're not going to make it through this."

Allison stiffened against him, defensive and determined. Joe held on tighter, refusing to let her go. She trembled in his embrace, her hands clutching at him, her head buried against his chest.

"What if she... oh, God, Joe. What if she does die?"

"I'll be here," he promised. "Right here. No matter what happens. We'll face it together."

Instinctively, she tried to shake her head. "I can't do that—"

"You don't have a choice," he informed her, stroking her hair and letting his shirt absorb her tears. "I'm having Tony drop my stuff over here this afternoon." When her head came up in protest, he just grinned at her. "You can't expect to stay here by yourself with that door broken."

"But your work..."

Joe shrugged. "Your other choice is to pack up Maggie's things and join me at my place. I wouldn't mind using up some of those bedrooms, but Maggie might miss her clouds."

"You can't stay, Joe. I can't ask you."

"Then don't. I still have a union job I have to clock in for every morning, but I'm going to be here in the evening. I'm going to help with exercises and bathtime and feedings. And when you go in on Monday, I'm driving you."

"No, really—"

He sighed in exasperation. "If you're going to keep that up," he informed her, "I see only one way to shut you up."

Allison straightened. "Joe—"

He silenced her with a well-placed kiss. Wrapping his arms around her so she couldn't escape, he gentled her protests, erased her doubts, numbed her arguments. She shuddered to silence in his arms, her mouth slow to respond, her body betraying her before she realized it.

Joe felt the first shudders of surrender ripple through her. He felt her lips ease open on a small groan. He'd bent to her in teasing. He stayed in earnest.

Her cheeks were damp, her lips salty and sweet. Joe tasted them, drank from them. He eased her mouth open and explored, savored, sated. He felt her hands light at his waist and pulled her tighter, tangling one hand into the silk of her hair, spreading the other across her back. She swayed against him, arched against him. She let her hands grow bolder, let her body speak for her. Joe answered blindly, filling his hands with her soft curves, filling his nostrils with her scent, spring and desire, filling his sight with her languorous body.

He'd known desire before. He'd wanted women, had pursued them, intoxicated by their looks, their walks, their bright plumage. He'd never known anything like this, a hot, hard ache that dug into his bones and wrenched a harsh groan from him. A sweet, drunken agony that soaked him and stunned him. His belly crawled with it, his head whirled with it. Desire mingled with need and succumbed to love and flavored every touch and whisper and taste with a yearning so powerful he could do nothing but sink straight down.

Joe swept Allison into his arms and carried her beyond the clouds and bells and chimes of Maggie's dream world to the big, soft bed Allison had slept in alone for all these months. And there he undressed her, lingering over every layer uncovered, praising the fullness of her breasts and tracing the silver threads Maggie had left behind along the sides of Allison's belly. He let her undress him, gasping at the havoc her fingers could play with a simple zipper, shuddering with the hunger of her mouth.

"This is what you give me," he whispered, cherishing her full, ripe beauty with hands and mouth and eyes. "I don't need any more."

"I can't give you enough," she objected, arching, whimpering with his touch, opening to him, inviting him, guiding him.

Joe followed, found the hot, honeyed folds deep inside her and delighted in her gasping, writhing response. He savored her eyes, the flush of passion that crept up her throat. He tasted it, laving the salty tang from her breast and dipping to taunt her nipples to attention. He tormented her, bringing her just to the edge of climax and then giving his attention elsewhere. He tormented himself, holding away from her until he could truly teach her satisfaction, until she was dancing and moaning with only his touch, begging for release and knowing that he would be there to offer it.

She begged, breathless and bold, her hands as shameless as his and far more clever. She moaned and sighed and sang, her eyes closed and her head back, her hair dark against the snowy pillow, her skin damp and glowing in the dim light. Joe smiled. He dipped his fingers again and guided her closer, to the very brink of oblivion when the shudders began to build. And then, as she clutched at him, as she writhed and wept beneath him, he joined her.

Her eyes flew wide. Her body closed around Joe's and welcomed him home. She wrapped around him, her eyes dancing and bright, her voice hoarse, her hands unquenchable. She lifted with him, soared with him, spiraled and sang with the white-hot release of climax, and then pulled Joe against her when he followed, breathless and gasping, burying himself deeply enough inside her she could never let him go.

Joe collapsed into her arms and let the warm afternoon air cool him. He wrapped a leg around hers and fitted his arm across her soft, round belly and floated on contentment. He felt her fingers in his hair and smiled. He was home. It hadn't taken a big house on the hill or the tumult of children. It had taken one woman's arms. One woman's quiet passion. He couldn't ask for more.

Beside him, Allison stirred.

"You surprised me," she admitted, and Joe thought he heard a smile.

"I told you," he answered. "My father didn't believe in taking chances."

"Not that," she allowed. "When you told me you were going to have to shut me up. I was afraid I was going to lose some teeth."

"Nah," he said. "Just some sleep."

Chapter 15

"**Y**a know," Allison admitted. "I'll be just as happy if I never see another hospital again."

On one side of her, Joe snorted. "I hear ya."

On the other, Brook shot Joe a suspicious look. "Don't you have a wife or something to check in on?"

Joe just shot her a dazzling smile. "No. As a matter of fact, now that Allison and I are getting married, I'm getting rid of my wife *and* my mistress."

Brook stiffened in outrage. Allison allowed her first smile of the morning...the first crack in her reserve in the twelve hours since Maggie had been admitted to the hospital. It was something she was going to have to share with the Down's support group. If you had to sit through your child's heart surgery, do it with two people who could make you laugh. It didn't keep your stomach from squeezing you like an overcooked sausage or your heart from skidding against your ribs. It didn't even stop the sweat. It just made you forget them for a minute.

"He's kidding," Brook begged Allison. "Isn't he?"

Allison turned guileless eyes on her friend. "Don't *you* think he should get rid of his wife and mistress?"

Brook looked very much as if Allison's hair were on fire. "I think you're both nuts."

Allison nodded without hesitation. "Now that's something I think we can all agree on."

Joe flipped through a few more pages of a year-old copy of *Newsweek* before throwing it back onto the pile in the corner of the waiting room. Across the floor several other sets of relatives paced and sat and whispered, their interactions carefully tempered as if one outburst would set the whole place off. Allison wouldn't have been surprised if that were true. She was only inches away from pandemonium. It was only Joe's wry humor, his hand that snuck over every so often to squeeze hers, his dark, deep eyes that kept her steady.

She still didn't quite believe he really meant to stay. But she didn't know what she would have done without him up to this point. The past six days had been a kind of oasis, a mirage in the wasteland of her recent life. They had all stayed at Allison's house, a temporary family complete with Dad coming home in the afternoons and Mom cooking dinner. Lucille had still demanded her share of Maggie's time, but she deferred to Joe with maddening regularity when it came to the little girl.

Joe had set up his drawing board in the living room and continued work on his new book, humming and smiling to himself. He'd practiced his sax before dinner, at first scaring the hell out of Maggie and then enchanting her with the cascade of notes he could produce. More often than not, now, Allison leaned out of the kitchen to hear Maggie's squeals matching Joe's notes with almost uncanny ability. He'd spent the day before teaching her the opening to "Rhapsody in Blue," both of them sounding like approaching ambulances. Maggie had kept her hospital roommate up the night before regaling her with it.

Maggie.

What *did* Allison pray for? Did she pray for her little girl to struggle through the surgery, just like she had all her other hospital stays, just as she did lessons and exercises and daily progress? Did she pray for respite, for peace for her daughter?

She was so torn, so tired of not knowing what to do. She was so tempted to let Joe really believe he belonged with them and simply lay her head in his lap and let him take over.

But Allison knew better. So she'd shared meals with him. She'd shared a bed with him. She would share this with him. And then when he decided he had to go, she'd let him.

"What did Thompson say about Dowd's new book?" Brook asked.

Allison fought a grin. "He said, 'Isn't this just a bit too realistic for fairy tales?' I was quick to remind him that if children are eaten and wolves boiled in a hot pot in fairy tales, then a small monster should be able to make friends with a waif."

"I bet he wasn't pleased."

"As a matter of fact, he relented very nicely."

"I think it's going to be a big seller," Joe piped up, now examining a magazine on guns. "There are a lot of people out there who need validation."

"I think that the Binkleys have always done that," Brook protested, sinking down farther into the shapeless chair and crossing her booted ankles.

"Not enough," Joe said. "They're just validating the insecurity of regular kids, not kids with real problems."

"Not waifs," Allison agreed with an absent nod.

Her eyes were on the clock, on the door. It had been over five hours already. Lucille had come and gone. Joe's parents had been by with food, and a couple of people from work had called to offer their support. It shouldn't be taking this long. She should have heard something by now, even from the usually distant Dr. Goldman.

She felt Joe's hand wrap around hers and turned a surprised smile on him.

On the other side, Brook was busy huffing. "For a carpenter, you sure like to think you know books."

Allison's smile broadened into delight. Joe's followed.

"You don't need to build a house to know if it's going to stand up," he philosophized.

Allison nodded. "I rely on his opinions all the time."

Brook almost came right off the couch. "Allison! Are you crazy?" She leaned forward to include Joe. "No offense, really. But we're having enough trouble with Dowd right now. The last thing Thompson needs to hear is that Allison has a blue-collar guru advising her on how Dowd should write."

"Don't you think that having Rose teach the monsters about compassion and love is a good idea?" Allison asked evenly.

Brook waved away the objection like a pesky fly. "I know you've been under a lot of stress lately, Allison, what with Maggie and then that thing with Frazier. Anybody could feel a little insecure about their work, a little harried."

Allison sank back into her own chair, her hand wrapped firmly in Joe's, delighted at Brook's outrage. "As a matter of fact, *Ralph Finds a Friend* was all Joe's idea."

Brook rolled her eyes. "Listen to me," she pleaded. "Not another decision, not another communication with Dowd until you and I can talk. Until Maggie's out of the hospital. Please."

"Be a little difficult," Joe allowed to no one in particular.

"I'm not talking to you," Brook snarled, and then turned back to Allison, who smiled dreamily into middle space. "I *am* talking to you, however. I mean it. You can't afford to lose this job. You can't make a great stand to protect Dowd and then forfeit him to a whim."

Joe's grin was irrepressible. "Brook."

Allison's attention was caught by a nurse in scrubs who'd appeared at the door to the waiting room. Allison's heart leapt, then tumbled when the woman turned to the family in the far corner and greeted them. Another patient treated and gone. Another interminable span of waiting.

Maggie had been so helpless, so small and limp and pale when they'd wheeled her downstairs. Allison couldn't bear to think of what she was going through.

"Allison, are you listening to me?" Brook demanded, tapping her leg. "I'm serious."

"No," she admitted, wiping her free hand against her pants. "I'm not listening."

"Brook," Joe tried again.

"I'm not talking to you, Joe. And please, stick to your hammers. Allison, don't let hormones blind you when nothing else has."

"He also decided that Unctious was going to fall in love with Wanda in the bathroom book," Allison said, still watching the door.

Brook came to a sick halt and looked over at Joe. "Oh, my God."

Joe nodded.

Allison watched the door. Finally, though, she turned to Joe, accepted his approval and faced her friend.

"Brook," Allison said.

"Don't talk to me," her friend retorted. "I don't know which of us is crazier. You, because of what you're doing, or me, because I'm probably going to let you get away with it."

"Brook."

"I know you're in love, girl. I've seen the difference in you since Joe's been around. Maybe he isn't what I would have wanted for you, but he's made you happy. Which makes me happy... kind of. But this—"

"Brook!"

"What?"

"Meet L. Wood Dowd."

Brook went very still. Her eyes narrowed and then widened. Her mouth opened and then shut. It seemed that she had nothing to say that would make any sense. Allison understood perfectly.

"If you hadn't been so distracted by all the pressure at work," she offered with a silly grin, "you probably would have guessed sooner."

But Brook couldn't take her eyes off Joe, who was bestowing his best smile on her. Brook finally settled for a stunned shake of the head. "Oh, no, I wouldn't," she disagreed, her voice as hushed as if she'd witnessed her first miracle. "You're both lyin' through your teeth." The protest was a token one at best.

"I decided to write the book about Rose after getting to know Maggie," Joe admitted. "I thought that little kids had as much right to understand handicaps as anybody else."

Brook shook her head again. She took a long considering look, very much like the one Allison had when she'd first been faced with the truth—except that Allison had to admit Brook's didn't take as long. Probably because Joe had his shirt on.

"You mean you sit in your house and draw monsters all day."

"All night. All day I build houses, just like I told you."

"No wife, no mistress."

"No wife, no mistress."

"Mrs. Henley?"

All three of them whipped around to find a nurse addressing them. She sagged with weariness, her scrubs wrinkled and sweatstained. Her mask hung from her neck and she held a surgical cap in her hands.

Allison jumped to her feet. "Yes? Maggie?"

The woman smiled. "I'm Dr. Goldman's assistant. He'll be in to speak to you soon. I wanted you to know that you have a real fighter. Maggie fooled us a couple of times in there."

Allison's heart stopped. Her chest froze with fear. "Is she all right?"

The woman ducked her head a little, a visual qualification. "Dr. Goldman will explain it to you. We had a rough time of it, I'm afraid. Maggie's in recovery now, but she's still not out of the woods. You know that."

"Did it work?" Allison demanded, desperate to twist the truth out of the nurse. She didn't even realize that Joe still held her hand until she tried to wring it. "Was the surgery successful?"

"The hole's been patched. If Maggie's electrolytes and rhythm stabilize, she shouldn't have any more problems."

Tears crowded Allison's throat. She slumped and felt Joe support her with hands that trembled. She tried to speak and couldn't.

"Could her mom see her?" Joe asked on her behalf, and Allison heard the tremble in his voice, as well.

"Just for a second," the nurse allowed, her features pursed with caution. "We told you how she's going to look, Mrs. Henley. Are you sure you want to?"

Allison nodded definitely. She had to see Maggie, to touch her and reassure herself with her daughter's presence. She had to see for herself that Maggie was out of surgery.

That it was over.

Joe led her down the hall after the nurse and provided a handkerchief when Allison couldn't see for the tears. He guided her through the shushing surgical doors and let her go when she reached out to touch Maggie's cheek.

The room was frightening, cold and sterile and noisy. Machines beeped and hissed. Patients moaned. Staff muttered and padded around on booty-clad feet. A sudden burst of laughter from the nurse's desk exploded into the harsh atmosphere like a bomb.

Maggie looked dead. Impossibly pale, flaccid, her arms and legs out like a little frog's. Allison wanted to bolster them, to support them just as she did at home to promote muscle tone. But Maggie had IVs in her arms, in her legs. She had tubes taped into her chest and into her throat, wires trailing from everywhere, a big machine pumping oxygen into her lungs. She was naked and tiny and helpless. Allison fought the sobs and stroked her daughter's cheek.

"Mommy's here, baby," she whispered over and over again, terrified at the chill of her child's skin, by the steady hum and click of equipment that breathed for her and monitored her heart. "Mommy's here."

Joe was beside her. She could feel it, a curious warmth in the chill of the recovery room. A strength that kept her up even without the touch of his hand. She turned to him, saw the glitter of unshed tears in his eyes and wrapped an arm around his back.

"She's going to be fine," she insisted, accepting his arm around her. Knowing now, finally, that Joe did love Maggie as much as she did.

"Mrs. Henley?"

Dr. Goldman. Small and wrinkled and frowning, clipboard in his hand. Allison straightened to attention, stifled her fears and hopes to hear his verdict.

"The surgery was a success, of course."

Allison felt Joe stiffen and stilled him. She was going to have to get him used to Goldman's frame of reference.

"The problem is, Maggie's electrolytes have been very unstable. I'm not really sure why, but we had a devil of a time getting her heart to start again after the repair. Irritable myocardium. Kept fibrillating on us. Truth to tell, I'm not sure it's finished yet."

Allison could hardly get the word out. "Meaning?"

He looked up at her then, a mixture of frustration, irritation and, finally, concern darkening his eyes. "Meaning that it's still going to be a very long night. Go get some food. Meet her up in the ICU."

"I'd rather be here—"

"In the way. No, you won't. Now, go on. We can page you if anything happens."

Joe guided her back out where she didn't want to be. She had to leave her baby in impersonal hands, in the care of people who didn't know that Maggie hated the taste of medicine, that she slept better on her left side and couldn't tolerate being turned too quickly.

"I hope he's good," Joe growled.

Allison barely heard him. "The best."

"Good. Otherwise, I would have had to deck him."

They ate. Allison moved about in a state of suspended animation, too overwhelmed by the hesitation in everybody's voice to function properly. Brook took care of business, and Joe took care of Allison.

"Code blue, CVICU. Code blue, CVICU."

Allison's head shot up. She knew the meaning of those words. Code blue, cardiac arrest team to the cardiac unit. To Maggie.

Joe held on to her hand. "They'd call you if it were Maggie."

"I want to go anyway."

Joe shoved a sandwich into her purse, picked up a glass of milk and led her out of the cafeteria.

They reached the unit just as medical people began to drift back out. Allison clutched Joe's hand as if he'd pulled her from the ice. She couldn't take much more. She just wanted to see Maggie; she wanted to make sure her daughter was still there, still quiet and small in that gray-and-white crib.

"Hi, Mrs. Henley," one of the nurses greeted her.

Allison heard the caution in the woman's voice and came to a halt.

"We were just going to get you," she said, and Allison knew.

"It was Maggie, wasn't it?"

The nurse smiled that same tired smile Allison was so used to up here. Her hair was mussed and her scrubs dotted with Betadine. "Her heart's a little irritable. We got it back. You want to go in?"

Allison nodded. Joe and Brook walked in with her.

Maggie didn't look any different. The crash cart stood next to the bed, a red tool cart for emergency drugs. Some of the drawers were half open, and the paddles had been shoved awkwardly back into the defibrillator. It had been used.

The scene was squeezing her, closing off her air. Bearing her down. Breaking her when nothing else had in the eight months.

"Hi there, little girl," Joe crooned, reaching out his own blunt, callused hand to rub at the downy cheek. "Stop scaring your mom like that, okay?"

His hand was so big against Maggie, so solid and hard, as if it would break something so delicate. As if he'd hurt her, crumble her in his grasp. Allison had never known a more gentle hand. A softer, more careful hand. She reached hers alongside.

Suddenly, Maggie stiffened. An alarm screamed. Chairs scraped out in the hall and a voice rose.

"Call the code!"

"Maggie!" Allison cried, struggling to get to her baby.

Joe grabbed hold of her and pulled her out of the way just as the team arrived.

"The waiting room," the nurse who'd greeted them before advised quietly as another nurse grabbed the little paddles and hit a button on the machine.

"No!" Allison screamed, fighting to be free of Joe's hold. "No, let me go! I have to be with her!"

Someone else arrived, blocking them from the crib. A big man in a collar. "Come on," he coaxed. "You don't want to be here."

Allison faced off with him. "She's *my* daughter. I've never left her yet."

"I'll keep her out of the way," Joe promised quietly. "We'll stand back by the corner where we can't bother anybody."

"It's not a good—"

"All clear! All clear! Defibrillating!"

Allison heard a little thump and then the team shifted so that she couldn't see Maggie again.

"We'll be fine," Joe promised, and pulled her back into the corner.

There they stayed, through that code and the four that followed. The sky slipped into black beyond the window and halogen lights turned the night orange. The hospital ticked along, nurses changing shifts and doctors cruising in and out. When Maggie was stable, Allison sat on a chair by her bed. When the machine stumbled and shrilled, Joe pulled her back, yanked the chair out of the way, and they waited back in their corner for yet another outcome. Allison watched as her baby fought back time after time from death, and it numbed her. She felt the torture of their efforts in her own body and didn't think she could hurt anymore.

Brook came and went, and later, Lucille came in to sit with them for a while. Tony brought crayon-drawn cards from all the nieces and nephews that Allison clutched in her hand until the colors rubbed off on her fingers. Sometime in the afternoon Joe force-fed her the sandwich, and another glass of milk, and cadged juice and crackers from the nurses. Allison never left Maggie, and Joe never left Allison. The nurses, old friends by now, sailed around the two of them as if they were part of the scenery.

It was close to midnight when the team trudged out after the fourth time. Allison didn't realize that Dr. Goldman had shown up. Suddenly he stood before her, his suit as rumpled as his scrubs had been, his eyes sharp and dark.

"We need to talk, Mrs. Henley. Why don't you come outside?"

Allison never took her eyes from Maggie. "We can talk here."

"You need to get a little rest," he objected.

"No," she disagreed. "I have to be with Maggie. I'll sleep later when she stabilizes."

There was a pause, a stiff silence that finally brought her attention around to him.

"That's what I wanted to talk to you about," he said.

"What?"

"She's not stabilizing," he told her. "We have her on more medication to stop the arrhythmias, to keep her blood pressure up. To help her heart work better. It's taking longer and longer to get her back from these episodes."

Allison just stared at him, long past comprehension.

Goldman sighed. "We can do this as long as you want," he assured her. "I've seen kids coded a hundred times. What I'm trying to tell you is I'm not sure it's doing any good. I want to know how long you want us to keep this up."

Allison did her best to follow his train of thought. "What do you mean?"

Goldman looked into Allison's eyes and she saw, for the first time, how worried he still was. She clutched the handrail of Maggie's bed, even Joe's support not enough.

"Maybe it's best for her to just let her go the next time," Goldman offered.

Allison looked down at her daughter, at the silent, still features that were usually so animated. At the soft hair, the tiny hands, the gossamer lashes that lay across porcelain cheeks. She remembered standing just like this the last time Maggie was in the hospital and wondering if she wanted what Dr. Goldman was now offering. Release, peace for her little girl. No more doctors, no more struggle. No more hurt and heartache.

What was best for Maggie?

What was best?

"No," she said, lifting certain eyes back to Goldman. "Your nurse told me that Maggie was a fighter. That means she wants to stick around. If Maggie's working this hard to live, I'm not going to refuse her."

"Mrs. Henley—"

She straightened, knowing that Joe's hand was on her shoulder, knowing that his strength and love surrounded her. "She's my daughter, Dr. Goldman. *My* daughter. And I say we fight to save her."

Goldman left without another word. Allison felt herself deflating, the sudden truth flooding her. Turning away from Maggie for the first time in hours, Allison buried herself in Joe's embrace.

"Good girl," he soothed, stroking her hair, wrapping her so tightly in his arms that she never had to worry about falling again.

"She's my baby, Joe." Allison sobbed, tears soaking his shirt yet again. "No matter what, she's my little girl. It doesn't matter that she has Down syndrome, does it? None of it matters. She's not a Mongoloid or a retard, she's Maggie, and I just can't give her up."

"You didn't," he assured her. "You didn't. I keep telling you, she couldn't have a better mother."

Allison lifted her face to find Joe's eyes glittering again. He ran a finger along her cheek.

"I almost didn't learn my lesson," she whispered, the truth terrible to bear. "I've watched children die right alongside of her and didn't realize how lucky I was that Maggie kept fighting back. What would my life have been if she'd never been in it? What would it be like if she doesn't come out of this hospital? I want her home, Joe. I want her back in her room where she can play with her mobiles and sing to me and spit food at me, and instead of surviving day by day, I cherish every moment. I want her back."

His smile broke her heart, because she knew that Joe hurt just as much as she did.

"Mrs. Henley," one of the staff whispered, walking in with a clipboard. They turned to her.

The lights were dimmed, the lights and switches from all the equipment like a forest of red eyes in the department. Hisses and whispers and trills were the night music of medical machines.

"Dr. Goldman asked me to speak to you again about signing a no-code order on Maggie."

Allison saw the hesitation in the nurse's stance. She saw the shadows in her eyes, half outrage, half agreement. Another person who saw handicapped children as only being a burden, as being robbed of something precious and therefore not due the same fight a normal person would have for life. Not a bad person. A misinformed one.

After all, Allison remembered somebody saying that last time in the emergency room. *She has Down syndrome. I mean, what are they trying so hard to save her for?*

But none of those people knew Maggie. None of them had seen her morning smile or the concentration on her tiny features when she'd rolled over that first time. None had had her nestle her head against their heart and known that there was no sweeter weight.

"She's already given her answer," Joe said, his posture betraying his own outrage. And then he told the nurse exactly what Dr. Goldman could do with the no-code order. Succinctly, clinically and finally.

Allison wanted to smile. She was going to have to teach him how to cope with ignorance a little better than that.

Allison met the nurse's eyes with the new certainty in her own. "Maggie wants to stick around. Who am I to argue?"

"You're sure?" the nurse asked softly. "We might try our damnedest and still lose her."

"Better to lose her than betray her," Allison said.

"She might come out of it more . . . affected than she is."

Allison smiled, finally sure. "It doesn't matter."

The silence enveloped them again as the nurse retreated. Allison wrapped herself into Joe's embrace and savored the wonder of her newfound realization. All of it, settling into place like a lost puzzle piece.

The truth. The sweet, solid, satisfying truth.

"You do love me," she wondered aloud.

He chuckled. "Don't be ridiculous. I'm just after your money."

"And Maggie?"

"I'm after her money, too."

Allison actually smiled. Then she closed her eyes and basked in the poignant comfort of his humor. "And if we have another child with Down syndrome?"

She heard the pause, the stumble over her tentative offer. She felt the tremor of possibility run through him. "We'd call her Rose."

Allison didn't think she had any more tears. "I'm sorry I doubted you, Joe. I'm so sorry."

"Don't be sorry. Just marry me."

"The minute the three of us get out of here."

Her eyes were closed. Joe's cheek was nestled against her hair, and she could smell him, smoky and dark, like jazz. His hands cradled her like a baby and his heart soothed her. She thought she might actually be able to curl up on a couch in the waiting room, as long as Joe was nearby.

Behind her, the alarms went off.

Chapter 16

Sunrise was a cliché. Allison thought of all the books and movies in which the protagonists held out for the dawn, when the danger would be over, the fear abated. The world set right. If only the sun would rise, we'd be all right.

She never understood it until she waited for that sun to rise.

Joe held her without moving that entire night. He was her pillow and her foundation. He made her laugh when she didn't possibly think she could, and cushioned her tears when there was nothing else she could offer. He sat through two more codes, silent and watchful and supportive, flinching each time Maggie stiffened beneath the defibrillator paddles. He sang to the little girl even knowing she couldn't hear him and told her Binkley Brothers stories that hadn't yet been written.

And now, as the sky paled toward dawn, he dozed in a straightbacked chair, his arms inexorably around Allison, his beard chafing her cheek, his eyes smudged and exhausted.

It had been five hours since the last episode. Five hours. They had begun to count, carefully, superstitiously, adding the minutes like a buffer between Maggie and death. Sandbags against a threatening tide. Allison and Joe and Brook and Tony and Lucille, and then the nurses, their eyes brightening by careful degrees from fatalism to caution to hope. The longer she goes, they admitted, the better her chances.

So Allison waited for the sun. She thought of every cliché about new days dawning and realized that the clichés had been built on solid belief. The dark was where monsters lived, where death ruled, where life was tenuous and mysterious. It was where reality kept hold only by the merest of threads because the eyes could fool in the dark and the ears misconstrue. The Binkleys didn't haunt in the dark for nothing. It was their world.

But the sun brought strength, sense, life. It bolstered heart rates and levels of consciousness. It soaked into closed eyes and forced them open. It stabilized and empowered. Allison kept her eyes to the window and watched the sky melt from night to morning, and prayed that the sun would awaken her daughter.

She prayed this time, knowing exactly what she prayed for. Knowing now what was important in her life and what she wanted. She also snuck in a few prayers of thanks for the gifts she'd been given, especially the ones she hadn't quite recognized before.

"I think my back is going to be permanently crooked," Joe growled above her.

"You should have fought harder for the couch."

He snorted. "Against Lucille? Never. She fights dirty."

Allison was surprised by the chuckle that bubbled up in her raw, scratchy throat.

"How's the fidget?" Joe asked, rubbing at his eyes with a hand.

Allison looked over to where Maggie lay silent and still beneath the white sheet, the tape from the endotracheal tube masking half her face, her arms still thrown out, her chest rising and falling with the machine.

"They say the arrhythmias are improving," Allison said. "She's beginning to fight the machine to breathe on her own."

Joe stopped rubbing to take his own look. "Sun's just about ready to come up. That's good."

Allison smiled to herself. It was nice to know someone else subscribed to universal superstitions. "Why don't you head out and convince everybody to go on home?" she asked. "I really think the worst is over."

He wrapped his arms around her again and gave her a companionable squeeze. "They'll go as soon as you do."

Allison scowled. "In a while."

Joe nodded against her. "Yeah. I know."

The day shift was coming on, laughter echoing in the work area. Greetings and jokes and taunts. The world coming to life. Come on, Maggie, Allison silently begged. Join us. Come back to me so I can spoil you rotten and let Joe spoil you worse.

Pulling her stethoscope from around her neck for yet another check, the night nurse trudged in the room. They'd all gotten pretty close since the moment she'd carried that permission to prevent resuscitation back out of the room unsigned. A single working woman, Susannah excelled at her work and offered comfort with pragmatic hands.

"Morning," she murmured with a tired smile. "How are you guys faring in here?"

Allison nodded to her, not even bothering to move from Joe's embrace. "We'll let you know as soon as you tell us how Maggie's doing."

Susannah bent to her work with an amazed shake of her head. "I have to admit that I didn't think she'd make it this far. She's really a tiger."

"Yeah," Allison admitted. "She is."

They waited, and Allison again flashed on scenes from movies. The doctor bent over the bed. The family gathered around, awaiting the verdict, hands clenched, eyes tormented, until the kindly old man straightened and proclaimed that the hero would be just all right.

Be just all right, she prayed. Confound Dr. Goldman and all the authorities and be fine. Alongside her, Joe held his breath, just as he had every time Susannah had come in to check Maggie, as if warding off bad news.

Susannah listened to Maggie's chest, checked eyes and color and limbs and the various attachments.

"It's about time you started waking up, little girl," she commanded as she worked, reminding Allison of Lucille. "Your mama's been sitting here all night long, and she needs to get some sleep. Come on, little Maggie. Let's see some kind of response."

She reached over and gently knuckled Maggie's sternum. Every time she'd done it during the night, Maggie had failed even to flinch. There hadn't been a reaction of any kind. Allison wasn't sure how many more times she could watch it.

They'd warned her. They had said that all those cardiac arrests might very well damage Maggie's brain. She might not wake up at all, even if she lived. Allison couldn't even comprehend it.

"Well, would you look at this."

Allison jumped up. Joe was right on her heels. Straightening from where she'd been poking at Maggie, Susannah bestowed a beaming smile that betrayed just how attached she'd become to the little girl.

"Say hi, Mom."

Allison bent over the bed and saw the most beautiful sight she'd ever thought to find. Maggie's eyes. Those fathomless dark eyes, so much like Joe's, so brown and sweet and funny. They were open, surprised, confused, a little bleary. But open. Allison sobbed.

"Oh, God, Maggie." It took everything she had not to just reach over and pluck her baby away from all the tubes and machines and hold her in her arms. She reached out a tentative finger and stroked Maggie's open palm. "Hi, my baby. Welcome back."

His arm tightly around her, Joe was suspiciously quiet. He reached out a hand that seemed to tremble just a bit and stroked the side of Maggie's face. Maggie looked up to him, and as groggy as she was, tried to smile.

"It's going to be all right," Allison said, reaching up to hold on to Joe's free hand with hers. Holding on to him, gathering him in, letting him encompass her and her daughter with his love. "It's really going to be all right."

Standing by the other side of the bed, Susannah shook her head in amazement and replaced her stethoscope. "I don't think she could have done it without you," she admitted. "Maggie's pretty lucky to have a family like you."

Allison looked up at Joe, her own smile challenging the sun. "Yes, she is," she agreed, submerging herself in those eyes, soaking in the love, the joy, the contentment. Knowing that this time she'd never come out. Knowing for the first time in her life what happiness was. What belonging was. "She's very lucky to have a family like ours."

Epilogue

A man should take his wife someplace special for their fifth anniversary. He should shower her with flowers and wine and jewels. Especially when his wife is somebody as special as Joe's. But Allison had demanded a different celebration, and she was one person Joe couldn't refuse.

Trudging up the steps to the house, he did his best to stretch out the aches from a hard month on a tough renovation. He was dusty and dirty and sweaty, and sporting a couple of slapdash bandages from where the saw had caught him daydreaming. He carried his lunch pail in one hand and a ragged bouquet of garden flowers in the other, but that was all he'd need. The real magic for this evening was inside.

"Daddy!"

Closing the beveled glass door behind him, Joe dropped his lunch pail and greeted his daughter with delight.

"Hey, munchkin, c'mere and give me a kiss!"

She collided with him full tilt, and he swept her up in his arms. A petite girl with mischievous eyes and boundless energy, Maggie had proved everybody wrong. She'd recovered from her surgery without a setback and gone on to challenge and torment Joe and Allison mercilessly. They'd danced when she'd sat up alone at nine months, and had a family party when she'd walked all alone at age two. Every achievement was met with joy, every struggle shared and lightened. She was more precious to him than any other child, but that wasn't something he was allowed to admit.

"Where's Mommy?"

"Up-tairs. With the twins."

"They been crabby today?"

She nodded vigorously. "Uh-huh."

"Well, then, we'd better have a party and put them in a good mood. Where's Benny?"

"Sleep."

They climbed the old, polished stairs, each running a hand over the rich, smooth texture. The walls had been re-papered and the ceiling painted. The furniture downstairs was regulation, some antiques, some plain overstuffed comfort. It was on the second floor in the sunroom, where the balancing equipment ruled. Beanbag furniture and ramps and packing-bead boxes. And still, on the third floor, a rocking chair and a drawing table.

"Allison?"

"Oh, good. Do something with these three, will you?" she demanded, stepping out of the twins' bedroom. "It's my anniversary, y'know. My date's coming soon, and I'm not even dressed."

Joe lifted his arms to show off the sweat-stained shirt and jeans. "Neither am I."

She smiled, and Joe fell in love all over again. "Yeah," she disagreed. "But I like you all sweaty."

He stopped to kiss her and took a second to muss up her hair. Maggie had already absconded with the flowers. Joe loved the look of his wife now, the small crow's feet that crinkled the corners of her eyes when she smiled, the soft, maternal fullness of her figure. The sweet, hot intensity that never quite left her smile or her commitments.

"Read to them," she commanded, and shoved a book in Joe's hands.

He sighed dramatically. "Again?"

She shot him a playful grimace. "They *like* Rose's story. They want to hear it again and again. I tell you, sometimes that Dowd character is a pain in the butt."

"I thought you liked him."

She smiled. "Only when he's sweaty." Then she disappeared into their room.

Joe headed for the rocker in the middle of the big, toy-ladened room. The minute the boys saw him, they hurtled over to climb into his lap. Joe gave them both fierce bear hugs, rubbing his bristly chin against their baby-soft cheeks and producing a chorus of delighted squeals. They were two years old, named after their grandfathers. Matthew and Michael, identical, definitely Burgetts in everything but their easygoing temperaments. They had large, green eyes, and were aggressively bright. Joe had been there when the two hearts had first been heard and coached Allison through the deliveries. He'd incorporated them into the Binkley Brothers saga, just as he had their sister and their new brother.

Benjamin. Three months old, born with Down syndrome, given up for adoption by a teenage mother who couldn't bear the burden. Gladly welcomed into the Burgett home and the greater Burgett family. Joe looked up to see that Benny's rose trembled at the edge of opening on the dresser by his crib. Just like Maggie's did in her room down the hall. Someday he'd teach his sons the tradition of the rose, the meaning, the special gift. Maggie already knew. She took pride in her position in the garden, and Joe couldn't ask more.

"All right, you guys," he announced. "Where did we leave off?"

"Halloween," Maggie chirped from her very own rocker next to Joe's.

Joe nodded. "Halloween, it is." He turned the pages to the correct pictures and began reading, even though he'd long since known the words by heart.

"'But Rose,' Ralph said. 'How could you get all that candy. You can't even fly.'

"Rose blushed all over her very pale skin. 'I knew the monsters would be sad because the Teachers took their candy. And they can't have Halloween without it. And they can't really sneak past teachers, who hear even the littlest of hisses. But I'm silent…except when I dream, of course. So I slipped under the closet door and carried the candy back out. I just wanted to help.'

"Ralph chewed on his claw a bit, trying to know what was best to do. All the monsters wanted to know who had rescued their Halloween. They wanted to thank the monster, to praise it for its great deed, for nothing was as feared by monsters as the dreaded Teachers. But he knew what they would say if a waif saved them. They would say she was just doing it to trick them out of scales. They would hunt her down and send her away where she could never share dreams with Ralph again. He would be alone with only monsters to talk to, and they would laugh at Ralph for being stupid and never talk to him again anyway. And Ralph was so afraid of being lonely again.

"He didn't know what to do."

"They were just afraid because waifs are diff-rent," Maggie announced from her chair. She rocked back and forth, just like her father.

"That's right," Joe allowed, nuzzling downy heads with his, smiling down at her very serious expression. "But is diff-rent bad?"

She shook her head. "Special."

Joe reached over and tousled her hair and thought how special she was. He thought how he'd wondered whether he could handle a child as special as Maggie. He wondered where he'd have been now if he hadn't taken a risk.

"Benny's special," Michael lisped.

"Yeah," Matthew echoed.

"You're all special," Joe corrected. "And that means we have a pretty neat family, huh?"

"Yes," Allison agreed from the doorway. "We do."

She hadn't changed. Joe had a feeling she'd been standing in the doorway all along, watching him read. Her eyes glittered in the light, and her smile carried five-year's worth of memories. Joe couldn't imagine loving her more.

He was wrong.

"So," she said, leaning a hip against the door frame. "You say you like the family life, Mr. Dowd?"

"I do, Mrs. Burgett."

She nodded, glowing. "Well, that's good. That's good."

"You?"

She nodded again. "Yes," she agreed. "I like it. I like it a lot."

Joe nodded right back, his arms full of children, his heart full with Allison. "Well, that's good."

Her smile grew geometrically. "It had better be. I'm pregnant again."

Joe's heart skidded. His quick retort died. "You are?" he demanded, his voice small and amazed.

She didn't move, didn't advance or retreat. Her smile held, grew, so that she took on a rare life he'd never seen before. "Happy Anniversary."

Very carefully, Joe put down the boys and approached his wife. Behind him, Michael picked up the book and began reading to Maggie. Maggie didn't particularly want to be read to and protested. Matthew went back to his trucks and began adding engine noises, which woke Benjamin up. Downstairs the front door slammed as the first of the family arrived for dinner.

Joe heard the music of his house and knew that even his dreams couldn't have been this magical. He'd seen Allison's eyes in his house, he'd heard her laughter. He'd never imagined her life and grace and quiet strength. He could never have manufactured the tide of love that kept rising in him as the days and weeks and years grew on them.

"It's going to be a very special baby," he told her, gathering her into his arms.

She lifted her face to his. "I know," she agreed. "It's going to have the best daddy in the world."

"No," Joe disagreed. "The best mommy."

"The best family," she decided. "Because the baby will be raised in a very special garden."

Joe forgot his family then. He forgot the dinner he and Allison had to get dressed for and the friends that were due any minute. He forgot the children squabbling behind him. He was too busy telling his favorite gardener just how much he loved her.

From *Ralph Finds a Friend*
by L. Wood Dowd

"Don't be silly," Mama Binkley objected. "Monsters don't have waifs for friends."

"I do," Ralph insisted, straightening as tall as he could. "Rose found my Halloween candy and risked her life to bring it to me. Rose is my friend."

He was trying very hard to be brave about this. After all, he was just a very small monster, and Uncle Ferocious was glaring down at him and snorting little puffs of smoke out his nostrils. That usually meant he was either upset or he'd had chili for breakfast.

Mama Binkley looked at Papa Binkley and shrugged, her scales rustling. "I don't know what to do with him. I think he's being very silly."

"I think he's being very brave," Uncle Ferocious decided.

Ralph took a chance and looked way up at his uncle and was surprised to find him smiling.

"I have a secret," Uncle Ferocious admitted. "When I was a little monster, I had a friend, too. A friend nobody else liked named Wilbur. But I wasn't as brave as Ralph, and I didn't say anything. My friend was chased deep into the Troll Woods and I haven't seen him since. But sometimes I wonder where he is.''

"We can go look for him," Rose offered softly. "A lot of lost friends live in the swamp at the edge of Troll Woods when no one wants them anymore."

Uncle Ferocious thought about that for a long time, causing a low cloud with all the smoke. Mama and Papa waited because no one interfered when Uncle Ferocious thought. Someone had interrupted once and caused a forest fire.

"I'll go see him," he decided. "I'll be his friend again. If Ralph can do it, I can do it."

Rose and Ralph walked Uncle Ferocious right down to the swamp, but they were too late. Uncle Ferocious would never find his friend again. Ralph and Rose stayed friends, though, through the years. Rose was invited to the Binkley house, and Ralph was allowed to sleep over in the Troll Woods.

He was laughed at by other monsters who didn't understand what a good friend Rose was, of course. They only knew she was a waif and that Ralph would wake up one day without a scale to his name. But Ralph knew better. And better than that, his family knew better. All of them, especially Uncle Ferocious, who said that Ralph was the bravest monster of them all, and that from this day on Rose was an official Binkley (although she didn't really have to lurk under people's beds if she didn't want to). And Ralph and Rose and all the Binkleys lived happily ever after.

Of course, the monsters who laughed at them got indigestion, but that's only to be expected, what with the awful things they ate.

The End.

* * * * *

**The wedding celebration was so nice...
too bad the bride wasn't there!**

Runaway Brides

Find out what happens when three brides have a
change of heart.

Three complete stories by some of your favorite
authors—all in one special collection!

YESTERDAY ONCE MORE
by Debbie Macomber

FULL CIRCLE
by Paula Detmer Riggs

THAT'S WHAT FRIENDS ARE FOR
by Annette Broadrick

Available this June wherever books are sold.

Look us up on-line at:http://www.romance.net

This July, watch for the delivery of...

An exciting new miniseries that appears in a different Silhouette series each month. It's about love, marriage—and Daddy's unexpected need for a baby carriage!

Daddy Knows Last unites five of your favorite authors as they weave five connected stories about baby fever in New Hope, Texas.

- **THE BABY NOTION** by Dixie Browning
  (SD#1011, 7/96)

- **BABY IN A BASKET** by Helen R. Myers
  (SR#1169, 8/96)

- **MARRIED...WITH TWINS!**
  by Jennifer Mikels
  (SSE#1054, 9/96)

- **HOW TO HOOK A HUSBAND (AND A BABY)**
  by Carolyn Zane
  (YT#29, 10/96)

- **DISCOVERED: DADDY** by Marilyn Pappano
  (IM#746, 11/96)

Daddy Knows Last arrives in July...only from

DKLT

Silhouette's recipe for a sizzling summer:

* Take the best-looking cowboy in South Dakota
* Mix in a brilliant bachelor
* Add a sexy, mysterious sheikh
* Combine their stories into one collection and you've got one sensational super-hot read!

Summer Sizzlers
MEN OF Summer

Three short stories by these favorite authors:

Kathleen Eagle
Joan Hohl
Barbara Faith

Available this July wherever
Silhouette books are sold.

In July, get to know the Fortune family....

Next month, don't miss the start of Fortune's Children, a
fabulous new twelve-book series from Silhouette Books.

**Meet the Fortunes—a family whose legacy is greater than
riches. Because where there's a will...there's a wedding!**

When Kate Fortune's plane crashes in the jungle, her family
believes that she's dead. And when her will is read, they
discover that Kate's plans for their lives are more interesting
than they'd ever suspected.

Look for the first book, *Hired Husband*, by *New York Times*
bestselling author **Rebecca Brandewyne**. PLUS, a stunning,
perforated bookmark is affixed to *Hired Husband* (and
selected other titles in the series), providing a convenient
checklist for all twelve titles!

FREE
Keepsake
Bookmark

Launching in July wherever books are sold.

FCT